A HOME CRAFTING MYSTERY

SOMETHING BORROWED, SOMETHING BLEU

CRICKET McRAE

WHEELER
CHIVERS

This Large Print edition is published by Wheeler Publishing, Waterville, Maine, USA and by AudioGo Ltd, Bath, England.
Wheeler Publishing, a part of Gale, Cengage Learning.
The text of this Large Print edition is unabridged.
Other aspects of the book may vary from the original edition.
Set in 16 pt. Plantin.

LIBRARY OF CONGRESS CATALOGING-IN-PUBLICATION DATA

McRae, Cricket.
    Something borrowed, something bleu : a home crafting mystery / by Cricket McRae. — Large print ed.
        p. cm. — (Wheeler Publishing large print cozy mystery)
    ISBN-13: 978-1-4104-2799-1
    ISBN-10: 1-4104-2799-4
    1. Women artisans—Fiction. 2. Soap trade—Fiction. 3. Large type books. I. Title.
PS3613.C58755S63 2010b
813'.6—dc22   2010027039

BRITISH LIBRARY CATALOGUING-IN-PUBLICATION DATA AVAILABLE

Published in 2010 in the U.S. by arrangement with Midnight Ink, an imprint of Llewellyn Publications, Woodbury, MN 55125–2989 USA.
Published in 2011 in the U.K. by arrangement with Llewellyn Worldwide Ltd.

U.K. Hardcover: 978 1 408 49315 1 (Chivers Large Print)
U.K. Softcover: 978 1 408 49316 8 (Camden Large Print)

Printed and bound in Great Britain by the MPG Books Group
1 2 3 4 5 6 7 14 13 12 11 10

This book is dedicated to libraries everywhere.

ACKNOWLEDGMENTS

I'm grateful to everyone who had a hand in this book: agents Jacky Sach and Kim Lionetti; my critique partners Bob and Mark; and the hard working crew at Midnight Ink — Bill Krause, Terri Bischoff, Connie Hill, Courtney Colton, Lisa Novak, and Donna Burch, among others. Meg and Arden, owners of the Windsor Dairy, were kind enough to answer my questions. They make the best raw-milk artisan cheeses imaginable. Anything I got wrong is my own fault. The staff at the post office in LaPorte, Colorado provided information about lost mail. Thanks also to my parents, supportive friends, and readers who continue to ask after Sophie Mae. And, as always, Kevin has offered unfailing encouragement. Thanks for having my back.

ONE

The shrill ring of the telephone startled me out of a sound sleep. My heart bucked, and panic shortened my breath as I stared wide-eyed into the darkness and felt around for the handset. The numbers on my bedside clock glowed 3:58.

Any call at that hour inevitably signaled grim news.

The phone tumbled, slammed onto the hardwood floor, and skittered beneath me. Brodie let out a single, sharp bark from Erin's bedroom down the hall. Swearing, I slithered out from under the sheet. Pajama-clad behind up in the air, I groped under the bed.

There: something, but definitely not the phone. I dragged the mystery item out and held it up to the pale gray light barely beginning to glow through the window.

A pair of purple lace panties.

So that was where those had disappeared to.

The phone reverberated again. I tossed the errant underwear in the corner and pressed my cheek against the floor. My fingers scrabbled against wood. Dust bunnies retreated to the far reaches as I touched hard plastic and teased the wailing handset into my grasp. I sat up on the cold floor and peered at the caller ID with bleary eyes.

It was my mother, calling from Spring Creek, Colorado.

"Anna Belle, what's wrong?" I demanded. "Is Dad okay?"

Her sorghum-laced voice floated over the line. "Good morning, Sophie Mae. I hope I didn't wake you."

"What? Of course you woke me. What happened?"

"You sound upset. It's too early in the morning for that, don't you think?"

I managed not to growl. However, my blood pressure dropped an infinitesimal amount.

"Why," I began, the words even and deliberate, "are you calling me at this hour if someone isn't sick or dying?"

"Oh, good Lord, Sophie Mae. You used to be such an early riser in the summer. It is, after all —" A pause as she no doubt consulted her watch. "Oh, dear. I didn't realize it's only five a.m. I'm sorry, hon."

"Four a.m.," I said.

"But . . . oh. I always seem to forget about the time difference."

"So nothing's wrong?"

"Well . . ."

"Can I call you back in a few hours?" I'd been working my tail off lately, making handmade toiletries and filling orders for my Winding Road Bath Products business, and I wanted a little more shut-eye before starting in yet again.

Plus, these days I wasn't in much of a mood to talk to my mother. Maybe I was a horrible daughter, but the frequency of her calls had increased lately as she tried to weasel her way into my wedding plans. Right now I didn't have the time or energy to try again to convince her that Barr and I wanted a small, simple ceremony. No wedding she was involved with would be either.

"Well, as long as you're up, I do need to talk to you," she said.

I sighed. "Right. As long as I'm up."

Couldn't quite keep the sarcasm out of my voice. Anna Belle Watson had no qualms about doing whatever she needed to in order to get what she wanted. Her polite, Southern belle demeanor softened her

11

manipulations, as did the accent toned by time to an alluring lilt. However, I wasn't one of her students or some untenured professor in the marketing department at Northern Colorado University. I was her daughter, even if she insisted that I call her by her first name, and I'd had a lifetime to see how she worked.

"Please," she said.

That, along with the tiniest quaver in her voice, gave me pause. "Are you sure everything's okay?" I asked.

"I want you to come home for a visit."

I blew out a frustrated whoosh of air and stood. Sliding on my ducky slippers, I began to pace in the limited confines of my bedroom. From the backyard, the murmurs of contented chickens already pecking at their layer ration rode the cool breeze that curled in through the open window.

"Seriously," I said. "I want a no-fuss, no-muss ceremony. I've already had one big wedding. That was enough for a lifetime."

A small sound on the other end of the line. Then another.

"Anna Belle?" I stopped short.

A sniffle.

Ohmygod. "Are you *crying?*"

Another pause, and then a quick, sharp laugh. "Don't be ridiculous." Sniff.

I pushed. "Tell me."

A pause, then, "You have to come home."

What on earth? Was this one of her tricks?

"Now," she said.

"Now?" The word came out as a squeak.

"Yes. As soon as you can." No sniffling and no hesitancy now, just hard demand in her voice.

I bristled. "Well, I don't know when that would be. It's hard to up and leave when you run your own business."

"I'm sure you can manage."

I thought of the rows of boxes on the counter in my workroom waiting to be filled with Winding Road orders. "Anna Belle —"

"It's about your brother."

Slowly, I sat down on the edge of my bed. Bobby Lee had been dead for eighteen years. I realized with a start he'd been gone half my lifetime. "What are you talking about?"

One evening, my brother had tossed a rope over the main beam in the great room of my parents' home and hung himself. Anna Belle had found him when she came downstairs for her morning coffee. Half a country away, in Seattle, I'd been sharing a dorm room with my best friend Meghan Bly at the University of Washington.

"He left a note," Anna Belle said. The

13

words punched through my memories.

"No, he didn't." My voice was quiet in my own ears. "We looked everywhere."

"He did. A letter, actually. And it's recently come into my possession. It . . . reveals something we didn't know before. Perhaps even the key to why he did it."

Sadness, curiosity and something very like fear rushed over me. "What does it say?"

"I'll show it to you when you get here."

"Anna Belle!"

"Come home for a few days, Sophie Mae. We need you."

"But —"

"Please."

Please? Again? I peered out the window at the high gray predawn — nope, no pigs winging their way above the rooftops yet. But they should be showing up any time now.

"It's been over a year," she said.

I closed my eyes. Dirty pool, Anna Belle. But she was right; it had been too long. On top of that, I knew very well that my mother wouldn't tell me what was in Bobby Lee's note over the phone. She had a bargaining chip, and she wasn't above using it.

Taking a deep breath, I stepped off the cliff. "I'll see when I can get away, check some flights, and get back to you."

14

"I'll tell your father. He'll be thrilled."

We Watsons had once been a normal — and very close — family. My childhood had been flavored with lively conversations over the dinner table about politics, religion, and current events. My mother was an opinionated intellectual who insisted Bobby Lee and I call her by her first name. My father, Calvin Watson, had a seemingly inexhaustible supply of fascinating stories from his days as an investigative journalist. Over and over they told my brother and me we could be or do anything we wanted.

Then Bobby Lee died, and everything changed.

"And honey?" my mother continued. "You might see if your new fiancé can come. Might be nice if we actually met him before the wedding, don't you think?"

"He's looking forward to meeting you both. I just don't know if he'll be able to change his schedule on such short notice." I said.

"I understand. As long as you can. So we'll see you soon?"

"Soon," I confirmed.

Her voice softened. "And I want you to know that I love you."

Flummoxed, I muttered, "Love you, too," and we said goodbye.

She hadn't said that to me for . . . I didn't know how long. Whatever she'd discovered about my brother, it had affected her deeply.

TWO

"You're going to Colorado with me," I announced.

The sounds of workmen banging away filtered around the corner to Meghan's office, formerly the old front parlor of the house we shared in Cadyville, Washington. The scents of ylang ylang and rose geranium essential oils drifted from the darkened massage room behind her, accompanied by the trickling sounds of the fountain. Brodie, his corgi muzzle gray with age, watched me from where he lay next to her desk. The constant noise from our house renovation set his canine sensibilities on edge, and these days he was never more than a few feet from Meghan or her eleven-year-old daughter, Erin.

My housemate's perfect eyebrow arched. "Colorado? Going to see your mom and dad?" Over the course of our lengthy friendship she had developed a great fondness for my parents.

I plopped into her big cushy guest chair. "Didn't you hear the phone ring this morning? It was Anna Belle, up bright and way too early, determined to chat with her only daughter."

She smiled. Dark curls swung around her delicate features as she shook her head and looked toward the ceiling. How nice that she found my mother's antics amusing.

"So why am I supposedly going on this junket with you?" she asked.

"Because now I have to go back home, and I'm not going by myself. Barr said he might be able to get off work for a day or so, but that's it. I just know Anna Belle is determined to plan a big wedding while I'm there."

She waved her hand as if dispelling a foul odor. "Bah. You're a grownup. Stick to your guns."

"Fine for you to say. She cried."

Shock replaced Meghan's smile. Her blue-gray eyes widened. "Anna Belle? Cried?"

I nodded. "Just a little. And she said 'Please.' "

She let out a low whistle. "Wow."

The shriek of a saw blade shuddered through the walls. Meghan and I winced. At our feet, Brodie whined.

"But all of that finally led up to what she really wants." I folded my arms across my chest.

Meghan looked pointedly at her watch.

Fine. "She found Bobby Lee's suicide note."

My housemate leaned forward and put her elbows on the desk. "Oh, God. Really?" She barely breathed the words. "What does it say?"

"She won't tell me." Frustration leaked out with my words.

A short laugh escaped before Meghan caught herself. "I'm sorry. I know it's not funny. Not funny at all. It's just that your mom is so . . ."

"Yeah. I know she is. But the truth is I do want to see them, and I haven't been back for a while." And I wanted to know — needed to know — what that note said.

A loud crash made the ceiling vibrate. My housemate's eyes narrowed. "This racket's making it impossible for me to work here. Clients can't relax, and I'm a nervous wreck."

"I know. It's awful. I'm sorry. But won't it be worth it?"

When Barr Ambrose had asked me to marry him, I'd balked. Not because I didn't love the guy to death, but because Meghan

19

and Erin Bly had become my close, if nontraditional, family. Luckily, Barr had anticipated my reluctance, and he and Meghan hatched a crazy plan to keep everybody happy. It was, in short, the perfect solution.

We bought into ownership of her large house and set to getting things changed around so Barr and I could have our own digs. The upstairs would be a one-bedroom apartment with a tiny kitchenette — Barr and I would still use the main kitchen most of the time, but it would be nice to be completely separate if we wanted — and we were adding two bedrooms to the main floor, as well as expanding the bathroom. My work area, office, and storeroom still took up the entire basement, and Meghan's office and massage room just off the front entryway remained unchanged. It was a huge project, but so far the contractor was on schedule. That in itself was a miracle, but it was still a real pain to live with.

"Of course. It'll be great," she said. "Not least because it means you'll be sticking around." A speculative look settled on her face. "When exactly are you planning this trip to Colorado?"

"The sooner the better."

She reached for her desk calendar, opened

it and ran her finger down a row of dates. "I've been booking light anyway, trying to schedule around when the workers are here. But it's getting so they're here all the time." A look up at me. "And Erin doesn't start school for two weeks."

"Day after tomorrow? Does that give you enough time?"

She considered. "I think so."

I tried not to look satisfied. "Excellent. I've checked flights already. There were some good last-minute fares online, so I'll go ahead and book three?"

She hesitated. A power saw screeched, and she grimaced. "Yes. Three tickets."

"You won't regret it. There's plenty to do around there, and you guys deserve a little vacay."

The screeching increased. Meghan gritted her teeth and nodded. "Talk about understatements."

I ducked out and headed down the narrow wooden staircase to the basement. When I'd talked to Barr, who was one of the Cadyville Police Department's two detectives, he'd been intrigued by the phone call from my mother. First off, he'd never met my parents and was curious about them. But the sudden appearance of a suicide note after eighteen years really

21

piqued his interest. Unfortunately, he'd been unsure whether he could get time off to come meet them, as he was scheduled to testify in a drug case some time during the next week.

My computer sat in the corner of my storage room, the online fares I'd found still on the screen. I quickly booked the tickets and then used my cell phone to call Cyan Waters, the teenager who worked for me several times a week. She was already familiar with how to fill and ship orders for Winding Road customers, and sounded happy to work some extra hours. In fact, she assured me that her sister Kyla — who'd also worked for me until recently — could help out if needed since she wasn't leaving for college for a few more weeks.

I turned to the shelves that covered the walls. Winding Road inventory packed them top to bottom. It was a relatively slow time of year, and I'd been good about keeping my stock high to avoid having to scramble for the upcoming Christmas rush. I'd have to fill the gaps once I returned, but that was okay. It was hard to complain about business being good.

Lye soaps in creamy earth tones stacked high along one wall. Other shelves held bottles and jars of bath salts, bath fizzies, foot scrubs, lip balms, lotions, air fresheners, and body oils. Another wall held raw materials: essential oils, butters, vegetable oils, solid palm and coconut oils, and jars of herbs and natural colorants. I closed my eyes, inhaling the plethora of heavenly aromas, and a quiet calm replaced the jittery anxiety I'd felt ever since talking to Anna Belle.

She'd refused to talk about Bobby Lee for years. Perhaps she simply couldn't bear discussing it when everything was still raw, and never quite got past that. The vibrancy of our family had faded until we had only the colorless shell of regular phone calls in which we said the same things over and over and the occasional visit where we walked around each other like ghosts.

I'd intended to go back to Colorado after graduating from college, but then I fell in love with a Washington boy. Mike Reynolds and I got jobs, got married, and got on with life.

Until he died, too.

But this phone call had been different from the others. Anna Belle had been different.

What message had my brother left behind?

The architecture of Denver International

Airport was supposed to reflect the outline of the Rocky Mountains, but the swooping white peaks looked more like a series of circus tents. Beside me, Erin strained against the seatbelt and craned her head to see through the scratched Plexiglas as the pilot guided the plane down the runway to the terminal. Pushing away, she flopped back in her seat with something that sounded very much like a harrumph.

"What's wrong?" I asked.

A scowl pinched her elfin features, so much like her mother's that she could have been a clone. "I thought Colorado had mountains."

I smiled. "Looks like we landed in Kansas by mistake."

She twisted in her seat to look at me with intelligent gray eyes. "Nice try. I'm not stupid."

"Try looking out the other side of the plane," I suggested.

To my right, Meghan dug her cell phone out of her pocket and turned it back on with a beep. There was already a message from her long-distance boyfriend, Kelly O'Connell. They were trying to coordinate a flight for him, so they could spend some quality time together. It was Sunday, and Barr was still hoping to manage a few days

24

off to join us later in the week. In the meantime, I'd be spending my quality time with Anna Belle and Calvin Watson.

At the top of the last escalator, our fellow travelers dispersed into the crowd of people waiting by the fountain in the main terminal. The shooshing sound of water muted their conversations. I searched the faces lined up behind the barrier but didn't see either of my parents. Meghan touched my arm and pointed. From a bank of chairs fifty yards away my father stood, waving his arm to get our attention. My mother remained seated, a look of mild interest on her face.

I waved back and guided Erin in their direction. She shook off my hand with an impatient gesture. I shot a questioning look at Meghan, who frowned, then shrugged.

"Hey you guys! How was the flight?" Dad embraced everyone with enthusiasm. I was glad to see Erin grin and hug him back. She was becoming hard to predict.

"We had to get out of the house before five this morning so we're a little tired, but everything went smoothly." I turned to my mother and smiled.

She stood and patted me awkwardly on the back, then greeted Meghan and Erin in turn. Dad put his arm around my shoulders and squeezed again. For a brief moment I leaned my head against his chest.

Anna Belle looked around at the group. "Let's get some double lattes, then, and hit the road." Ever efficient, she turned on her heel and led the way to the coffee bar. Over her shoulder she tossed, "Sophie Mae, I like your hair short like that. Shows off your pretty green eyes."

"Um, thanks."

"You should have cut it like that years ago."

Beside me, Meghan grinned.

As we followed behind my mother like a string of baby ducks, I examined my parents. In the last year the lines on my father's lean face had deepened, and a few more white strands accentuated Anna Belle's smooth copper hair. Other than that, little had changed. As always, they both were prime specimens of physical fitness.

Anna Belle's cropped pageboy framed a face that had once graced magazine covers. Her stint as a model had been short, intended only to make money for college. She'd always drilled into Bobby Lee and me that physical beauty was ultimately meaningless. Of course, she was right, but Anna Belle Watson could better afford that attitude than most, with her high cheekbones and dark, intense eyes. It also looked

26

like she spent more time than ever in the gym. Muscles defined her bare arms and roped up her tanned calves to the hem of her Bermuda shorts.

Feeling like a pale lump of dough, I turned my attention to my dad. Lean and only slightly taller than Anna Belle, he had a thick blonde mane and clear hazel eyes. An electric-blue-and-chartreuse floral shirt topped his khaki shorts — one of the many Hawaiian patterns in his extensive collection. His gait was loose and easy as he walked beside her. In fact, he looked remarkably calm, and I wondered what that was all about. He'd mellowed over the years, as had my mother, but he had always been a man with fire in his belly, intense and curious and interested in everything.

Especially when my brother was alive.

In line at the coffee counter, Anna Belle asked, "What does everyone want?"

She took our orders and presented them to the barista in a succinct and slightly impatient list. My mother seemed to be in a real toot to get on the road. A few minutes later we were armed with various forms of caffeine, green tea for my father and a lemon granita for Erin. Our suitcases were circling on the conveyer when we got to the baggage claim station, and we rolled straight out to the parking garage.

On the way, Anna Belle culled me from the herd, her hand on my elbow guiding me far enough away that the others couldn't hear her mutter, "Your father doesn't know about the letter."

I looked my surprise at her. "Why not?"

Ahead of us, Dad turned in our direction, a quizzical look on his face. Anna Belle pushed me back toward the group. "I'll explain later."

You sure as heck will, I thought.

THREE

"We're here!" Erin jumped out and stood on the sidewalk with her hands on her non-existent hips, face tilted toward the azure sky.

I rubbed my gritty eyes. My neck screamed as I turned my head to look out the window; Meghan's shoulder had proven an awkward headrest on the ride to Spring Creek. The last vestige of air-conditioning slipped out Erin's open door and the dry summer heat wrapped around me like a python. Anna Belle was already on the front step, keys jingling in her hand. The hydraulic support of the hatchback wheezed open behind me.

I peered out at the house I'd grown up in: brick mixed with oatmeal-colored siding, two stories high and featuring a fully fin-ished basement courtesy of my father's hard work. The yard boasted a tiny patch of grass, but was mostly landscaped with drought-hardy plants like Russian sage and sunset hyssop, interspersed with puffs of blue fescue grass. Zinnias brightened the spaces in between, as did the two identical ceramic urns that flanked the front door, planted with verbena, lobelia, and geraniums. Red Colorado flagstone, artfully arranged river rock, and chunky boulders provided structure: high desert xeriscaping at its best.

It was always a bit of a shock to return to Colorado after living in the verdant green of the Pacific Northwest. I could feel my sinuses crinkling from the dry air, and blinked rapidly to prevent the moisture in my eyes from wicking into the atmosphere.

Oh, and it was hot, too. August hot. And I don't care what they say about a "dry heat" — once you hit 95 degrees, it just doesn't matter anymore.

"Nice nap?" Meghan asked.

I wiped the sheen of sweat from my forehead with the back of my hand. "I guess."

My mother beckoned Erin to the front door. Dad started unloading luggage behind me. The ache spread up my neck and settled behind my eyes. At least it went with the coffee-sour stomach.

I did not want to go into that house.

Why my parents hadn't moved was beyond me. How could they stand living there after what had happened? The one time I had the temerity to ask, Anna Belle had changed the subject.

Meghan opened her door and stepped to the pavement. I took a deep breath and followed her.

"Here, Dad, let me take that."

My former bedroom was larger and had a king-sized bed, so Anna Belle put Meghan and Erin in there. That left Bobby Lee's old room for me. I found the prospect less than thrilling, but kept my mouth shut in the name of common sense. Our childhood rooms were both run-of-the-mill guest bedrooms now. Had been for years. There wasn't a trace of either of us in the entire house anymore, except for the cluster of photos on the bookshelf in the great room. My inner child found that disconcerting, but the grown-up part of me said to stop being such a big baby.

Still, while I unpacked I expected a vestige of my brother in his old room, if only in the feel of the air against my cheek. But there was nothing — just taupe walls, blue Venetian blinds, a navy chenille bedspread, and a distressed pine dresser with a stinky fake gardenia candle on it. A cheap framed print of Picasso's *Don Quixote* dominated one wall.

Kitty Wampus, my parents' orange Abyssinian cat, sprawled on my pillow, shedding at will. I shooed him off and tried to shake some of the fur off, but it clung like Velcro. I sneezed and tossed it back on the bed. From the floor, the offending feline began to purr and do that cute squinty thing they do. Then he jumped back up and curled on the pillow again.

I sighed. Sneezed again. And sighed again.

Leaving the cat to his snoozing and shedding, I unpacked my toiletries in the bathroom I would be sharing with the Bly girls. I smiled when I saw the bar of Winding Road Alligator Soap, so named because it contained extra oils to soften dry skin, awaiting us in the shower. Then I peeked into my parents' bedroom, thinking Anna Belle might be in there.

I wanted to know about that note. But all I found was a perfectly neat and uninhabited room.

From the bottom of the stairs I could see through a corner of the kitchen to the big sliding glass door that led to the back patio. Out in the yard, my parents were showing their kitchen garden to Meghan and Erin, who seemed to be listening with interest. I slipped around the corner of the stairwell and down three more steps into the great room.

Over the last eighteen years Dad and Anna Belle had updated the furniture to light earth tones and rearranged everything a multitude of times. They'd painted the walls a dusty mushroom color, and the front yard, visible through the two plate-glass windows, had changed and matured since the time when I'd lived there. Long ago, sleek maple blinds had replaced the heavy brocade drapes. The light fixture had changed from a brass-and-glass chandelier to an artsy, blown-glass affair. The slightly sunken living space, open to the kitchen above except for a long counter, felt airy and light, relaxed and welcoming.

But when my eyes followed the cord up from the overhead light, it affixed to that same wooden beam. The one that stretched across the vaulted ceiling all the way into the kitchen. Stained dark, as it always had been.

Stop it, Sophie Mae. Just stop it. It's only a beam. Only a room. Dad always told us that things don't have meaning unless you assign it to them.

Ha. Great in theory. Not so easy in practice, though.

Perhaps I had a more vivid imagination than Dad and Anna Belle. Or perhaps over time they'd simply grown used to living with it.

"You have to promise to keep this between us for now." My mother held an envelope between her first two fingers, over her shoulder as if I were a little kid who might try to grab it away from her.

"Too late," I said.

Her eyes narrowed.

"I didn't tell Dad, if that's what you're worried about, at least not yet. But I can't fathom why you haven't."

She ignored my implied question. "You told Meghan."

I nodded. "Of course I did. Didn't know it was such a big secret."

"Well, I'm glad she came. And that she brought Erin. That girl is smart as a whip. She's really growing up."

Meghan, Erin, and my father were downstairs in the kitchen putting together bison-and-bell-pepper kabobs to grill on the patio. When my mother had touched my arm and jerked her chin toward the stairs, Dad had been mixing up a marinade and chatting with my housemate about the necessity of balancing oil with acid to elicit the most tenderness from the lean red meat. Anna Belle had a few signature dishes, but Dad had always been the real cook in the family.

Now my mother and I sat on my bed. Kitty Wampus had moved on to deposit his fur elsewhere, so we were truly alone. The scent of garlic wafted up from downstairs, vying with the cloying scent of the faux floral candle on the dresser.

I eyed the envelope. "So why haven't you told Dad? Is there something in the letter you don't want him to see?"

She pressed her lips together. "I have my reasons."

I got up and removed a Winding Road clove-and-cinnamon air freshener from my suitcase and put it next to the candle. Sat back down. "Like what?"

"I do my best to keep your father's stress level down."

"Oh, for heaven's sake, Anna Belle. He's a grown man. Besides, he's the most easy-going I've ever seen him. Or is there something about his health I should know?"

Her lips compressed again. "He's fine. Been doing some . . . experimentation lately, but that's his business."

My eyebrows climbed up my forehead. Experimentation? My thoughts bounced from Timothy Leery to gravity boots to

Xanax. I opened my mouth to ask more, but Anna Belle shook her head. "You should ask him about it. He can explain it much better than I."

"But —"

She held up the letter again, still by the corner. Like a dog being offered a piece of bacon, I shut my trap and waited expectantly.

At least I didn't drool.

A moment of hesitation, then her hand shot toward me. Gingerly, I took the envelope. Stared. It was addressed to Tabby Atwood. She'd been Bobby Lee's girlfriend at the time he'd done the deed. It looked like the top had been carefully slit open with a very sharp knife.

I looked back up at Anna Belle. "Tabby gave you this? I thought you two weren't speaking."

Anna Belle's tongue crept out to her lower lip. "Not exactly."

I squinted. "Meaning?"

"She never received it."

Bending closer, I examined the envelope. "It's been postmarked. Oh, wait. I see: *Return to sender.*" The scrawled words were small and nearly unintelligible. I met my mother's eyes. "The postage is only twenty-nine cents. It's postmarked the day Bobby

Lee died."

"I know. The postman brought it with the rest of the mail a week ago Saturday. I imagine it's been in the dead letter office this whole time, and they finally got around to delivering it." She licked her lips. "Now that we're ready to see it."

I gaped at my mother. *Now that we're ready to see it?* Did she just invoke fate? Acknowledge an order to the universe that went beyond science?

Good Lord. So to speak.

Shaking off my wonder, I turned my attention back to the envelope. "But this was returned. It was addressed to Tabby, and you've opened it. Does that count as mail fraud?"

She shrugged. "Fraud schmaud. Those Atwoods didn't want it, and if you think I wasn't going to read what may have been my son's last words, you'd better think again."

Good point.

Downstairs a clatter of dishes warned of an imminent call to dinner. A sense of urgency overcame me. With shaking hands I extracted a single sheet of paper from the envelope and took a deep breath. I swore I could hear my brother's voice as I began to read.

Dear Tabby,

Don't worry, I haven't told anyone. And I know it wasn't your fault. It was a stupid thing to do, and I don't know why either one of us went along with it. Still, we did. I know this is a strange way to say it, but I don't want you to blame yourself. I'm doing more than enough of that for both of us. I can't handle the guilt. I can't handle what would happen if my parents found out. I couldn't bear the look in their eyes. I've thought this out very carefully, and this is really the best thing. For all of us.

I love you.
BL

That was it. Not much of a letter after all. Just a note. A suicide note, sent to his girlfriend. I stared at the paper without really seeing it. They had done something. Something bad. Something so secret that he'd couched his last words to Tabby in such a way that no one else would know what he was talking about.

But Tabby would.

I returned the note to the envelope and handed it to my mother. "Does she know about this?"

Anna Belle shook her head. "As you said,

we're not speaking."

"But this — don't you think it's worth burying the hatchet to find out what Bobby Lee meant?"

"It doesn't matter what I think. After the, uh, incident at the funeral, Tabby hates me. I'm certain she wouldn't be interested in helping me, even with finding out what this note means. Maybe especially not with finding out what this note means."

I chewed on a cuticle, considering. "You're probably right. It implies Tabby was a part of whatever happened that made Bobby Lee —" I stopped. Looked closely at my mother. This was the most we had really talked about my brother in eighteen years.

Her return gaze was clear, if a little irritated. "That's why I want your help."

Uh oh. "No . . ."

"You have to find out what happened."

"That's why you hornswoggled me into coming out here? What on earth do you think I can do?"

"The same kind of thing you've done in your little town up there in Washington. You always were an inquisitive girl. Took after your father that way."

"I haven't seen Tabby since the funeral. Now you want me to just march up to her and ask her what crazy trouble she and

Bobby Lee got into way back when?"

"Of course not. She wouldn't tell you anything then. You have to come at her sideways."

"Sideways."

"You know — roundabout. Be her friend. Gain her confidence."

"Right. In a week."

"However long it takes."

That sounded ominous. "You know what a ridiculous idea this is, don't you?" I asked.

Her face pinched. "Maybe. But I don't know what else to do, and I want to know why he —" she took a deep breath. "I need to know. We need to know."

I nodded and heard myself say, "I'll try."

"And once we understand what happened, we can tell your father," she said.

My eyes narrowed. "You have another reason for not telling him, something besides shielding him from stress. What is it?"

FOUR

A layer of worry deepened the lines in my mother's face. I waited. She seemed to make a decision. "Back when it happened I kept trying to figure out why Bobby Lee would do such a thing. Finally, your father told me we'd never know for sure, and to stop making myself crazy. And more pointedly, to stop making him crazy."

"Really?"

Dad had always been the curious one, the one who needed to get at the truth no matter what the cost. He'd built a career on it.

As if she'd read my mind, Anna Belle said, "It's different with family, you know. And, of course, he was right. It was all second guessing and imagining terrible scenarios. But now we have this. This is real. I just . . . I guess I don't want him to tell us to let it go, to try to stop us from finding out what happened."

I protested. "He wouldn't do that."

41

Silently she searched my face, looking for compliance.

This time I pressed my lips together.

Dad's voice drifted up the stairs. "Anna Belle? Sophie Mae? Where did you two — oh, there you are." He stood in the doorway. "Catching up?"

"Exactly." My mother stood and smoothed the bedspread. The letter had disappeared. "Are we ready to get cooking?"

"Ready, willing, and able," he said. "The risotto is nearly done."

"Yum," I said. I'd sorely missed Dad's Parmesan risotto.

On the way out of the bedroom I grabbed the gardenia candle and put it on the hall table. Following my father down the stairs, I asked Anna Belle in a low voice, "Do you know how to reach Tabby Atwood?"

Dad apparently had ears like a wolf. He turned around on the bottom step. "Tabby Atwood is Tabby Bines now."

"She married Joe?" I asked in surprise.

He nodded.

Beside me, my mother murmured agreement.

Dad continued, "They own a dairy east of town. No hormones, all organic. Tapped into the whole community-supported agriculture movement."

"Good Lord," I said.

"Pretty good milk, too." He continued around the corner into the kitchen.

I turned to Anna Belle. "A dairy."

Her lips crept up in a satisfied smile. "And you are about to learn more than you ever wanted to know about cheese making."

"Mmm. Cheese. I love cheese."

"An added bonus."

"They give classes?"

"They don't. Tabby does. And, as Sophie Reynolds, you're registered for one tomorrow morning."

I shook my head, amazed at my mother. Oh, well. If nothing else, at least I'd learn something.

"And when you get home we'll go over some ideas I have for the wedding."

"Anna Belle —"

But she was already around the corner. Boy, my mother could really move when she wanted to.

As we carried the kabobs out to the grill on the patio, I still couldn't get over the fact that Tabby had married Joe Bines. Joe and Bobby Lee had been best friends since junior high school, managing to get into trouble fourteen ways from Sunday. Back then I'd found him to be a real pain in the behind. No doubt he'd grown up like everyone else and had turned into a nice, normal guy.

At least I hoped so.

Monday morning I came downstairs to find Meghan and Erin packing bacon, lettuce, and tomato sandwiches, fresh peaches, and lemonade into a soft-sided cooler.

Meghan looked up when I entered the kitchen. "Morning! Anna Belle left the granola out on the counter, and there's yogurt in the fridge. She and your Dad had some work to do at the university, so they're already gone. They rode their bikes and left us their cars — wasn't that nice?" She grinned. "I'll flip you for the Audi."

I waved my hand at her. "Take it. I'm fine with the Subaru. But right now, I'm starved." I opened the refrigerator door and stared at the contents. Packed stem to stern with all manner of comestibles for the visiting hordes. "Sleep well?" I reached for an apple to round out the granola and yogurt on offer.

"Sure did," Meghan said.

I peered over the top of the door at Erin. "You?"

She shrugged. "Sure."

I continued to look at her.

"What? It's sleep, not rocket science."

Just ignore her, I told myself. This sudden crankiness is just a phase.

Meghan broke the minor tension hanging in the air. "I wish you could go hiking with us."

"Me, too," I said, swinging the door closed. "But duty calls. You'll just have to try to have fun without me."

Erin snorted under her breath. I ignored her some more.

After Meghan and Erin left, I crunched through some breakfast while considering how to approach Tabby Bines. Anna Belle had suggested "roundabout" as the technique of choice, but that would take time — and someone better at prevarication than I was. The other problem was that if I got into Tabby's good graces, even developed a friendship, I'd be shown up as a big fat liar as soon as I tried to casually ask about the contents of the letter. That would only blow up in my face.

No. Better to be straightforward about it if things went well. I'd show the letter to Tabby today if I got the chance. For all I knew, she'd tell me what the heck Bobby Lee had been talking about, and my mission would be accomplished. We would finally know the truth behind my brother's death.

Problem was, I didn't have the letter. Anna Belle did. And my parents had already left for the university.

The door to Anna Belle's den was closed, but not locked. A psychological barrier only, but she had always believed it to be an effective one. She thought no one in the family went in there when she wasn't around.

Of course, she was wrong.

When I was a child, Anna Belle's den had been a source of hidden treasure in the form of her secrets — with the added excitement that I'd have been grounded or worse if she'd ever caught me. Bobby Lee and I had sneaked in on dares a number of times, though never together: Someone had to stand guard. And we'd snooped — in drawers, behind books, under cabinets. Bobby Lee found the racy romance novels tucked under the seat cushions of the loveseat. I discovered a packet of love letters from a high school boyfriend in a flat metal box behind the ancient set of Encyclopedia Britannica. But my find had seemed too personal to share with my little brother, so I'd professed utter failure that day.

I opened the door and went in. Bright stripes of sunlight spilled through the half-drawn wooden blinds, alternating with bands of shadow across sofa, desk, chairs, and floor alike. Particles of dust danced in the narrow shards of light. The air smelled of lemon furniture polish and another one of those phony flower candles, this one trying to be rose but not quite succeeding. I wrinkled my nose at my mother's jaded sense of smell.

The sudden caw of a crow on the other side of the window gave me a start, and I realized I was tiptoeing. Anna Belle would still have a fit if she knew I was in her den, especially if she knew what I was about to do.

First I checked her desk drawers. No letter. Nothing in the file cabinet, either. Hands on hips, I considered the shelves of books. Once I'd found a credit card in a book with the title *Your Money or Your Life*. Another time I'd discovered a picture of my grandmother, arms folded and a frown on her face, in *My Mother, Myself*.

I looked at my watch. At least a thousand books lined the walls. Then my eyes lit on the ancient set of Encyclopedia Britannica.

Well, duh.

The box with the old love letters was still there. The envelope with Bobby Lee's letter wasn't.

Damn.

I replaced the box and stood back to scan

the rows of book spines. Mostly nonfiction, loosely grouped by subject matter. Self-help titles dominated one long shelf.

There. *Night Falls Fast: Understanding Suicide.* I took it down and flipped through the pages.

Nothing.

As I slid the book back into place, the one next to it caught my eye. *The Empty Chair: The Journey of Grief After Suicide.*

Bingo. My brother's letter was tucked inside the front cover.

I replaced the volume and slid the envelope into my tote bag, thinking about all those self-help books. Could they have anything to do with the changes I'd seen in my mother on this trip home? As acerbic as ever, she nonetheless seemed less aloof, more accessible than usual. It struck me that Anna Belle might have been dealing with my brother's death all along with the aid of books like these. She always had been a do-it-yourselfer.

As was I. Finding out what had tipped Bobby Lee over the edge would be my self-help.

My closure.

At least that was the plan.

FIVE

Outside, the sky was that amazing mile-high blue that verges on purple. An arching lenticular cloud hovered on the far eastern horizon, but otherwise the sun beat relentlessly down upon pavement, flora, and fauna alike. Inside Dad's Subaru Outback, I cranked the air-conditioning as high as it would go.

Traffic on College Avenue had worsened since I'd lived in Spring Creek, but it still didn't take long to get to the post office downtown. Only one other person stood in line ahead of me, and in no time I was talking with a clerk. When I told her about Bobby Lee's letter being returned after eighteen years, she looked puzzled.

"Eighteen years?"

"My mother assumed it had been in the dead letter office."

She shook her considerable mane of dark hair and squinted at me through thick eyeliner. "I don't think so, honey. First off, we don't call them that anymore. Now they're Mail Recovery Centers, and if something ends up there it's because it was undeliverable and couldn't be returned to the sender. That return address is still the residence where your parents live?"

"Yes."

"Well, then it would have been returned back then, not treated as a dead letter."

"I see." I wasn't exactly surprised at this news, since I never really bought into the dead letter theory that seemed to satisfy my mother. Something about a letter showing up like that was suspicious — especially one that happened to be a suicide note. Over the years I'd learned not to trust coincidences.

"And," she continued, "if it had gone to the Mail Recovery Center, it would have been opened to try and determine the identity of the sender and returned if possible. Or else burned."

"Burned? You burn letters you can't deliver?"

"Sure." She leaned over the counter, and I took a step backward. "What would you have us do with them? Build a monument?"

"Er, no." Sheesh. Settle down lady. "So what do you think happened?"

"Beats the heck out of me," she said.

"Do you think someone might have an idea? Maybe your supervisor?"

She sighed, but disappeared into the back and returned with a portly man with a salt-and-pepper buzz cut and unfortunately large ears. He hooked his fingers through the belt loops of his dark trousers and hitched them up.

"Agatha here says you've got a question about the Mail Recovery Center."

"Well, sort of. Actually, I'm wondering if you might have a theory about how this letter ended up being returned after eighteen years."

Intelligence lit up behind his eyes. "Eighteen years? That might be a record. Let me take a look."

I handed over the letter with reluctance, as if he'd take it and run away.

He held it up, turning it this way and that. "There are tales we hear every once in a while about letters that got stuck under a cabinet or a copy machine and then were found and sent on their way."

"Do you think that happened here?"

He glanced at me. "Those are just stories. But sometimes they find letters in mailbags or machinery that hasn't been used for a while."

I perked up at that.

He shook his head. "But those items are stamped 'Found in Supposedly Empty Equipment' and sent on their way."

"Really? You have a stamp that says that?"

"Yup. But lookie here. This was returned to . . ." He held the envelope at arm's length and peered at it, ignoring the reading glasses poking up out of his shirt pocket. ". . . returned to Bobby Lee Watson back when first-class stamps cost twenty-nine cents."

Now he put on his glasses and looked at me over the top. "I take it you're not Bobby Lee."

"He was my brother."

My use of the past tense was not lost on him, and he nodded. "Ah. I'm sorry."

"Thank you." But I was distracted. The Bines had lived in the same house for several years after Bobby Lee died. Tabby had been there for at least another year, and after she moved into her own place her parents could have easily passed on any mail that came for her. But someone had hand-written the words *Return to Sender* on the envelope.

The post office supervisor gave it back to me. "I'm sorry. I don't know what to tell you."

"That's okay. This information has actually been very useful." I thanked the clerk who had helped me in the first place and made my way out to the parking lot, still thinking.

My trip to the post office took longer than expected, as did the drive to the T&J Dairy. I turned off the county road, glancing at my watch as I drove toward the cluster of buildings at the end of a long gravel driveway.

The Bines lived in a big farm-style house at the top of a little hill. They'd painted it white with forest-green trim. The colors were reversed on the barn, chicken house, and three other outbuildings which marched in a circle around the house. The siding showed wear, and lighter shingles spotted the roof in several places where it had been patched after rough weather. There were no mild seasons in northern Colorado, despite three hundred days of sunshine a year.

A line of cottonwoods wandered across the landscape behind and below the house, no doubt tracing the path of a river or significant stream. Several brown cows with white markings lay in the morning sun, fenced from the road with split rails instead of the ubiquitous barbed wire. The rheumy eyes of a bony old specimen watched with calm interest as I shifted the Subaru into

Park. My tennis shoes hit the gravel in the parking lot at the bottom of the hill, and I stretched briefly before reaching back into the car for my tote bag. Chickens of all sizes and colors gabbled at one another conversationally, bocking and scratching in a large rectangular enclosure built off one end of their coop. A thick animal smell hung over the whole place, potent but not unpleasant.

The hand-lettered sign stuck into the ground read *Classroom,* and the arrow on it directed me to a small, square outbuilding by the parking lot. Dark green with white trim, like the rest of the outbuildings. Tabby had just begun talking when I entered.

"Sorry I'm late," I said, stowing my tote bag in a corner and then joining the others.

Surprised recognition flickered across her face as she nodded her welcome at me. "No worries. You're right on time."

When Bobby Lee first told me he was dating Tabitha Atwood, all he could talk about was how amazing her eyes were. They still were: ice blue and intelligent. Now a fine web of crow's feet fanned from their corners, and the years and sun had added lines around her mouth. The rest of her skin was taut and tan. White-blonde hair swooped down from a denim scrunchy into a short ponytail, and her gaze ricocheted between the class participants as she spoke, constantly gauging reaction and understanding from her six students. But her eyes kept returning to me. She'd recognized me the moment I walked in, and no doubt wondered why I was back in town.

The interior of the small space was clean and bright. The open windows front and back encouraged air circulation. A long folding table stood in the center of the room, and equipment both recognizable and mysterious, instruction handouts, a microwave, and a two-burner hotplate littered the surface. A miniature refrigerator hummed in the corner.

"Today we're going to be making mozzarella," Tabby said. "It'll be ready to eat today, as opposed to cheeses that need to age for a significant amount of time in order to develop flavor. By definition, then, fresh cheeses taste quite mild."

My mouth started to water. Beside me, an older woman with gray dreadlocks nodded her agreement at our instructor. Next to her stood an outdoorsy-looking couple, and on my other side a drab, bespectacled woman in her mid-twenties hung on Tabby's every word. Given their similar features, I guessed the heavyset blonde beside her was her mother.

Tabby donned a pair of rubber gloves and waved us over to where a stainless-steel pot of milk sat on the hot plate. "From the same milk you can get any number of cheeses — the difference comes from the kind of culture or bacteria introduced, the coagulating agent, and the amount of heat applied to the milk and for how long. Oh, and then there's the aging process."

We crowded around the pot as if it held gold bullion.

She continued, "Now, we'll add a little acid to the milk, and then some rennet, and then heat it to around one hundred degrees — I'll always be talking Fahrenheit when I mention temperature — to coagulate the curds. Then we heat the drained curds in the microwave a few times to extract more of the whey. In the end we get to stretch the mozzarella like taffy."

We all exchanged dubious looks when she mentioned pulling cheese like taffy, but I was game. Unfortunately, all the talk about curds and whey started "Little Miss Muffet" chanting in the back of my brain.

Gesturing toward the thermometer attached to the side of the pot, Tabby said, "We'll add the citric acid when the milk has warmed to fifty-five degrees."

Sat on a tuffet.

What the heck was a tuffet, anyway?

She handed the dreadlocked lady a measuring cup with a little water in the bottom and told her to mix the citric acid into it. The citric acid was a white crystal that looked like salt. It was familiar to me, since I used it to make bath bombs. There was a five-pound bucket of it in my storeroom. It was food grade, so there was no reason not to use it to make mozzarella at home. A frisson of excitement ran through me at the thought of pizza made with Meghan's homemade dough, sauce canned from our garden tomatoes, a chiffonade of fresh basil, and homemade mozzarella.

I wrenched my attention back to what Tabby was saying.

"You can usually find citric acid at the grocery store with the canning supplies. Often people add it to tomatoes when they preserve them, to ensure the acid level is high enough to safely can them in a water bath."

We always used lemon juice for that, I mused to myself.

"You can also use lemon juice," Tabby said, "since that's citric acid in its original form. Some people use lemon juice to make mozzarella, too, but we're using the crystals in order to ensure we get the exact amount of acid that we need. Go ahead and stir that in now."

The dreadlocked woman did as she was told. We all peered eagerly at the milk in the pot. Nothing happened.

Tabby handed another cup with water in it to me, along with a small bottle of brown liquid. Following her instruction, I carefully added seven drops to the water.

"This is liquid rennet," she said, "and I find it to be the most reliable for cheese making. Traditional rennet comes from the stomach lining of very young cattle, but you can also get vegetable-based rennet. Some people even use a kind of nettle tea. You can get what we're using today online, or I have some available for purchase. In a pinch, you can use plain old junket from the grocery store instead, but the resulting texture will be a little different. Okay, let's take a look at the temperature. We'll add the rennet when the milk reaches ninety degrees."

The addition of the diluted rennet gave the milk a kind of grainy texture. While we waited for the temperature to increase to just over a hundred degrees, Tabby gave us a little lecture on the history of cheese through the ages. Man puts milk in a leather bag made from a calf stomach, jostles it around as he rides his horse all day in the desert, goes to drink it and finds cheese instead. From there on the conversion of milk to cheese became more complicated, complex — and tasty.

"Oh, look!" I said, pointing to the pot. A white mass was pulling away from the edge, leaving a rim of clear liquid next to the stainless steel.

Tabby smiled. "Perfect. Just what we want it to do." She checked the temperature. "Almost there. Then we'll let it sit a few minutes and drain the curds."

Eating her curds and whey.

Once the curds and whey were separated, Tabby told us to don rubber gloves. "This is going to be hot to handle, folks."

We took turns heating the cheese in the microwave, stretching and pulling it each time.

"No wonder string cheese is so stringy," I said to the tomboy brunette standing beside me.

She folded her chunk of cheese and then stretched it back out. "Look how shiny it is, too. I love fresh mozzarella, but it's so expensive."

"I bet it would be a lot cheaper to make yourself," I said.

The subject changed to our favorite

59

cheeses, and as we worked the rest of the group joined the discussion.

And I waited.

Along came a spider,
Who sat down beside her
And frightened Miss Muffet away.

Six

The other class participants gathered their belongings and trickled out to the parking lot, chatting amongst themselves and carrying their cheese samples. I hung back, puttering and poking at the contents of my big tote bag until Tabby had finished a long goodbye to Gray Dreadlocks, whom she apparently knew. When the door finally closed, Tabby turned to me with a slightly wary expression.

"Aren't you . . . ?"

I nodded. "Sophie Mae Watson. Well, Reynolds now. Soon to be Ambrose."

Sophie Mae Ambrose. Had a nice ring to it. Still, it would be strange to give up my dead husband's last name after all this time. And Reynolds was the name I used in my business. Did I really want to change my name after Barr and I were married? Would he balk if I didn't?

Tabby's forehead wrinkled. She examined

me for a long moment, and something akin to regret deepened the lines around her eyes. "You look so much like Bobby Lee."

That hung there in the air for a while, neither of us quite sure what to do with it. Then she cleared her throat and said, "You're back in Spring Creek, then?"

"Just for a visit. My mom and dad, you know."

Her expression hardened at the offhand mention of my mother, and I quickly moved on. "But I love to cook and to make things from scratch. My friend and her daughter wanted me to hike up Horsetooth Mountain with them today, but when I saw you offered this class, I couldn't resist."

Another long pause then, "I make several artisan cheeses, mostly bleu varieties, but generally people don't want to go through the hassle of doing that themselves — inoculating, pressing, and curing. We'll get a few people for that class, but this fresh cheese class always fills up. Sometimes we make mozzarella, sometimes feta or paneer."

"More and more people are interested in doing this sort of thing for themselves," I said. "I'm a soap maker, myself. I sell handmade toiletries on the Internet from my home in Cadyville, Washington."

"Soap! Now that sounds like fun. I'd love

to learn more."

"A lot of the same things apply: temperature, chemistry, time. But no bacteria. At least we soap makers work pretty hard to avoid that."

"I bet," Tabby said. "Bacteria can certainly be bad — or really, really good. After all, it's what keeps our digestion working. Are you interested in making mold-ripened cheese?"

"Of course," I said. "When is that class?"

"Day after tomorrow. Just show up if you decide to take it. You can pay me then."

She was going to slip away, and however much I might like the idea of making my own cheese, I hadn't had a chance to talk to her about anything important yet.

"I heard you married Joe Bines."

She paused in the act of reaching for the door handle. Looked over her shoulder. "Your mom tell you that?"

Uh oh. "My dad, actually. When he learned I was coming out here this morning. You know, so I wouldn't be surprised when I saw you, I guess."

She watched me babble with an amused glint in her eye.

I wanted to kick myself, but kept going. Couldn't let her escape yet. "So anyway, is he around?"

"He's out delivering milk."

Joe, the milkman. Go figure.

"You guys have any kids?"

"A daughter. She's fifteen."

"Wow. That makes me feel old."

She laughed. "Tell me about it. She's a good kid, though. Nuts about horses. Pretty good rider, too."

"How is Joe?"

"Ornery as ever." She seemed to be loosening up a little, her gestures and facial expression relaxing the more we talked.

"Do you guys ever talk about . . . Bobby Lee?"

Her shoulders hunched and her chin tucked in. So much for loosening up. Too bad. I only had a week to figure this thing out, and I didn't have time to dink around.

"I'm sorry, Tabby. I didn't mean to hit a nerve," I said.

She looked at the floor. "That's okay."

I pushed harder. "I mean, I think about him a lot. Since you and Joe and Bobby Lee were so close when it happened, I just wondered."

Her eyes met mine, wariness and anger flaring behind them. "It wasn't my fault."

"Oh, God. I know that. And let's get something out in the open here. My mother knows that, too. She was just hurt and bewildered when she said that at the funeral. She's always felt bad about it."

Okay, so maybe I shouldn't have spoken for my mother. She had, after all, accused Tabby of killing her son. I remembered the day well. My mother had been a mess: a precisely coiffed, Southern-belle-with-perfect-manners mess. Not many people would have known, but when she lost it and yelled at Tabby in front of everyone, I hadn't been the least bit surprised.

The Watsons and the Atwoods hadn't spoken since.

But my attempt to explain Anna Belle's actions fell flat. Tabby made a "pffft" noise and looked away.

"I was pretty upset then, too," she said. "But you didn't hear me accusing your mother of being responsible for her son's death. And you know what? I dare say she was a lot more responsible than I ever could be, the way she judged everything he did, the way he had to live up to all of her crazy expectations."

The hair rose on the back of my neck as my daughterly pride came to Anna Belle's defense. I opened my mouth to protest.

Then I remembered the letter. Painful though it was, I had to admit Tabby wasn't entirely wrong. Bobby Lee had said he couldn't face my parents if they discovered what he'd done. Tabby either already knew that, or had instinctively figured it out. That part of the letter must have hurt Anna Belle a lot to read. Was it one of the reasons she insisted on keeping my father in the dark?

"Okay," I said. "Fair enough."

She looked surprised.

"Any chance we could get on the other side of the whole funeral thing?" I asked. "I'd really like to come back for that other class, learn more how to make cheese before I have to go back to Cadyville."

She considered me, chewing on her lower lip. "You should definitely come for the mold-ripened cheese class. Are you interested in knowing more about soft cheeses? Cultured milk products? That kind of thing?"

I couldn't keep the big smile from spreading across my face. "I'd love to know more."

"How long are you going to be here?"

"A week."

"There's only so much I can teach you in a week, but I can cover enough to give you a firm base."

"Really?"

"Sure. How 'bout you come by for two hours tomorrow morning, and we'll cover bacterial cultures. Then you can hit the mold-ripened cheese class on Wednesday with everyone else, and then come back for another two hours on Thursday to learn more about hard cheeses like Cheddar and Parmesan."

"Sounds good. How much do you charge for private lessons like that?"

She shrugged. It was a deliberately casual gesture. "Regular class fee."

Whatever that was. Anna Belle hadn't said how much she'd paid for the class I'd just taken, but I felt my head nodding in vigorous agreement. I had a feeling Tabby could use the money, plus I loved the idea of learning more about the ins and outs of cheese making

"Okay, then. We're set. I'll see you tomorrow." Finality in her tone.

Rats. Trust me to lose track of the reason I was really there. My hand crept into my bag, and I fingered the envelope that held Bobby Lee's letter. "I brought something to show you."

Curiosity flicked across her face as she looked at her watch. It was quickly replaced with alarm. "Oh, God. I'm sorry, Sophie Mae. I have to run."

Ack! "This won't take long," I said, desperation leaking out between the words. "It's important."

"I don't —"

"Please." Taking a deep breath, I reached into my bag and extracted the envelope. After a brief hesitation, I handed it to her.

Her eyes widened as she read the handwriting, and she shot me a bewildered look. "What is this?"

"It's a letter that was returned to my parents' house. According to the postmark, Bobby Lee sent it to you the day he died."

She blinked. "I don't understand. Your mom and dad have had it all this time?"

"It only came in the mail a week ago. I'm as baffled by that as you are."

She bent closer, eyes traveling over the writing on the envelope. Then she grimaced. "My mother."

"What?"

"This handwriting?" She pointed to the words *Return to sender.* "It's hers. She kept this from me." Bitterness laced her tone.

"Why would she do that? Didn't she like Bobby Lee?"

Her eyes met mine. "My folks were a little . . . overprotective. They thought Joe and your brother were bad influences at the time, but I think she probably sent this back because she didn't want me to be any more upset by Bobby Lee's death than I already was."

That actually made some sense.

Tabby removed the single sheet and unfolded it. I watched carefully as she read it. Tears shone in her eyes when she laid it down on the counter.

She blinked them dry and swallowed audibly. "I can't believe I didn't get to see this until now."

I felt a little sick to my stomach. This digging into the past was making a real mess, and a part of me wished I'd left everything alone. Too late though. I was up to my neck in it.

Barely breathing, I asked, "Tabby? What was my brother talking about in the note? What had he done?"

Her one-shouldered shrug was nonchalant. "Haven't got a clue." But her eyes slid off to the side when she said it.

"Sounds like something pretty major."

"We were teenagers. Everything was major."

"You know what I mean. He wrote that so you would know what he was talking about and no one else would." My hand crept out and took possession of the letter and envelope again.

Tabby watched me return it to my tote bag. "I can't help you. I'm sorry."

Can't or won't, I wondered.

But I couldn't let it go. "What about Joe? Do you think he'd know?"

Her lips pressed together, and her eyes seemed to search the air above my head. Then her gaze met mine. "I don't see how he could."

"Will he be home soon? I could wait."

She shook her head with a rueful twist to her mouth. "I have to go. I'm already late picking up my daughter from her riding lesson."

Quickly, she turned and opened the small refrigerator in the corner of the room. "Here — take this with you." She shoved a small plastic container at me. "It's piima-cultured butter. So you can get a taste of what we'll be doing tomorrow morning. Eleven o'clock work?"

"Um, sure."

She was already out the door, and I followed her to the parking lot. Lickety-split she jumped in a black jeep and drove away. A red pickup and older blue minivan were still in the parking lot. A metallic noise drifted down from the barn. Someone was still on the property.

Well, duh, Sophie Mae. A place like that was bound to take a lot of work. No doubt Joe and Tabby had a hired hand or two around to help. Slowly, I got into Dad's car and turned the key in the ignition. Hot air winged out of the vents as the air conditioner revved up. It magnified the manure smell tenfold, making me cough.

Was Tabby really in that much of a hurry, or was she trying to get away from me? I didn't know her well enough to tell. Still, she seemed game to give me another cheese-making lesson. Maybe she simply needed time to process this blast from the past.

At least I could still ask Joe about Bobby Lee's note tomorrow, even if Tabby didn't exactly encourage me. If anyone besides Tabby knew what Bobby Lee had been up to before he died, it was his erstwhile best friend.

Plus, Meghan would be thrilled if I learned how to make cheese. There was a dairy near Cadyville where we could get quality milk.

And Erin would — well, I didn't know. It was hard to tell with her anymore.

I circled the tiny parking lot and turned onto the dirt driveway. Dad's Subaru kicked up a cloud of dust that followed me out to the county road.

SEVEN

The front door was unlocked when I got home, but no one seemed to be around. I'd just settled at the kitchen table with a big fat sandwich — sourdough piled with shaved turkey, Muenster, tomato, cucumber, and avocado, all dripping with spicy chipotle mayonnaise — when I heard a sound downstairs. Curious, I abandoned my sandwich and slipped down to the basement, expecting to find Kitty Wampus getting into something yet again. Abyssinians were infamous for being able to open doors and drawers, and his reputation was worse than most.

Instead, I found my father had turned into a pretzel.

"What on earth?" I walked into the rec room and flopped onto the old brown sofa. Many an hour of my youth had been spent lounging there, watching television or gabbing for hours with my friends. It still smelled faintly of our old black lab, long gone to his happy hunting grounds.

Slowly Dad returned to a recognizably human shape. He smiled at me. "Scorpion pose." Standing now, he raised his arms straight up and bent at the waist, touching his palms to the floor. "Intense forward bend. Try it."

I shook my head. "Huh uh. My back hurts just watching you."

Unfolding again, he rolled his shoulders back and took a deep, audible breath. "Okay."

"Um, Dad?"

"Yeah?"

"You all right?"

His gray shorts hung loosely on him, but he had always had a runner's physique. Or, more accurately, a bicyclist's physique. Pure ectomorph. His bare chest sprouted gray hair, but was defined by lean muscle.

He sat cross-legged on the floor. "I'm fine."

I chewed on my lip and considered him. "You seem different."

His head dipped forward. "Maybe."

"Are you taking any medication?"

His head tipped to the side.

"Tranquilizers?"

He laughed. "Is that what you're worried

73

about? No, nothing like that."

I drew my legs under me on the sofa. "High on life, huh."

"Sort of. You know how much I used to ride my bike?"

I nodded. "Sometimes for hours."

"Right. Well, it kept me sane. It really did. Then my knees started giving me fits, and I couldn't ride as hard as I liked. I was miserable. And by that I mean not only was I miserable, I was difficult to be around."

"I bet." I wasn't trying to be mean, but my dad was an intense guy. The bike riding had definitely bled off some of his energy, and I could only imagine how cranky he got after he had to cut back.

His lips twitched. "Right. Well, Anna Belle was worried. I think she was a little sick of putting up with me, too. She came up with the idea of trying yoga. I did, and it really helped. My knees are much stronger, and it turned out I loved it. As a result, I started looking into some other Eastern practices. Now, believe it or not, I meditate daily."

"I'm actually a little jealous. I've tried to meditate — guess I don't have the patience. The closest I get to that state of mind is when I'm spinning or doing something soothing and repetitive like wrapping soap."

"There's a lot to be said for that." He

74

hesitated, then, "I've been studying Buddhism lately, too."

"Really?" I laughed. No wonder Anna Belle had had that look on her face when she'd told me Dad was experimenting. "Doesn't that kind of go against the whole agnostic thing?"

"Less than you'd think. The meditation clears my mind, and what I've learned so far has given me a whole new perspective on life."

"And Anna Belle approves."

"She sees the results. I'm mellow as a cello and fit as a fiddle."

I rolled my eyes and stood up. "Well, that's good enough for me."

"You can come join me any time you want to, you know. I spend a couple hours a day down here rearranging my carcass or meditating."

"Thanks. I'll think about it." I turned to go.

"Did you find out anything about Bobby Lee's letter?"

I whirled back to face him. "You know about that?"

He smiled.

"Anna Belle didn't want me to tell you about it," I said. "For the record, I disagreed with her."

"It's okay. She's afraid I won't want her to pursue it, but I don't feel that way at all."

"So you know what the letter says?"

"I might have happened across it."

Did Dad know about the hidey holes in my mother's den? I couldn't quite bring myself to ask him. Instead, I leaned against the door frame. "So what do you think?"

He took a deep breath. "I think my son had some problems with depression. I think he had some problems with his girlfriend. I think he was searching for some big answers, and then I think he did something he was ashamed of. Something he thought his mother and I would condemn him for. I think it all got to be too much for him to handle."

My hand crept to my mouth, and I found myself looking at my father through a watery veil.

He continued, "I also think his sister, who takes after her investigative-journalist old man, is going to get to the bottom of what happened. I just hope in the end your mother will be able to move on from the self-imposed limbo she's been living in for the last eighteen years."

I blinked, and felt wetness splash down my cheek. I swiped at it with the back of my hand. "I'll do my best. I promise."

His eyes radiated warmth. "Of course you will, kiddo. That's all she wants. And if there isn't an answer, there isn't an answer. That's okay, too." He closed his eyes, and I got the impression I'd been dismissed.

Softly, I left the room.

There was an answer. I just knew it. And I'd find it.

Kitty Wampus was nowhere in sight when I returned to the kitchen, but he'd eaten all the turkey and cheese out of my beautiful sandwich and dragged the rest halfway across the table. No doubt he'd beelined out the cat door and was dozing under the lilacs in the backyard, fat and happy. My stomach growled as I surveyed the mess.

"Stupid beast," I muttered, gathering what was left of my lunch and dumping it in the garbage. "Evil creature. I hope you get heartburn from that spicy mayonnaise."

A sense of restlessness joined my hunger. The remainder of the afternoon stretched ahead; I might as well make use of it. I still had the letter, and plenty of questions to go with it.

Time to find the people who could give me some answers — and maybe hit a drive-through on the way. A quick look at the phone book gave me the information I needed.

First stop: a guacamole cheeseburger. I scarfed it down as I drove, licking the sauce oozing out around the edges before it could splatter onto my lap.

I didn't know whether the Atwoods were retired or not, but it seemed worth taking the chance that one or both of them would be home. I knew the general area where they lived, a few miles northwest of town, near the tiny town of Bellevue. The Subaru turned that direction almost of its own volition.

As I drove and chewed, I formulated what to say.

EIGHT

Tabby's parents lived in a pale blue, ranch-style home set near County Road 54E. Two llamas peered out from the other side of a wire fence, apparently companions to the old sway-backed horse in the far corner that turned his head to watch my progress down their driveway. The yard was a riot of bright zinnias and purple coneflowers, punctuated by explosions of indigo Russian sage. I got out of the car and inhaled the heat, blinking in the bright sunlight.

An enormous gray cat ambled around the corner. It walked right up and rubbed against my bare leg. I reached down to scritch it behind the ears and wild rumbling erupted deep in its chest.

"Mrow!"

"Mrow to you, too," I murmured, then stood and braced myself for what I was about to do.

Celeste Atwood opened the door almost

immediately, so I suspected she'd heard me get out of the car and had watched from behind the gauzy curtains as the cat greeted me. She was sun-faded and weary-looking. Thick glasses with tortoise-shell frames magnified her ash-brown eyes. A yellow camp shirt and white slacks hung on her thin frame. Her smile was small, uncertain.

"Hi. Are you Celeste?"

"I sure am."

"My name is Sophie Mae Reynolds. I know your daughter, Tabby."

She waited, an expectant look on her face.

"Could I ask you a few questions?"

Puzzlement took over. "What kind of questions?"

I hesitated, then took the plunge. "I'm Bobby Lee Watson's sister. My family recently came into some information about what happened back . . . when he . . ." I didn't finish.

Alertness sparked in her gaze, mingled with alarm. For a long moment neither of us spoke, the air between us thick with the past. Then she pushed open the old screen door with a creak.

"Come in."

Inside, ostriches were everywhere. *Everywhere.* Glass ones, ceramic ones, stuffed, stone, carved, big, little, anatomically accurate, fantastical, green, pink, orange — every color of the rainbow and then some. They covered every surface, sat on the sofa and chairs, and paintings of long-necked birds populated the walls.

"You must like ostriches," I said. Nothing like stating the obvious, Sophie Mae.

"I have a fresh pot of coffee in the kitchen."

I followed her into a bright yellow-and-orange kitchen. A floor fan in the corner whirred back and forth. The dish towel had an ostrich on it. The napkin holder was a carved wooden ostrich. Celeste poured hot coffee into mugs with purple ostriches sporting cowboy hats and lariats on them.

"Thanks." I raised the mug. The balloon coming out of the bird's mouth read, "Slow up there, Pardner!"

Celeste got right to the point. "What do you want?"

I was so distracted by the total ostrich weirdness that it took me a moment to regroup. With an effort, I turned my attention to the matter I'd come to ask her about.

"I don't suppose your husband is around," I said. It made more sense to talk to both of them at the same time if possible.

"He's dead."

Oh, God. "I'm sorry, I didn't know."

81

"That's okay. It was five years ago. Heart attack."

"I'm sorry," I said again, and wanted to kick myself. As a woman living alone she probably kept his name on the phone book entry as a precaution.

She shrugged. "It happens."

I barreled on. "Do you remember what happened eighteen years ago?"

She looked at me like I was crazy. "Of course I remember."

"Sorry," I said again. Ack! "Anyway, a funny thing happened a couple of weeks ago."

"Funny?"

"Well, not funny like ha-ha. More like odd. My mother received a letter. Or rather a letter was returned to the house. It was from Bobby Lee."

She looked at me like I was crazy again. "I don't understand."

"Bobby Lee wrote a letter before he died. He sent it to Tabby, but it came back to our house as undeliverable mail — eighteen years later."

She licked her lips.

"Someone wrote *Return to sender* on it." I pulled the envelope out of my bag. "See?"

Celeste got up abruptly and retrieved the coffeepot. Some of the dark liquid splashed onto the kitchen table as she topped off our ostrich mugs.

"Well, isn't that strange." She wouldn't look at me. "What does this mystery letter say?"

"It refers to something that happened, something Bobby Lee was involved in. He seemed to assume Tabby knew about it, too, though I don't know whether she was personally involved or not."

Talking about what my brother had assumed brought him into the present in a new and disconcerting way.

Celeste returned the coffeepot to the burner and sat down again. She ran her fingertips over a knothole in the pine table-top. "That doesn't sound very specific."

"It's not. That's one reason why I'm here. Do you have any idea what he might have been talking about?"

Meeting my eyes, she shook her head.

"Tabby never said anything to you at the time?"

Another shake of the head. "We went through a bad patch, her and me, when she was a teenager. She wouldn't talk to me about your brother — when he was alive, either."

Ah, mothers and daughters.

"All's I know is Tabby was taking classes

83

at NCU — wanted to be a vet — and he'd taken a year off before going to college. I think it might have been a problem for them."

Hmm. Tabby hadn't mentioned that. "Were they fighting?" I asked, remembering Dad said something in the basement earlier about how Bobby Lee was having problems with his girlfriend.

Celeste's shoulders rose then slumped. "I guess. I heard her yelling on the phone a couple of times. Pretty sure she was talking to Bobby Lee. Could've been one of the other boys, though. There were three or four of them head over heels for that girl. The phone rang off the hook."

"But she was only dating Bobby Lee, right?"

"Oh, yes. The others were just her friends. You know . . ." she said, looking into a distance that wasn't there.

"Yes?" I prompted.

"There was another death around then. Someone Tabby's age. Accident. Not anyone I knew. No one I thought Tabby knew." She glanced at me and shrugged.

"What happened?"

She shook her head. "I don't remember now. Something about the cold weather. It was a long time ago."

84

Another death. The town of Spring Creek wasn't that large. More than likely at least one of the Tabby/Joe/Bobby Lee trio had known him. Her?

"The accident you mentioned — was it a boy or a girl?" I asked.

"Boy. No, girl. I don't remember. Sorry. I shouldn't have mentioned it." Tabby's mother took another swallow of coffee. The steam fogged her glasses. The fan in the corner barely stirred the air.

Was she being deliberately unhelpful? I couldn't tell.

"I have one more question," I said.

Resignation twisted the corner of her mouth. "Okay."

I paused, searching for the right words. "Did you already know Bobby Lee sent Tabby a letter?"

"No." The word came quickly.

Too quickly.

I cocked my head to one side. "Really?"

"I told you. Tabby didn't confide in me."

Hmmm. I pushed the envelope across the table. My brother's loopy scrawl affected me like a painful tooth. It hurt to look at it, but I couldn't seem to stop. But now I pointed to the *Return to sender* notation. "This doesn't look like a teenaged girl's writing. It looks like an adult's."

She stared at it for a long moment, then suddenly blinked and leaned toward me. "I don't know anything about that letter. Sorry."

"Tabby told me it's your handwriting."

Her eyes flicked back to the words, and the tip of her tongue worked against her lip.

"Why did you send the letter back?" I asked.

Celeste exhaled. "I just did, okay? She was already a mess. There wasn't anything Bobby Lee had to say that Tabitha needed to see right then." She rose to her feet. "Now, I'm sorry, but I gotta get to work over to the liquor store. If I'm late they'll dock me."

Slowly I pushed back from the table. She led me to the front door and opened it with a decisive gesture.

"One more thing," I said.

Big sigh. "What?"

"When did you send it back?"

She looked confused. "What do you mean when? When I got it."

"You didn't keep it for a while?" Like eighteen years. "Maybe it took some time to decide to return it?"

There came the look doubting my sanity again. "No. I knew right away she shouldn't see it."

And yet, Celeste hadn't destroyed it. Would I have, under the same circumstances?

"Thanks for your help," I said, utterly baffled.

"Sure." The door shut in my face, and the cat immediately wrapped itself around my ankles as I turned away. I stumbled and almost fell.

"Mrow."

I glanced back at Celeste Atwood's closed front door, then down at the tabby. "You've got that right."

Where the heck had that letter been all this time?

It would be an hour or so before everyone gathered at the house again. Enough time to check out some old newspaper stories.

The Spring Creek Public Library was near Old Town Square, surrounded by older homes and streets lined with well-established trees. Along with a small museum and expansive, park-like area complete with playground and picnic benches, it took up an entire city block. Out front, three apparently homeless men lounged on sunny benches, looking as content as the cat in Celeste Atwood's driveway earlier.

I found the reference desk upstairs and

asked for help in tracking down newsworthy events from eighteen years ago. Soon I was seated in front of a microfilm machine, trolling through copies of the Spring Creek *Courier* starting two weeks before Bobby Lee sent the letter.

By the time half an hour had passed, my eyes were burning from scanning headlines on the screen. It had been a pretty boring period. I bypassed sports and national news, focusing on local stories that might have had an impact on Bobby Lee and his friends. Not much caught my attention, and I had to wonder if I was missing something important. I told myself it was just a first pass; the archives would still be here if I needed to come back and spend more time.

At the end of an hour I'd read sixteen days' worth of newspapers from the middle of November and culled four possible events that fit Celeste Atwood's vague description, though only two of them actually ended in death. After all that reading, the four items that piqued my interest happened within a twenty-four-hour period.

A young woman had fallen in a nearly frozen river east of town. The owner of the property had rescued her and driven her into town, but she died of hypothermia on the way.

A sixteen-year-old girl had been attacked by a mountain lion in the Poudre Canyon, but survived when her uncle threw a rock at the big cat and hit it on the head. From what I could tell, he was a bit of a local celebrity for about a week, but the girl was badly mauled and required plastic surgery.

A young man riding a bicycle in the early morning hours had been hit by a vehicle which had then sped off without stopping. No one had found him for an hour, by which time he was half frozen and could barely talk. He was in the hospital for two days before succumbing to his injuries.

And a woman had severely beaten another young man who'd sneaked into her bedroom and tried to steal her underwear. She was quoted as saying, "They were my granny pants, too! I just don't get some people." He'd required hospitalization, but survived to raid panties another day.

Hurrying, I printed out copies of the articles, thanked the reference librarian for her help, and hightailed it out to the Subaru. Unfortunately, I'd forgotten to put the foldout shade in the front window, so it was broiling inside. Cursing, I started the engine and gingerly turned the burning steering wheel toward home with my fingertips.

NINE

My mother was on me like white on rice the second I walked through the door. Looking over her shoulder toward the kitchen table where Meghan and Erin sat talking and eating cookies, she hissed, "I have to talk to you," and strode toward her den. Bewildered, I followed behind. As soon as I cleared the threshold, she clicked the door shut behind me.

"Good Lord, Anna Belle, what's wrong?"

She turned to face me, and alarm trilled through me at the look on her face. I'd rarely seen her so upset.

"It's gone."

"What?"

"Bobby Lee's letter. It's *gone.*"

Uh oh.

"Someone *took* it, Sophie Mae." Her voice shook.

Oh, God. There was just no way out of this. My lips pulled back in an apologetic grimace. "It's okay. I have it."

She stared at me.

"It's safe," I reached into my tote bag and handed it to her. "See?"

Taking it, she gazed down at the envelope for a moment. "But . . ." Her eyes met mine. "How did . . . ?"

"I needed to show it to Tabby."

Anger flared behind her eyes as she assimilated what I'd said. "You took it out of the house? Without even asking me?"

I nodded. "You'd already left. I needed to be able to show her, to see if she'd tell me what it meant."

She walked to the bookshelf. Turned. "And how exactly did you know where to find it?"

My inner child whimpered, but I squared my shoulders and said, "I followed a hunch." I shrugged. "Turned out I was right."

Surprise warred with the anger on her face. Then they gave way to an expression of amused admiration.

Now I was confused.

Her lips quirked up in a half grin.

"What's so funny?"

"If only you could see your face. You look like you did when you were eight years old, and I caught you sitting on the floor of your closet eating a whole bag of Oreos."

Great. "Well, I'm glad you're not upset."

Her eyes hardened. "Oh, I'm upset all right. You had no right to come into my private space and snoop around. I didn't raise you that way. What were you thinking?"

But her earlier smile mitigated her current scolding, and I answered truthfully. "I told you. I needed that letter to show Tabby. Do you or do you not want me to get to the bottom of what happened eighteen years ago?"

Her lips pressed into a thin line. A long moment of silence as she weighed how to respond. Then, "You could have called me, asked where the letter was, told me you wanted to take it."

I bowed my head. "You're right. I could have called." Old habits had dictated my actions. "I should have."

"And I don't suppose it occurred to you to take a copy of the letter, instead of the original?" She nodded toward the combination printer/copier in the corner behind her desk.

"Er," I said, feeling more chastened by the moment.

She stepped over to the machine, opened it, and placed the letter and envelope on the glass surface. As the copies printed, I said, "I took it to the post office, too. To ask about how it could have taken so long to come back."

"I want to hear everything. Here." She handed me copies of the note and the envelope.

We heard the front door close, and my father's voice filtered through to the den. He sounded enthusiastic about something.

Anna Belle looked at me expectantly.

I turned and opened the door. "Come on. Let's join the others."

Behind me, she made a small sound of protest, but had no choice but to follow me to the kitchen.

"This is so incredibly yummy," Meghan said, taking another bite of bread and butter.

"Who knew something so mundane could be so tasty?" my mother added, licking her lips.

We sat around the table, sampling the cultured butter Tabby had given me. I'd picked up a loaf of rustic ciabatta at the Spring Creek Bakery on the way home. Dad was at the counter, dressing the trout a friend had given him with lemon and dill. That's what he'd been so excited about:

scoring the fresh fish. Erin had gone upstairs to change out of her hiking clothes. Bright sunburn swooped across Meghan's perky little nose, and her freckles stood out in stark relief. Anna Belle had just finished lecturing her on the strength of the sun at high altitude and broken off a piece of the aloe vera plant on the window sill for my friend to rub on her burn.

"So did you make this?" Meghan asked me now.

"No. Tabby did, but tomorrow I'll learn how."

"You know, Europeans regularly culture their butter." There was a tang of self-satisfaction in Dad's voice.

"And we don't in America? Then where does cultured buttermilk come from?" Meghan asked.

"In most cases, the buttermilk itself is cultured, rather than the cream before it's churned into butter."

Erin entered the kitchen and plopped down on a chair. "You *churned* butter today? God, Sophie Mae. Don't you think this whole pioneer woman thing is getting out of control?"

"Actually, I didn't. Maybe tomorrow, though I'd be surprised if we use a churn. More likely a food processor. Not exactly like sitting on the front porch working a dasher."

"What's a dasher?"

"The handle thingie that you move up and down in a traditional butter churn."

"See what I mean?" she said. "You know what a dasher is. Do you know how weird that is?"

"Hey!" I protested.

She shook her head. "I'm going down to that park I saw at the end of the block. See if I can find someone normal to hang out with." She stood.

"Ahem," Meghan said.

Erin paused. "I mean, is it okay if I go down to that park?"

Meghan hesitated, then nodded. "Okay. But be back in an hour."

Erin shrugged. "Whatever."

Meghan watched her go, and then we heard the front door open and close. She turned back to us with a frustrated expression. "I don't know what's gotten into her."

Anna Belle laughed. "Years. And there will only be more. Brace yourself."

"Oh, come on. I wasn't that bad, was I?" I asked.

"You never got into any serious trouble, but boy did you have some attitude on you when you were growing up."

Meghan snorted. "Like that's changed."

I made a face at her, then looked at Anna Belle. "Gee, I wonder where I would have learned attitude."

A smile flitted across my father's face. "It sounds like you got a chance to do a little extra credit work at the dairy. How is Tabby?"

"She seems happy. Has a fifteen-year-old daughter."

Meghan looked sympathetic.

"And she's going to give me private classes on cheese making, so I'll be at the dairy for a while every day. And day after tomorrow, I'm going to take the mold-ripened cheese class."

"Can I come?" Meghan asked.

"I don't see why not. Tabby said it hardly ever fills up."

Her eyes twinkled. "Excellent."

"I showed her Bobby Lee's letter."

My mother's eyes widened in alarm, flicking sideways to my dad.

"It's okay," I said to her. "He already knows about the letter."

She blinked, then whirled around. "You do?"

His lips twitched. "Uh huh."

She looked pointedly at me.

"What? I didn't tell him. He already knew

96

before we got here."

Her attention returned to him. "Calvin! How long have you known? How did you find out? Why didn't you say something?"

"Pick one," he said.

"One what?"

"Question." His smile widened.

"But . . . how — oh, never mind." Anna Belle scowled at us both. I couldn't blame her. By now she must suspect she didn't have any secrets left. I wondered whether Dad had read the old high school love letters. Even I hadn't stepped over the line that far.

Dad settled at the table with us. "Tell us what you found out, Sophie Mae."

So I did, including my visits to the post office, Celeste Atwood's house, and the library, and what I had discovered.

Which, after I'd gone over everything, wasn't much. "So I spent most of my day trying to track down information and came up with a big fat zero. Sorry."

Dad shook his head. "That's not true. You found out Tabby's mother returned the letter and Tabby knew nothing about it. And you found out Tabby herself either doesn't know what Bobby Lee meant, or won't tell you. Believe it or not, that's progress."

"The mystery of how that letter appeared

out of nowhere has only deepened, though," I said.

Anna Belle drummed her fingernails on the table, looking out the window.

"What are you thinking?" I asked.

Her attention came back to us. "You said you printed out the newspaper articles you found at the library?"

I got up and removed the pages from my bag. "Right here."

She held out her hand. "Let us take a look at them. Maybe we can help."

Handing her the printouts, I said, "I hope so. I need all the help I can get."

My mother stood. "I'll see what I can do. And then, after dinner?"

I waited.

She smiled. "We can go over the progress I made on your wedding plans while you were gone today."

"What? Anna Belle!"

She left the room, and I turned to Dad and Meghan. "Did you hear that? She's planning my wedding without me."

Meghan laughed. "There are people who would pay for that service, and here you are, getting it for free. Now, what kind of cheese did you make today?"

"Mozzarella," I grumbled.

"Really? Can we do it at home?"

I launched into a detailed description of the process while my housemate listened with interest, my mother's wedding-related antics hovering in the back of my mind.

TEN

Not until after a dinner of grilled trout, green beans, and caprese salad — made with tomatoes and basil from Anna Belle's kitchen garden and the tennis-ball-sized round of fresh mozzarella I'd brought home from class — did I have a chance to follow up with my mother regarding my wedding.

But first I stopped by my old bedroom to say goodnight to Erin. I found her sitting in bed, Kitty Wampus draped across her legs. The beast cracked one eye when I came into the room, then gave a languid stretch and returned to full slumber.

Erin barely glanced up from her Philip Pullman novel when I sat on the edge of the bed.

"Hey," I said.

"Hey," she mumbled.

"I bet you miss Brodie, huh." Her corgi was staying with our neighbor, Mrs. Gray, while we were gone.

She shrugged. "I guess."

That was weird. She loved that dog.

"Erin."

She looked up at me from under her eyebrows without raising her head.

"Are you mad at me? Did I do something?"

"No."

"Then why are you acting like this?"

Big sigh from Erin. "Acting like what?"

"Well, like you're mad at me."

Yet another shrug. I felt like putting her in a straitjacket.

I leaned over and kissed her on the cheek. "Listen — when you want to tell me, I'll be here to listen. Okay?"

Our eyes met for a few moments. Raw vulnerability shone from hers. "I'm sorry I haven't been very nice."

"Can you tell me what's going on?"

She blinked and shook her head. "Nothing."

"Erin —"

"Can I read now?" She returned to her book, effectively ignoring me.

I leaned back and watched her for a few moments. Yes, something was definitely up. It almost made me feel better to know that, because it meant that this bright and funny girl had not somehow morphed into a rude pre-teen. This wasn't about attitude, or at least not only about attitude.

She'd tell me or Meghan when she was ready. But she'd better be ready soon, because I was getting tired of being treated like an enemy.

As I'd expected, Anna Belle was working at her desk. I cleared a pile of books off one end of an old carved bench and sat down, leaning my back against the wall.

"What are you working on?" I asked.

She pushed the pile of papers aside. "Finals. Marketing 101. Summer course."

I took the bull by the horns. "You mentioned something earlier about wedding details?" There: my voice was calm, my words carefully chosen to sidestep conflict.

She dropped her red pen on the desk blotter and leaned back in her chair with a satisfied look on her face. "Not much. Just checked on the schedule of a certain judge who lives near that perfect venue we've talked about. Oh, and I talked to a friend of mine who's a florist, and she had some very nice suggestions for arrangements." Suddenly she was gushing. "What do you think of gerbera daisies? Have you decided on your colors? And are you planning to wear white? I know it's not strictly traditional for second weddings, but more and more people are doing it, you know. It's perfectly acceptable."

She launched to her feet and began pacing behind the desk while I looked on, slack-jawed. "We really have to get the invitations put together first. Good Lord, Sophie Mae, you haven't left much time for planning, now have you? I'll tell you what: Get me a guest list by tomorrow, and I'll get right to work on ordering the invitations."

"Stop," I said.

"At least we won't have any problem booking the Horseshoe Guest Ranch, given it belongs to your future in-laws, but —"

"Stop."

This time she stopped. Stared at me. "Now, you weren't serious about not having a real wedding, were you?"

"Absolutely. Positively. Is there any other word I can use to get that through your head?"

Her excitement and high energy disappeared, as if all the air had been released from her balloon. "I talked to Cassie Ambrose, you know. She's thrilled at the idea of you and Barr getting married at their place."

I sighed. Barr's family owned a guest ranch a few hours north, in Wyoming. For weeks now Anna Belle had lobbied for us to get married in the main lodge. I'd seen pictures of the ranch on their website and had to admit it looked beautiful. I had yet to meet any of Barr's family — we hadn't even been dating for a year before getting engaged, and we hadn't had a chance to make it back to Wyoming during that time. However, I frequently spoke with his mother, Cassie, on the phone, and I loved her to death.

No, the sticking point with getting married at the Ambrose's Horseshoe Ranch wasn't the facilities or Barr's family. It was his brother Randall's girlfriend who had worked at the ranch for years.

Who happened to be Barr's ex-wife.

And looked freakishly like me.

We'd had our difficulties before — one encounter involved a handgun — and I just couldn't imagine having to deal with Hannah on my wedding day. Still, I didn't say anything to Anna Belle about that. For one thing I didn't think she'd be all that sympathetic, and for another, I felt like a big baby.

I let out a slow, deep breath. "I'll talk to Barr about it."

Her eyes brightened at that and the corners of her mouth turned up. "Excellent. Now, about those gerberas . . ."

■ ■ ■ ■

"So that's all I know so far," I said. After Barr updated me on the house renovation, I'd filled him in on my day.

There was a pause on the other end of the line, and then he said, "Are you sure you want to pursue this thing?"

"The cheese making?"

"No," he said. "Not the cheese making."

Okay, so I was being deliberately obtuse. His question had taken me off guard, though. I sighed. "I want to know why Bobby Lee did it, really I do. It's just . . . there's something almost obscene about digging around in his life, trying to unearth his secrets." If not obscene, then at least selfish.

But what Bobby Lee had done had been selfish, too.

"Do me a favor, okay? Don't do this only for your mother," Barr said.

"Of course not. Believe me, I'm doing it for myself. Did I ever tell you that I tried to find out what happened back then? I talked to his friends, searched his room from top to bottom, checked out the places he secretly stashed things — all trying to figure out why he'd done it."

"I didn't know that."

"I've always wondered, Barr. I wasn't very good at finding things out then. But this time maybe I'll be able to provide some closure — for myself and for my parents." Even I could hear the bouncy note I'd injected into my voice. It sounded totally fake.

"I'm afraid you'll find out things you don't want to know," Barr said.

"I understand that, and you might be right. But I still have to do this. No way I'm going to stop now. There's a story behind what happened, and I couldn't live with myself if I didn't track down what it is."

He was silent for a few moments. "Okay. I won't try to stop you. In fact, I'm proud of you. If anyone can get at that story, you can. Be careful, though."

A warm glow passed through me. "I miss you."

"I miss you, too."

"Are you going to be able to come out here? Meet my folks and all?" I wanted him there by my side.

"Day after tomorrow, darlin'. Wednesday. Everything's set up with Robin and Sergeant Zahn." Robin Lane was the other Cadyville Police detective. "But I can only stay for a few days before I'm due back. Besides, I

106

want to keep an eye on the construction at the house."

"Oh, Barr, that's great! I mean, I wish it could be for longer, but I'll take what I can get." I couldn't keep the excitement out of my voice.

"I thought everything was going well."

"It is. I still want you here. I need all the allies I can get. Besides, I happen to like you."

"Ah. Well, back atcha. Good thing we're getting married, eh? And it sure sounds like you're making great inroads on the wedding plans."

"Umm. Who have you been talking to?"

"My mother, of course."

"Who's been talking to my mother," I said.

"Also, of course."

"Barr?"

"Yeah . . ."

"Do you want to get married at your family's ranch?"

"Ah," he said.

"Ah, what?"

"Hannah."

"Hannah," I confirmed.

"Is she a deal breaker?" he asked.

I considered. "We'd talked about simply going to the courthouse in Washington and keeping things easy. Now it sounds like you'd really prefer to get married in Wyoming."

A few moments passed before he said, "I'd like to, but I won't insist."

That gave me pause. It was one thing to blow off my mother or his mother, but not Barr. He was doing an awful lot for me, selling his house and moving in with Meghan and Erin and me. The least I could do was agree to have our wedding on the ranch where he'd grown up.

Ex-wife or no ex-wife.

I'd just have to buck up and do it. "Okay, then. It's a deal. I can handle Miss Hannah, don't you worry."

"You sure? I'll talk to my brother. And to Hannah, if you'd like."

Yeah, because that had worked so well in the past. Ha.

"That's okay," I said. "It'll be fine."

We progressed on to silly sweet nothings for a while, then said goodnight.

On my way to bed, I stopped by my old bedroom again. This time I found Meghan in bed reading one of Dad's cookbooks. Beside her, Erin snored softly. Her mouth was slightly open, and Kitty Wampus had moved up to curl inside her arm.

I smiled. "The altitude takes it out of you for the first few days you're here."

"So does hiking up a mountain," Meghan said. "I'm about to nod off myself." She took off her half-glasses. "Any idea why this child of mine is so grumpy all of a sudden?"

I shook my head. "Hormones?"

"I don't think so. Her behavior is so out of the blue. She's always been such a good kid."

Sitting on the edge of the bed, I gave Meghan a hug. "She still is. Don't worry. It'll be okay."

"I'll see if I can get her to open up when we go up to Estes Park tomorrow. What will you do while we're gone?"

"Remember? I'm going over to Tabby's to learn more about milk cultures."

She squinted at me. "And? Besides following up on this new obsession with all things dairy?"

"Naturally I'll try to talk to Joe. See what he has to say." I shook my head. "I still can't get over that letter showing up after eighteen years."

"Yeah. Pretty weird, huh."

"Convenient, even."

"Hmmm. For whom?"

"That's a very good question."

"Any ideas?"

"Not yet. I'll see you in the morning. When are you leaving for Estes?"

"Right after breakfast."

"It's beautiful up there. You're going to love it. Maybe you'll even get to hear Flora's ghost play the piano in the Stanley Hotel."

Meghan grimaced at the mention of one of the many ghosts said to haunt the stately and historic hotel. "No wonder it inspired *The Shining*."

"Oh, c'mon. It's not like you're going to stay the night," I said. "That's when they're all supposed to come out and play."

She yawned. "Erin wanted to, but I nixed that idea."

"Spoil sport."

"Of course. But I want to get back a little early. Kelly's flying into Denver tomorrow afternoon. Your mother said he could stay here." She tossed that out casually, but couldn't keep the note of joy out of her voice.

"That's great! And Barr just told me he's flying in on Wednesday." I gave her another hug. "You'd better get some rest. Sleep tight." It would be a crowded house for a few days, but we'd manage.

I left her to her book and went down the hallway. After climbing into bed, I wheeled the dial on the clock radio to NPR and cracked open a book on meditation Dad had recommended. But I found myself distracted over and over again, my gaze drifting from the page to wander around the room.

Last night Anna Belle's redecoration had been all I could see. Tired and feeling a little bamboozled, I'd tumbled into slumber with only fleeting thoughts of Bobby Lee.

Perhaps it was the earlier talk of ghosts and haunting. Perhaps I just wasn't as tired tonight. Or maybe talking about him with his old girlfriend had brought my brother not only to the foreground of my mind, but right into the room with me.

"Bobby Lee?" I whispered.

ELEVEN

The only response was a mild breeze rustling the lilac bush outside my open window. Well, of course that was the only response. What was I, ten? Still, I found myself closing my eyes and listening carefully to the leaves muttering against each other. They began to tell stories, and I saw Bobby Lee walking down a dirt road. He was holding hands with a girl, and she was holding hands with another boy, and he . . .

The knock on the door sent me a foot into the air. Uninvited, my mother entered the room to find me wide-eyed, palm pressed to my chest where my heart was trying to hammer its way right through my ribs, thankyouverymuch.

"What's the matter with you?" she asked.

"Nothing."

"Nothing, my foot. You look like you've seen a ghost."

I swallowed. "Must have fallen asleep

reading. You startled me."

She held me in her gaze for a few more seconds, then seemed to accept my explanation. "I wanted to say good night before going to bed. I'll take a look at those newspaper articles before I go to sleep." She turned back to the door.

"Good night, Anna Belle," I said.

She paused. Spoke without turning around. "And thank you. I wanted to say thank you."

"I haven't done anything yet."

Now she threw a look over her shoulder. "Yes. You have. You've decided to help me find out what happened."

"I'm doing it for me, too, you know. And Dad."

She hesitated. "I know. Good night."

" 'Night."

But the door was already closing behind her.

I got up and shut the closet door before turning off the light. As a kid I'd never believed in monsters under the bed; the closet, though, that was a different thing. And being back in the house I'd grown up in always made me regress in new and creative ways. I could hardly wait to see what other aberrant behavior from my youth would surface in the next few days.

Bleah.

Instead of listening to the leaves tell more stories, I found myself drifting off while thinking of Barr. Marrying Barr. A life with Barr.

I slept like a baby.

The smell of pancakes on the stove teased me awake. As I hurriedly threw on shorts and T-shirt, I envisioned my dad's summer breakfast specialty: raspberry-studded buttermilk pancakes doused with thick maple syrup. Sure enough, when I hit the kitchen the first thing I saw was Erin tucking in to just that.

She looked up at me with cheeks stuffed like a chipmunk.

I laughed and sat down. "Pretty good stuff, huh Bug?"

Nodding emphatically, she reached for her fork again.

"Slow down." Meghan's tone was mild as she turned a page of the *Denver Post.* She had donned a white cotton skirt and blood-red tank for their day out. Her sandals matched the tank top.

"Morning," I said to my parents, bustling around the stove together. As I watched, they bumped hips and smiled at each other. I blinked in surprise and then couldn't help grinning.

"Good morning, dear." Anna Belle set a cup of steaming coffee in front of me. Dad, wearing a fuchsia-and-orange Hawaiian shirt, followed right behind with a plate of pancakes.

Tearing my gaze from the jarring color combination, I leaned forward to take a big whiff. Tried not to moan. "Oh, man. I've missed these."

"Good," he said.

I looked up at him in surprise.

"You should always miss something. It's good for you."

"Some of your Buddhist philosophy?"

"Nah. Just a plain old Calvinism."

Smiling, I unfolded my napkin and laid it across my lap. Dad had always couched his rules for living as "Calvinisms." I hadn't heard any new ones in a while, though.

Pancakes packed into my belly, Meghan and Erin sent on their merry way to spend the day in Estes Park, Anna Belle off to the University for a faculty meeting, and Dad in the basement twisting his way through a yoga workout, I settled down at my laptop. My Winding Road e-mail inbox overflowed with requests, orders, and questions. Two hours later I'd dealt with the majority of them, called Cyan to talk about what she should work on for the next couple of days, and enlisted her sister's help with a particularly large wholesale order for lip balms and bath salts which had to be packed up and sent out by the end of the week.

It was comforting to know I could leave town for a few days and, between working remotely on the computer and having reliable helpers, Winding Road Bath Products would continue with business as usual. It was with a feeling of accomplishment that I poured another cup of coffee and went out to look at the kitchen garden. Anna Belle had landscaped and planted it for aesthetics as well as edibility, interspersing herbs and flowers with the vegetables to add texture and repel pests. Basil and calendula peeked out from beneath heavy heirloom tomato vines and purple pole beans climbed a trellis behind bright red, yellow, and orange peppers. Purple, yellow, and red potatoes were hilled within small retaining walls built of red flagstone. Dark red nasturtiums tumbled over the tops of the walls, spilling down among the feet of cucumber plants tied to a teepee of bamboo poles. A border of spiky onions and blue-and-white pansies marched around the whole garden and an eggplant here, a trio of leeks there, frilly kale snugged up to a big-leaved red cabbage

— all added to the effect of an ornamental perennial bed.

Bobby Lee had always loved to work in the vegetable garden with Anna Belle.

I longed to dig my hands into the soil, to gather some of the harvest for dinner, or to simply sit on the ancient wooden chaise lounge and listen to the buzzing of the bees, but a glance at my watch made me drain my cup and move back toward the house. I only had time for a quick shower before driving out to the dairy for my next lesson.

All clean and shiny, my hair fluffed into some semblance of order, and slathered with sunscreen, I donned a gray skort and peach-colored T-shirt, slipped into my most comfortable pair of sandals, grabbed my tote bag, yelled goodbye to Dad in the basement and ran out the door. Anticipation itched under my skin as I started the Subaru and automatically flipped on the air-conditioning. In less than half an hour I'd be showing Joe Bines the copy of Bobby Lee's letter.

Maybe, just maybe, I'd learn the truth at last.

But then Barr's words of warning came back to me as I made the twenty-minute drive to the T&J Dairy. What the heck was I doing? Who knew why anyone committed suicide? Maybe we'd never know. And if I did uncover the reason Bobby Lee did what he did, would it change anything? What if I were churning the waters needlessly, muddying what little peace time had granted us all?

I tried to imagine turning around and going back home, dropping the whole thing. But I couldn't.

I just couldn't.

The Subaru pulled a plume of road dust behind it as I navigated the lengthy gravel drive leading into the dairy. A milk delivery truck with their logo — a stylized intertwining of Tabby and Joe's first initials — dominated one corner of the small parking lot, next to the square outbuilding where Tabby had held class the day before. A battered red truck and the Jeep Tabby had driven the day before were parked on either side of it. No milk deliveries this morning, I guessed.

Good. I crossed my fingers and dared to hope Joe Bines would tell me what had happened then and there. I could go home, tell my parents, and we'd all get on with our lives.

Three small goats greeted me when I climbed out of the car, lined up in a row of pure cuteness. They trotted their adorable selves right up and let me scratch their heads and pet their soft, floppy ears. Of course, they were probably just begging for food. I knew that look — at home Brodie was a grand master.

For once I remembered the sun shade for the front windshield and abandoned the kids to find it in the backseat. I had just adjusted it the way I wanted and was backing out of the car again when something brushed against my behind.

Surprised, I whirled around. A much larger goat had joined the smaller ones. She . . . he? I bent down. Couldn't tell. It didn't have horns though. Girl, then. She blinked at me, then let out a loud bleat. I jerked back in surprise, then smiled.

"Are these your babies? Don't worry, I'm harmless." I turned my back to her and started walking up to the farm house.

The blow to my posterior sent me flying, arms outstretched. The tote bag sailed off my shoulder, and I landed face down in the dirt.

Well, it was mostly dirt. There was some other . . . matter mixed in. The kind of stuff farm animals tend to leave behind, which I could see quite clearly because it was inches away from my face.

Ewwww.

I pushed myself up and managed to get back on my feet. Brushing off my hands, I spun around. Rubbed my rear end and glared at Mama Goat. "What did you do *that* for?"

Her response was a placid gaze.

"Git," I said and stomped my foot.

She took a step toward me.

I ran at her, flailing my arms. She turned tail and ran off, the three little ones trotting behind.

"Stupid goat," I muttered, and began returning scattered items to my tote. The copy of the letter was streaked with dirt. I gave my mother a mental nod for taking back the original. I brushed off the muck as best I could and continued up the slight hill to the house.

Sure enough, Joe answered the door when I knocked. He wore Wranglers and a long-sleeved chambray shirt, even in the heat. He looked worn for a man three years younger than me. Ridden hard and put away wet, as they say. Lined, sun-damaged skin stretched across his prominent cheekbones and hooked nose. He surveyed my face for mere seconds before recognition dawned.

When he opened his mouth the same

nasal tones I remembered assaulted my ears. "Well, if it isn't little Sophie Mae Watson. Not as little as you used to be, though, are you? Look like you went a few rounds, too. Didja win?"

Excuse me? Was Joe actually commenting on the fact that I weighed exactly seven and a half pounds more than I had in high school? I mean, maybe I wasn't quite as . . . coltish as then, but I wasn't exactly a cow, either.

All of that must have flickered across my face — after all, I was terrible at maintaining any kind of a poker face — but Joe Bines just leered and showed off the dark tobacco stains on his teeth.

"I see some people haven't changed a whit," I said. "Is Tabby around?"

"Nope. She's helping out at our girl's school. She'll be back in a few, though. Come on in." He stepped back from the doorway, and I entered the house.

It was tidy and scrubbed and smelled like fresh bread. Rye bread with lots of caraway seeds, if I wasn't mistaken. I followed Joe into the kitchen, and sure enough, two lovely loaves sat cooling on the center island.

I perched on a stool and brushed at the dark smudge across the front of my T-shirt. "What's your daughter's name?"

Joe leaned against the counter and continued to run his eyes up and down, finally stopping at my boobs. "Delight," he said to them.

"I beg your pardon?"

"Her name. Delight."

"Oh. That's, um, pretty."

"It was Tabby's idea. I think it's stupid."

I hoped his daughter didn't know that.

Suddenly, he looked me in the eye. "Why are you here?"

Wow. And people said I was abrupt. Well, when in Rome . . . "I'm trying to find out why Bobby Lee killed himself."

He squinted at me. "Little late for that, don't you think?"

Stifling the urge to turn around and leave, I said, "Did Tabby tell you about the letter he wrote? The suicide note?"

He stared at me. The moment stretched into thick discomfort. Finally Joe said, "He didn't leave a note."

"Turns out he did." I slid my hand into my bag.

Joe began emphatically shaking his head. "No, that's not possible." He held up a palm. "What does it say? No, he wouldn't do that." It was like he was not only talking to himself but answering himself as well. To my ear, both sides of the conversation sounded pretty darn scared.

Obviously Tabby hadn't told her husband about the note. My hand came back out of the bag, empty.

"My parents just found it," I said, fudging the truth a teeny tiny bit. "It's very revealing."

His Adam's apple bobbed convulsively. He opened his mouth to speak, but nothing came out.

Oooh. The jerk knew something, something big. I wasn't about to tell him I didn't know what the heck Bobby Lee had been talking about or that Tabby had professed ignorance.

Placing both elbows on the Formica, I leaned forward. "Maybe you'd like to explain? Tell me your side of things?" I wanted to prime him with one of the newspaper stories, but if I picked the wrong one he'd know I was bluffing. For that matter I didn't know if any of them were relevant.

"I don't care what the hell it says, your brother's a liar."

Hot anger crept under my scalp, and I felt my face redden. "Is that so."

He shook his finger at me. "Don't you go around spreading any lies, either, Sophie Mae. That would be very bad for your health."

My jaw dropped. "Are you actually threatening me?"

His fingers curled into fists, and my heart bucked against my ribs. Fear crawled up my neck. Joe looked ready to explode.

"Okay," I said in a desperate, conciliatory tone. "I believe you. And it was all a long time ago. None of that matters now."

The sound of the front door opening filtered into the kitchen. It loosened his fists but did nothing for the tension in the air between us. When Tabby walked in her first words were, "What's going on?"

We were both silent.

"Joe?" Her tone held accusation.

He glared at me for a few more moments, then turned on his heel and left the room. Tabby ran after him. I heard their voices, low but sharp in the front room. Less than a minute later the front door slammed.

Tabby came back into the kitchen, let out a whoosh of breath and put her hands on her hips. "What did you say to him?"

"I'm sorry. I had no idea he'd react like that. I asked him about Bobby Lee's letter."

Her nostrils flared. "I wish you'd stop going around showing *my* letter to everyone."

"I'm not showing it to everyone." In fact, I hadn't revealed the contents to anyone. The postal supervisor had only seen the envelope.

"My mother called me last night. She wasn't happy you dropped by and asked all those questions."

Too bad, I thought. "I went to see if she could tell me more about why the letter was returned eighteen years after it was sent. I only showed her the envelope. And I didn't show it to Joe, either. Still, he seemed to assume it said something incriminating about him."

Concern flickered across Tabby's face, then was gone. "I'll set him straight later. Now, are you going to give it to me?"

"I'm sorry, but it's not my decision. My mother has the original now, and you know she'll never give it up. What I want to know —" I put steel into the words. "— is why Joe became so frightened."

But she just shook her head, completely ignoring my insistent tone. "No idea."

"Like hell."

She shrugged. "Sorry."

Right.

I tried a different tack. "I'm sorry I upset him so much."

Her shoulders slumped. "Yeah. Me, too," she breathed.

"Is he . . . does he get violent?"

A pause, then she shook her head. "Not

125

with us. He's gotten in a few bar fights over the years."

"Charming."

She frowned. "He's my husband. The father of my daughter. And he's a good dad, he really is."

He's a total ass, I thought but didn't say. "You love him." It was the only explanation I could think of for why they were still together. I may not understand it, but I could accept it.

So her sharp laugh startled me, especially juxtaposed against the sudden sadness on her face. "Love? Not really. He used to interest me. Bad boy syndrome, I guess. But I grew out of that." She leaned on the counter and put her chin on her hand. "I was crazy in love with your brother. After he died, I swore to myself I'd never hurt like that again. But we have a bond, Joe and I, and we've built a life together. It's a pretty good one. We get along okay, and I have the dairy. And then there's Delight. She's everything to me."

This intensely personal turn of events felt uncomfortable. Still, I couldn't help repeating, "But you're not in love."

She reached for the refrigerator door. "Sometimes being in love is overrated."

TWELVE

My breath hissed in through clenched teeth, and I tried not to jerk my hands out of Tabby's grasp. My palms stung where I'd broken my fall outside, but that was nothing compared to the pain from the alcohol working into the cuts.

"I can't believe Billy did this." Tabby's head was bent over her work as she disinfected my minor wounds. "I'm so sorry."

She dabbed the cotton ball on my knee where another abrasion had drawn blood, and I sucked in my breath again. I felt like I was twelve and had fallen off my bike, the way she was mothering me. Still, her ministrations weren't that surprising. After all, she was a mom.

"It's no big deal," I said. "I thought it was a girl goat, though. It didn't have horns, and I couldn't get a good look at its, er, other indicator."

"We removed his horns. Billy likes to

butt," she said. "Despite their reputation, not all goats do that. But when they're kids they play at it, and if you push them back they'll get worse and worse." She looked up at me from under her brows. "Naturally, Joe pushes back. Thinks it's cute."

"Do you milk them?"

"Sometimes, if a nanny is in season, and I have a craving for feta or chevre, but my main focus is cow's milk. There." She stood up. "That should keep you alive for a while. Have you had a tetanus shot?"

"About three years ago."

"Should still be good. Have to be careful about that stuff around animals. Lockjaw's nasty."

She left, shutting the door behind her. I washed my hands and face and ran a comb through my short, messy mop. Though futile, I also dabbed at the dirt smudged across the front of my T-shirt. Thoughts of my upcoming nuptials crowded to the forefront of my brain as Tabby's words continued to resound in my mind. Were Barr and I rushing things? We hadn't even been together a full year, and here we were getting married.

What if we fell out of love and ended up like Tabby and Joe?

I shook my head at the woman in the mirror. According to Tabby, she and Joe had never really been in love. She'd said something about a bond. Had Bobby Lee's death brought them together in the first place, and then they'd built a life on that horrible event? It seemed sad if not downright dysfunctional. But who was I to criticize?

And my fiancé wasn't Joe Bines. Barr was intelligent, kind, thoughtful, strong, and handsome as all get out with those deep brown eyes and chestnut hair graying at the temples.

Relax, Sophie Mae. This is the real deal.

Now if I could only manage to get through the wedding ceremony itself without incident.

Sanitized to the best of my ability under the circumstances, I entered the kitchen again to find Tabby unloading bottles and jars from the refrigerator.

"Is Bobby Lee's letter the only reason you're here?" She asked. "Or are you actually interested in learning about cheese making and milk cultures?"

Her sudden bluntness threw me for a moment, and the accuracy of her question scraped a nerve. Perhaps she regretted her earlier honesty about her marriage. People often say that it's easier to confide in someone you hardly know, but I'd found that inevitably a feeling of vulnerability settles in afterward.

Quickly regrouping, I answered. "I loved learning about making mozzarella yesterday. I definitely want to know more."

She held my gaze for a few moments, then gave a slight nod. "Okay. I was planning to tell you about cheese cultures and how different bacteria work to create different kinds of cheeses. But now we don't have as much time as I'd like, and you'll get a lot of that information if you come to the class tomorrow." The last word lilted up as a question.

I inclined my head. "I'll be there, and my friend is planning to come, too. She's a terrific cook and has quizzed me about everything I've learned so far."

Tabby smiled. "Good." She sounded pleased, even after our tense words. Did she actually want to teach me, or was she simply happy to get another class fee? I wondered how lucrative a small dairy could be.

"I'm going to show you how to make yogurt and kefir and piima cheese today. Quick and easy and tasty." Now her words had taken on a teacherly tone. "Do you like kefir?"

"Um, I don't know. I've never had it."

Tabby pulled a jar of milk out of the fridge. It had a weird mass floating in it that looked like fish eyes, or tapioca pearls, all mooshed together. These were the kefir grains, she told me, and then gave me a taste of the kefir itself. I was a little hesitant at first, but the kefir was yummy — kind of like drinkable yogurt.

"It has bubbles," I exclaimed after the first sip.

She nodded. "The grains ferment the milk. It's a way to preserve it, and a tiny bit of alcohol is actually created, as well as that subtle carbonation. You can use the grains to ferment other things — fruit juice, for example. But once you do that you can't use the same grains for milk anymore."

"Where do you get the grains?"

"They grow slowly, and you can divide them. I got mine from a friend a long time ago. As long as you keep them active, they'll last for years. I'll sell you a batch if you're interested. Or you can find them online."

She chattered on, and I let her.

So much for intensely personal.

I thought of Bobby Lee, writing that cryptic letter to the girl he loved — and then taking that final step.

So much for love being overrated.

It didn't take long for Tabby to show me how to make yogurt — it was so easy I couldn't believe we didn't already make our own at home. All you did was heat the milk to a hundred and fifteen degrees, add a little commercial yogurt to the milk and let it sit on the counter in a thermos for six to twelve hours. At least that's what she told me I could do, because she had a fancy yogurt maker and used a packet of starter culture.

"You'll get a thinner yogurt than you might be used to," she said. "Commercial manufacturers add thickeners. This is the real deal, though."

The real deal sounded good to me.

"You can always strain it through a coffee filter if you want it thicker," she added. "Strain it for long enough and you'll have yogurt cream cheese."

The piima was more of a starter culture that had to be replenished periodically, like sourdough. "It'll last for years, just like the kefir grains," she told me.

She showed me how to add a few table-spoons from a jar of cream that had already been cultured — it was the consistency of thick sour cream after the piima had a chance to work its magic — to a new jar of cream and mix it in.

"Then you put it in a dark cupboard for twenty-four hours to let it stew, before popping it in the fridge. Again, none of this stuff works very well with ultra-pasteurized milk, so you have to find someplace where you can get either lightly pasteurized or raw milk."

"Won't the cream sour?" I asked. Leaving it unrefrigerated for a whole day seemed kind of weird to me.

"No, the room temperature encourages the culture to grow. It'll continue to grow, though more slowly, in the fridge. And it'll last for several weeks, which the uncultured cream wouldn't."

"Our half-and-half lasts a month."

She pointed a finger at me. "It's ultra-pasteurized. That kills all the bacteria, good and bad, as well as a significant portion of the nutrition."

"Yuck."

"Normally, the lactic acid in milk kills any bad bacteria, so ultra-pasteurization is kind of overkill. But it's good for shipping and shelf life, so it works best for the big corporations. Even light pasteurization damages many nutrients, including conjugated linoleic acid."

"Conjugated what?"

"CLA for short. It's an important omega-six fatty acid. The most nutritious milk is hormone free, comes from grass-fed cows and isn't pasteurized at all. Unfortunately in a lot of states it's illegal to sell raw milk, so you have to purchase a share in a dairy cow in order to get it."

Mental note: Cheese making or no cheese making, we would find a good source for milk when we got home.

Then we made butter from the piima cream, using a standing mixer. Again, it was ridiculously easy. We whipped the cream in a standing mixer as if for dessert topping, but kept whipping beyond stiff peaks. After awhile it became grainy with tiny butter solids which soon combined and stuck to the beaters, separate from the buttermilk. Then it was a matter of rinsing the solid mass in a clean towel and squeezing out any remaining buttermilk. Finally we added a little salt and packed it into an old-fashioned butter mold.

Tabby gave me more of the butter, and a jar of buttermilk along with a recipe for salad dressing. Then she gave me a sample of piima cheese she had made by culturing whole milk and straining it, much like yogurt cheese. It was soft and spreadable. "Add a few herbs and serve it with crackers," she said. "Or spread it on bagels or sandwiches."

My big tote bulging with all those goodies, I wrote her a check and got ready to go.

"I'll walk down with you. I have to get something from the classroom and then check on the mold house."

"The what?"

"It's where I inoculate my specialty cheeses and let them age. It was tricky to get the humidity right, but now I can make a unique variety of bleu and other mold-ripened cheeses."

I wanted to know more, but by now we were walking down the driveway toward the parking lot. Time was running out.

"Tabby?"

Something in my voice must have tele-graphed the change of subject, and she shot me a look. "What?"

"I looked up some newspaper articles from around when Bobby Lee died, to see if I could find out what he was talking about in that letter."

I took a couple of steps before I realized she'd stopped behind me. Slowly, I turned back to face her.

Tabby stood stock still, hands on her hips. Her voice was emphatic, her words care-fully enunciated. "You have no right poking your nose into something that was between your brother and me."

"So you do know what he was talking about!"

She shook her head. "I didn't say that. But whatever it was, he didn't write to you about it. He wrote to me."

Then maybe your mother shouldn't have sent the damn letter back to us, I thought. But I keep my mouth shut.

"Leave it alone," Tabby said. "Just let it go."

"But he was my brother —"

"If something happened back then, do you really think it would change anything to dig it all up? Do you somehow think you can bring him back? Because you *can't.* All you can do is hurt other people."

I stared at her, dismayed.

"I'll see you tomorrow in class," she said, rotating on her heel. Without another word she walked around the back of the classroom building where she'd taught us how to make mozzarella.

What the heck? I felt closer than ever to the truth, yet strangely more reluctant to learn what it was. I was sure both Tabby and Joe knew what had happened. In fact, I bet they'd known all along and had managed to keep it a secret. What if they never told anyone? The thought was crazy-making, and I shook it off. Even if they wouldn't reveal what they knew, the truth was still there for me to discover.

Keeping an eye out for cranky goats, I continued between the delivery truck and the red pickup toward the Subaru. I had just put my tote into the backseat when Tabby's high-pitched scream echoed off the outbuildings.

THIRTEEN

Joe Bines was sprawled on his side amidst chunks of broken glass. A thin trickle of scarlet threaded through the pool of bright white cream spread like a corona around his head. A shaft of afternoon light slanted behind the classroom building to illuminate the waxy, translucent skin of his face.

His eyes were closed. His chest was perfectly still.

Beside me, Tabby sucked in a shuddering breath as if to compensate for her husband's lack of respiration. Then, before I could stop her, she shouldered me aside and fell to her knees, reaching for Joe's shoulder.

I opened my mouth to say God-knows-what — Don't do that? To comfort her? To swear? — but snapped my jaw closed again in silence as she turned him over and I saw the other side of his head.

Let's just say it wasn't round anymore.

Tabby recoiled, scrabbling back like a

drunken crab. She almost fell, but I grasped her arms from behind and managed to steady her. Slowly, she stood and leaned back against me. Her rapid breathing mingled with the murmurs of turtledoves in the nearby trees.

Gradually, she calmed. I released her, and she turned to face me. Her ice-blue eyes echoed a resounding sadness. "Joe really did it this time."

I raised my eyebrows. "Did what?"

She closed her eyes and shook her head.

My eyes returned to the dead man, surrounded by shards of the murder weapon: a glass bottle of heavy cream, by the looks of it. I sighed. My tendency to find dead bodies had apparently followed me across state lines all the way to Colorado.

It was getting so I felt like I should come with a warning label.

The sheriff's department arrived quickly without benefit of lights and sirens. Tabby and I perched on the edge of one of the landscape timbers that defined the dairy's small parking lot. We stood up as two men simultaneously exited their respective vehicles and warily approached.

I stepped forward and nodded a perfunctory greeting. "He's around the corner there."

The two men consulted each other with a look then turned toward the sound of a siren approaching from the west. A green-and-white ambulance roared down the road toward us. The driver slid to a stop on the gravel, barely missing the Subaru. She boiled out of the cab and started toward the deputies.

Raising my hand, I called, "There's no big hurry."

"I think you'd better let us be the judge of that," said the first deputy.

The two of them looked like Jack Spratt and his . . . life partner? Short and stout and tall and thin. Both men were clean shaven and wore navy Smokey the Bear hats.

"Of course," I said, chastened.

A man hopped out of the passenger seat of the ambulance, and all four of them went around the corner. Tabby and I stayed put. I sure didn't want another look at Joe, and no doubt she felt the same way.

I looked sidelong at her. Her hands were tucked into her back pockets, and her shoulders slumped forward under the invisible burden of her husband's death. She stared down at the dirt with red-rimmed eyes, unblinking.

"Are you okay?" I whispered.

She nodded but didn't say anything. I encircled her shoulders with my arm and squeezed. There was no response, and after a few minutes it felt awkward enough that I let my hand fall to my side.

Two vans arrived. Their occupants were hatless and one wore a dark jumpsuit. Crime scene investigators? I pointed to where the others had gone, and one of them nodded. They went around the corner, too.

Then another county vehicle came down the road, a big Suburban this time, and the small parking lot was officially full. The SUV stopped. The door opened. Cowboy boots emerged below it, and a large man stepped out. He had thick ginger hair streaked with gray and a luxuriant moustache topped his lip. Broad shouldered, thin hipped, and wearing sunglasses, he looked like a quintessential lawman. He reached back into the car and drew out what had to be a non-regulation hat. Not Smokey the Bear for him, no sir. He clapped the brown Stetson on his head and started toward us.

Tabby watched his approach with wary eyes. He stopped in front of her and nodded. "Ms. Bines."

"Sheriff Jaikes," she said.

Under that thick moustache he had thin

141

lips and a receding chin. He removed his sunglasses to reveal small, watery blue eyes. "Hear you've had some trouble here."

"Somebody killed Joe."

He stroked that barely-there chin. "Shot him?"

She shook her head.

"Looks like they hit him with a bottle of cream," I said.

His eyes cut my way, then returned to Tabby. "Who did it?"

"I don't know," she said.

"Hmmm. We'll find out, don't you worry."

Beside me, Tabby only sighed.

The sheriff's attention turned to me. "I don't believe we've met."

"Sophie Mae Reynolds," I said.

"Friend of Tabitha here?"

I glanced at her. "I'm visiting my parents in Spring Creek, and Tabby's teaching me how to make cheese."

"Visiting from where?"

"Cadyville, Washington."

"I see." He watched me. There was considerable intelligence behind those pale eyes. It didn't take long to make me squirm. I tried a smile, but even I could tell how weak it was.

Thank goodness a flurry of voices attracted our attention. Jack Spratt and his buddy came back from the side of the outbuilding, spied Sheriff Jaikes, and came over.

The first words out of Jaikes' mouth were, "Separate these two and conduct preliminary interviews. Where's the body?"

"Right around the corner there, Boss," the skinny deputy said.

The sheriff tipped his hat to us. "Ladies." And off he went to survey the mayhem.

I got Jack Spratt, whose real name turned out to be Inspector Thomas Schumaker. We spoke in his car, with the motor running and the air-conditioning on full blast. That right there made me like him. It was soon clear he knew the Bineses, especially Joe. I got the feeling Tabby had glossed over Joe's "bar fights."

First he asked me to tell him everything that happened. I did my best to keep it simple, ending with, "and then I called 911 on my cell phone, and Tabby called her mother."

"Her mother?"

"To ask if Celeste could leave work and go pick up Tabby's daughter from school."

"Ah." Schumaker mopped his flushed face with a graying handkerchief. The air-conditioning didn't seem to make much of a dent in his overheated state. I wondered whether men got hot flashes.

"You didn't leave the body after finding it?" he asked. "Neither one of you?"

"Well, we didn't sit beside it, but we stayed there by the building, waiting for you." Except for when I got my tote bag out of my car.

"Both of you."

"Uh huh."

"And you both saw him leave the house late this morning."

"Yes."

"Both of you."

"Yes."

"And you and Tabby were together the whole time up at the house."

I nodded. For Pete's sake, was this guy thick or something?

"And then you both came down here and found the body together."

"Yes." I tried not to grit my teeth. "She was out of my sight for less than fifteen seconds."

"Hear or see any vehicles come or go?"

I tried to think. "The window in the kitchen was open, and I heard a lot of traffic. Most of it was on the county road, but someone could have driven in here, I guess. The drive and the parking lot are far enough

144

away from the house that I might not have noticed. Tabby would be more tuned into the sounds of coming and going here at the dairy."

He made a couple more additions to his notes. "You didn't help her kill him, by any chance."

"What!"

He held up a hand. "Just checking. Because it sure looks like you give her a solid alibi." Skepticism leaked out around his words. "Mind telling me why your shirt's dirty and your hands are all scraped up?"

I looked down at my hands sitting in my lap. The scratches from earlier were red against my pale palms. "It was a goat."

"Pardon me?"

My not-so-friendly billy goat was eating weeds over by the chicken house. I pointed. "That one. It came up behind me while I was walking up to the house from the parking lot here and, well, butted me."

Beside me, Inspector Schumaker struggled not to laugh.

"Right in the tush. Sent me flying. See? My knee's skinned, too. He hit me hard."

A quick snort, and he had himself under control.

I felt myself flush bright pink, but did my best to ignore it, hoping he would, too.

"Now why on earth would Tabby Bines want to kill her husband?"

He hesitated, weighing what to say. "How well do you know the Bineses?"

"Not very. Tabby used to date my brother back in high school, and Joe was his best friend. But I haven't seen him since my brother's funeral."

He considered the word *funeral.* "You used to live here?"

I nodded.

"What was your brother's name?"

"Bobby Lee Watson."

"I see." Pity crossed his face. "That was a very sad business." He made another note.

"You remember what happened?"

"Yes, ma'am. I was going to Northern Colorado University, finishing up my criminal justice degree. I recall —" He realized who he was talking to and clamped his mouth shut.

"What?"

He shook his head. "Doesn't matter."

As if of its own volition, my hand slipped into my tote bag and retrieved the envelope with the copy of Bobby Lee's letter in it. I gave it to Schumaker. "This recently came into my family's possession. It's why I came back home, frankly, and I'm trying to find out what it means. Any help you could give

146

me would be great." Mixed feeling about getting the authorities involved crowded my thoughts. What if Bobby Lee had done something criminal? Anna Belle would have a fit if she found out.

He gave me one long look, then took the letter out and unfolded it. The inspector's eyes narrowed as they moved down the page, then flicked back to the top as he began to read through it again.

Sheriff Jaikes rapped on the window with his knuckles. We both jumped, and Schumaker reached for the door handle.

"Can I have my letter back, please?"

He scanned it one last time before handing it to me. Opening the door, he got out. I did the same.

Jaikes spoke. "What's taking so long? Pickel's been done with the wife for ten minutes."

Deputy Pickel. I just managed not to snort.

"Trying to be thorough, sir."

Jaikes scowled. "Please get back into the car, ma'am. Schumaker, come with me."

I was happy to slide back into the cool front seat, at least until the inspector removed the key, which turned off the air conditioner. He shrugged at my sound of protest. "Sorry, Ms. Reynolds. You understand."

Bah.

The sheriff and his two deputies consulted, notebooks open. I peered at the bells and whistles tacked all along the dash, the computer within easy access of the driver. I wondered whether the inspector could type and drive at the same time. Probably. That couldn't be safe. Maybe he played solitaire at stoplights.

The interior of the vehicle was an oven by the time they were done and Schumaker came over and opened my door. Apparently Tabby's story matched mine, because they let her go back up to the house. She threw me an agitated look over her shoulder as she walked away. Sheriff Jaikes gestured me out to the parking lot.

"I take it we're done?" I asked.

The sheriff frowned. "For now."

"Do you have any idea who might have killed Joe? Did Tabby tell you anything useful?" I already knew I hadn't.

But my question only earned me twin basilisk gazes.

"I mean, it sounds like he had a history. Enemies. And it was probably someone he knew, right? Because, being hit from that angle, on the side of his head like that, he

148

probably would have been able to see his assailant. Unless they surprised him, and he turned toward them. Which way was he facing? Could you tell from the blood spatter . . ." Seeing the looks on their faces, I trailed off. They were lawmen, for heaven's sake. What was with the horrified expressions?

"You appear to have a real taste for the macabre," Sheriff Jaikes said. "Most ladies would be happy to remain ignorant of the more, uh, graphic details of a violent death."

Not only implying that I should lay off the questions, but that I wasn't a lady.

"Sorry," I said.

"That's okay." A bit of condescension in his voice there. "You have yourself a real nice evening, all right?"

The sheriff walked away. Tall and lanky like Barr, only with those massive shoulders. And, unlike Barr, he had an attitude I didn't particularly care for.

Schumaker swiped at his face with the soppy handkerchief again. "You're free to go, but please don't leave town."

I put my hands on my hips. "Oh, for Pete's sake. You can't make me stay here without arresting me, and it doesn't look like you're going to do that. I have a flight booked out of here on Sunday." Which didn't leave me much time to get to the bottom of Bobby Lee's death. At least I didn't have to concern myself with who killed Joe Bines.

Unless . . . were they related?

In my experience, life was filled with a lot more cause and effect than coincidence. But after eighteen years? That might be a bit of a stretch.

Schumaker looked unhappy. "I'll have your statement typed up tomorrow. Come in and sign it in the morning."

I sighed. "Where do you want me to show up?"

He gave me directions, and then began to rejoin his comrades.

"Inspector Schumaker?"

He stopped and swiveled his shoulders toward me.

"About my brother?"

"Not now." He glanced toward the sheriff. "But bring that letter when you come in tomorrow to sign your statement. I'd like to take another look at it."

That sounded ominous. A part of me regretted mentioning anything about my brother. On the other hand, Schumaker had started to tell me something when Bobby Lee's name first came up. Then he'd stopped himself. Perhaps given a little more time I could convince him to help me find the truth.

I nodded my agreement, and he walked away. It took me five minutes to maneuver Dad's car out of the sea of county vehicles.

FOURTEEN

It was after six by the time I got home feeling hot, sticky, sore and not a little cranky. Voices drifted through the open windows from the backyard, but I slipped quietly up the stairs. A quick spritz of a shower later, I donned a flowing skirt that fell below my skinned knee and an airy, paisley-patterned blouse. Then I liberally slathered on my homemade mosquito repellent. That time of day the little blood suckers were bound to be thick outside. The combination of clove, rosemary, lemongrass, castor and neem oils would keep them at bay. I grabbed the bottle to share with the others.

Downstairs, I opened the sliding glass door and stepped out. Oblique light cut across the backyard, and the green scent of new-mown grass combined with the savory aroma of grilled meat from a neighbor's barbecue. The fact that I hadn't eaten anything other than a glass of kefir since breakfast roared to the front of my mind accompanied by a predictably Pavlovian response in my mouth.

Everyone was intent on a lively game of Bocce. My parents were playing against Meghan and a rugged-looking man with thick black hair and a bounce in his step. Erin sat at the tile-topped patio table, watching with a scowl on her face. She looked over at me and blinked to acknowledge my presence, then returned her attention to the game. The satisfying clack of one Bocce ball connecting with another elicited a groan from my father.

I eyed the pile of corn on the cob, silk removed and rewrapped in their husks, awaiting the grill. I could only imagine what that perfect summer food would taste like dripping with Tabby's piima-cultured butter. And Dad had mentioned chicken for dinner. I envisioned lots of tender dark meat, slathered with the sticky, spicy sauce my Southern grandmother had taught Anna Belle to make when she was a child. Mmmm. Maybe add some fresh sliced tomatoes, glowing red and still warm from the garden, sprinkled with a pinch of kosher salt and freshly ground pepper.

I mentally shook off the culinary fantasy and walked over to put my hand on Erin's shoulder. "We can play the winners."

She glanced up at me, then back down. "I don't want to play."

"Erin," I said.

"What?"

I sighed. "Never mind."

From across the yard, Dad raised his hand in greeting. My mother followed suit, a glass of red wine in her other hand. She liked to adhere to tradition when it came to Bocce. Meghan flashed white teeth at me, all giddy because her beau had finally arrived. He saw me and approached, towing her by the hand.

"Kelly!" I gave him a big hug. "It's so good to see you!" He was a handsome man, half Irish, half Cherokee Indian. His olive skin and light eyes were a devastating combination. They'd certainly bewitched my best friend.

"Hey, Sophie Mae. You look great."

I ducked my head at the compliment. "Hurry up and win. Or lose. Whatever. You won't believe what happened at the dairy today."

Meghan looked the question at me. Kelly cocked his head to one side. Across the yard Dad and Anna Belle were talking. She pointed at something in her kitchen garden and laughed.

I said, "Someone bashed Joe Bines over the head with a bottle of milk."

Concern and alarmed warred in Meghan's tone. "Is he going to be okay?"

"Er . . . not exactly."

She blinked, and realization dawned across her features. "He's *dead?*"

"Um . . . yeah."

Muttered exclamations at that. "When did this bashing take place?" There was danger in Meghan's voice.

"When Tabby and I were up at the house making yogurt."

Her mouth opened. Closed. Opened again. Closed. She put her hand over her eyes and hung her head. Kelly stared at me like I was a particularly interesting bug.

"Hey, I didn't kill him!"

Apparently, I said that a little too loud, because Anna Belle's head whipped around. Her eyes narrowed as she strode toward us. Dad followed at a more leisurely pace.

"You're late," she said.

I sighed. "I know. Someone killed Joe Bines while I was at the dairy. I had to stick around and talk to the sheriff and his minions." Well, technically I'd only spoken to one minion.

Dad joined us.

Erin said, "Sophie Mae found another

155

dead body."

His eyes widened.

We all sat down around the table, Bocce ball forgotten. I filled everyone in on my afternoon. When I'd finished, a long silence ensued as everyone assimilated the new information.

"Let's get the chicken and start dinner," Meghan said. Her expression had gone from unhappy to horrified to resigned as I spoke.

Erin rolled her eyes. "But I want to hear more."

"You've heard it all," I said. "Besides, I'm hungry."

"Me, too," Kelly said.

Erin glared at him, turned on her heel and stalked inside. Meghan looked an apology at both of us.

"So you're at it again," Kelly said to me.

I grimaced. "I was only trying to find out what happened around the time my brother — you know."

He nodded.

"You should get a license, do it for real," he said.

He was a private investigator in New Jersey, still talking about moving his P.I. business out to Washington so he and Meghan could be together. Problem was, he had a couple of long-term clients in New

Jersey who kept things lucrative for him there, and he didn't have any client base in Seattle. So they still had a few things to work out. At least they'd managed to meet halfway for a few days together.

"Of course," he continued, "you don't have to have a license to be an investigator in Colorado."

That got my attention. "Really?"

"Oh, for heaven's sake," Anna Belle said. "Don't tell her that."

But he winked at me. "Really. So what does this Joe guy's murder have to do with your brother?"

"Not a thing, to the best of my knowledge." Still, I couldn't help but wonder.

Something must have shown on my face, because my mother narrowed her eyes. "What did you do?"

"Nothing! I mean, I told him about the letter but didn't show it to him. He seemed to think Bobby Lee had incriminated him in some way. Got a little nutso about it, really. Then Tabby came in and I dropped it, figuring I could brace him again later." I slumped. "Guess I lost my chance."

"So he would have been able to tell us what Bobby Lee was talking about if you'd shown him the letter." Anna Belle sounded frustrated. Hard to blame her.

My shoulders rose and fell. "But he wouldn't have. I could tell, because if I'd shown him the letter he would have known it didn't really say anything specific. No way would he incriminate himself." I shook my head. "He was always a real jerk, and that didn't change at all. In fact, I think he's worse."

"Was worse," Meghan said.

"Was worse," I agreed.

No, Joe wouldn't be insulting anyone anymore. But was that why someone had killed him? Or had telling him about Bobby Lee's letter pushed a potential killer into fast forward? Only three hours had passed between when I talked to Joe and when we discovered him with his head bashed in.

But maybe that had been enough.

Even better than fresh garden tomatoes, Dad, in a fit of culinary experimentation, had created a beautiful platter of zucchini carpaccio: paper-thin rounds of the summer squash in overlapping layers, sprinkled with olive oil, lemon juice, salt and pepper, then topped with parsley, shaved Parmesan, and a scattering of finely chopped pecans.

"What a good idea for using up the glut of zucchini," I said. "There aren't nearly enough recipes for it this time of year." It

158

had also been a terrific acidic accompaniment to the sweet corn and predictable tang of barbecued chicken.

Dessert was light: fresh peaches and mixed berries tossed with a sweet balsamic vinaigrette. We were just digging in when something nudged my bare foot.

Craning to look under the table, I saw Kitty Wampus looking at me expectantly.

"You don't like fruit," I said to him. "You like turkey sandwiches, remember?"

Then I felt the movement and saw something lying on the concrete next to my heel. I shrieked and jumped up, scrambling away from the table.

"Wampus! Bad cat. *Bad* cat."

Of course, by now everyone was looking under the table.

Dad laughed. "It's just a vole. He's not a bad cat; he's just a cat. They all do that."

"All cats do not drop half-dead rodents on my feet!"

Meghan said, "It means he likes you best."

"Great." I shuddered. "Next he'll leave a rat on my pillow. The one where he likes to sleep and *shed.*" I sighed. "I miss Brodie."

Kelly gently scooped up the little creature. "This guy'll be okay. I'll put him out by the garden."

"Thank you," my mother said.

Kitty Wampus watched Kelly walk away with the vole. Probably noting where to retrieve it later.

Anna Belle had been uncharacteristically quiet, especially in light of my news about Joe's murder. I sat back down and asked her, "Is everything all right?"

She exchanged glances with Dad. Even though it was brief, the look was pregnant with meaning. Neither of then said anything.

Oh, no. Now what?

Meghan, bless her heart, picked up on it. "Kelly, it's a beautiful evening and I could use a walk. Erin, come with us. You can show us that park down the street."

"No, thanks," Erin said. "I'm done with dinner. Can I go inside and read?"

"Um, sure," Meghan said.

Without another word, Erin rose and went inside.

But Kelly stood with alacrity, always ready to spend some time alone with Meghan. They went around to the front of the house, and I turned back to Dad and Anna Belle.

Raised my eyebrows and waited.

Finally, Dad said, "One of those articles struck a note with me last night, but I didn't realize why until I was meditating this morning."

Eager, I leaned forward. "Which one?"

"The one about the girl who died of hypo-thermia."

"Did Bobby Lee know her?" I could hardly keep the excitement out of my voice.

"Well, maybe," he said.

I made an impatient noise.

My mother spoke for the first time. "The girl belonged to a cult your brother was interested in."

I blinked. "What?"

Dad said, "It wasn't really a cult."

"Yes, it was," Anna Belle said. The muscles around her eyes and lips tightened, and she looked about ten years older.

"Bobby Lee was . . . involved . . . a *cult?* Since *when?*" I squeaked, flabbergasted. "No one ever told me any of this." I flapped my hands. "My brother joined a cult?"

FIFTEEN

"Of course he didn't join a cult," Anna Belle said. "We wouldn't let him."

"It wasn't a cult." Dad sounded exasperated. "There was a pastor who had a little place outside of town. Called it Rancho Sueño. Sometimes he'd let kids — teenagers — stay there. Runaways, recovering addicts, abuse victims, like that."

"Kids," Anna Belle said. "Who were probably from good homes and wouldn't have run away at all if it weren't for the persuasive powers of Mr. Dunner et al. He went door-to-door. Targeting teenagers."

Dad explained. "I think most of the kids that the pastor — his name was Ogden Dunner — helped were referred by his church members. But he came to our house once. He was working the neighborhood, spreading the word — you know how it is."

I nodded. "Saving the masses, one doorbell at a time."

"Bobby Lee was home. He let him in. Your mother came home to find them in the kitchen talking like old friends."

Oh, dear. That wouldn't have gone over well with my mother.

"He was trying to lure my son into his cult."

My father leaned forward. "Oh, for Pete's sake, Anna Belle. It. Wasn't. A. Cult."

"Well, whatever it was, it certainly piqued your brother's interest for a while, along with Joe and Tabby's," she said. "They should have all been busy with college, learning how to make something of themselves in the world. But Bobby Lee had to take a year off after high school, work in a print shop, for heaven's sake. And Joe had decided not to go to school at all. Got a construction job and moved out on his own. Tabby was the only one taking classes, and they didn't take up nearly enough of her time, in my opinion."

I stood up and began pacing back and forth on the patio. "So Tabby and Joe were involved with this God Rancho place, too?"

My mother's lips pressed together. "Rancho Sueño. Dream Ranch. They certainly spent a lot of time out there for a while."

"Celeste Atwood mentioned that Tabby and Bobby Lee might not have been getting along. Was this before or after that started?"

She sat back in her patio chair. "Before. I think Joe Bines came between them later. If anyone deserved getting murdered, he did."

"Anna Belle!"

She waved her hand in the air. "Oh, I don't mean it. But I'd always wondered what happened between Bobby Lee and Tabby. He never had a chance to tell me."

"So this Rancho Sueño thing was earlier?"

My mother said, "Your brother's involvement? Oh yes. At least six months before. We caught wind of it, and sat down with Bobby Lee. Had a long talk with him and convinced him not to go back there."

"We forbade him to go." A layer of sarcasm underscored my father's words.

"And he obeyed?" I didn't know whether to be more surprised that Bobby Lee was involved with Rancho Sueño or that my parents had thought he'd do what they told him.

"Of course he did," Anna Belle said.

"Probably not," Dad said.

She glared at him.

"What?" he said. "I'm only stating the obvious. We brought them both up to make their own decisions."

"It was that girl," she said. "If he kept going despite our express wishes, if he defied

164

us like that, then it was because of that girl."

"The one who died?" I asked.

She looked startled. "Of course not. I'm talking about Tabitha Atwood."

"Oh. Then what does the dead girl have to do with Bobby Lee?" I asked.

"Nothing." Anna Belle crossed her arms. "Nothing at all. She fell in the Cache la Poudre River where it ran through the Dunner property."

I looked at my dad.

He shrugged his shoulders. "The only reason we brought it up at all is because it was something that happened around the time of your brother's death. Of all those articles — and I checked the newspapers from around then again, and those were the only items that caught my attention, too — that was the only one even remotely related to Bobby Lee. And I do mean remotely. This town isn't that big — more of a two or three degrees of separation thing than the usual six."

Anna Belle scowled at both of us.

"I'm sorry," I said to her. "It was messy then, and it's messy now. But we'll figure it out."

"If," my father said, and we both looked at him. "If there is something to figure out. It's possible we'll never know why Bobby

165

Lee made the choice he did."

Choice.

I was sure my expression echoed Anna Belle's. She said, "Don't make a big deal out of nothing. Your brother was smart, and he understood what that pastor was all about. I don't care what your father says —" She shot him a pointed look. "— but Bobby Lee wasn't taken in."

"I agree," Dad said. "I don't think he went because of Pastor Dunner. But it's possible Tabby did. And he cared for her. A lot. He may have continued to go out to the Ranch without our knowledge out of concern for her."

Anna Belle closed her eyes. "Of course, Calvin. You're right." She opened them again, directing her gaze at me. "If he went against our wishes, it was for her sake."

"Is that why you accused her of killing him? At the funeral?"

She ran a palm over her face. "I don't know."

"We weren't thinking about any connection to Rancho Sueño," my dad said. His bitterness shouldn't have surprised me, but I'd already grown used to his new aplomb. "And now it may be too late to find out." He took a deep breath. "We have to be content with the idea that we might never know."

I smiled at him, encouraging him to let go, let it be, be happy. *Omm* and all that stuff.

But I wasn't about to be content with that, and from the look on my mother's face, neither was she. Tomorrow I'd make another trip out to the dairy to see what I could see.

In the meantime, I had to go call Barr and tell him I'd found another dead body. He wouldn't be happy.

Not happy at all.

Wednesday morning I showed up bright and early at the Sheriff's Department, itching to talk to Inspector Schumaker. Wouldn't it just figure, then, that he'd make me wait almost half an hour before summoning me from the little waiting area by the front door.

He led me to a conference room. A long utilitarian table surrounded by molded plastic chairs dominated the middle of the room. The air felt muggy and smelled of carpet shampoo. The gray walls imposed a subdued atmosphere, as did the tinted window film that muted the sunlight coming in from the east.

"Ms. Reynolds, have a seat. I've got your statement all typed up."

I settled my slightly bruised posterior in one of the charcoal-colored chairs and placed my empty latte cup on the table.

In the chair opposite, Schumaker looked up at me from under his brows. His forehead was already shiny with perspiration. "Check this carefully. Very carefully. If anything is off, or if there's something you've remembered overnight, you be sure and tell me, all right?"

"Of course," I said and reached for the pages he held.

He pulled them back from my grasp.

"Any changes at this point I'll put down as an earlier case of miscommunication. Understand?"

I sat back. "Inspector, just what are you getting at?"

He held my gaze for a long moment. "This statement, as it stands, gives Tabitha Bines a thorough alibi."

"Okay."

"If it turns out that she left for a while, and you don't tell us?"

"Yes," I prompted.

"Well, it would be like you were lying about her being there. In effect, Ms. Reynolds, you would be considered an accessory to murder if it turns out she killed her husband and you, um, misrepresented her whereabouts in this statement."

That kind of made my breakfast bacon and eggs do a flip flop. I wracked my brain, trying to remember whether Tabby left at all during our milk culture lesson.

No, but I had. Only a few minutes, though, spent in the bathroom to freshen up after she'd bathed my cuts with alcohol. It hadn't been long enough for Tabby to slip out, certainly not enough for her to kill Joe, had it? No. Still, the thought that I might somehow be prosecuted . . .

Then I remembered her reaction to finding Joe dead, the look of horror on her face. I just didn't think she was that good an actress.

"I was in the bathroom for about three minutes," I said to Schumaker. "It would be great if I could check your accuracy, though."

He frowned at my implication that he might have written something down incorrectly, but he handed me the statement. "Add your potty break to the bottom of the last page and initial it."

I perused the pages carefully, taking a long time to make sure it was absolutely accurate. It was. I added a sentence, signed it with the pen he gave me and pushed it back across the table.

He sighed and gave the slightest shake of his head as he looked down at my scrawled signature.

"If I didn't give her an alibi, would you arrest her?"

Suspicion crossed his face.

I held up my palm to him. "No, I'm not changing my mind. But I don't know Tabby that well, nor Joe, and I was just wondering why she'd be a suspect in his murder."

"Wives are always suspect."

I thought of my upcoming nuptials. Barr would be delighted to hear that. Of course, as a police detective, he'd no doubt agree.

Schumaker withdrew a handkerchief from his hip pocket and mopped his face. Today it was dark blue. He folded it carefully before replacing it. "Besides, anyone married to Joe Bines would have ample motive to kill him."

Surprised that he'd make a statement like that to a civilian, especially someone involved with the case, I asked, "Why?"

He considered me. "Joe had what you might call a relationship with law enforcement. Real troublemaker: fights, gambling, a little low level drug dealing for a while. Tabby was wild when she was younger, especially right after your brother died, but she settled down and flew straight once they started up that dairy and she had that little girl."

"Sounds like Joe had a lot of people who might have wanted to kill him."

Schumaker cocked his head to one side. "I've checked on your background, too. Apparently you've had some success bringing a criminal or two to justice."

Tamping down a smile, I said, "There have been a few situations."

He snorted. "So I hear. Talked to Sergeant Zahn, up there in Cadyville where you're from."

I winced. "Great. I can't believe you're talking to me at all after that."

He grinned. "You'd be surprised. He seems to really respect you."

My eyebrows climbed up my forehead.

"Of course, he doesn't like how you get in his way." Schumaker leaned forward. "Now, you're not going to get in my way, are you?"

I shook my head. "Of course not. I just want to find out what was going on with my brother."

"Uh huh. And there's no chance that Joe Bines' former relationship with your brother is anything I have to worry about?"

"Worry about?"

"I'm not going to find out you have a motive to kill him, am I?"

I shook my head again. "No sir. I haven't seen Joe for almost two decades."

"I'll take you at your word," he said. "For now."

"You never told me why you think Tabby would kill Joe."

"And I'm not going to. This is you not getting in my way."

I allowed a tiny smile. "Okay, okay. But will you tell me something else?"

He barked a short, humorless laugh. "Probably not."

Well, all I could do was try. "Do you remember someone named Ogden Dunner? He had a place east of town he called Rancho Sueño?"

Schumaker grew still. "Why are you asking?"

I considered. Took a leap of faith. "There was a death out there, just before my brother killed himself. A girl fell in the river. It was November. She died on the way to the hospital."

His gaze never wavered from mine. I went on. "The newspaper didn't say anything more than that, but my parents told me that at one time Bobby Lee was . . . attracted to Rancho Sueño. My mother called it a cult."

"Bah."

Obviously Schumaker agreed with my

father's assessment of Pastor Dunner's activities.

"They also said Tabby and Joe spent a lot of time there."

"Is that so? Hmmm. Well, I haven't looked at that one for quite a while. The case has been closed a long time."

"Closed?" I asked. "So it was open at one point."

He hesitated then said, "They're all open, until they're not."

"What exactly happened?"

The silence stretched between us as he reflected on what to tell me — if anything. Finally, he spoke. "According to Dunner, that night his son — name's Ray — and some other kids went down to the river."

I scooted to the front of my chair. "How many kids?"

"Five, including the girl who died."

"You talked with them?"

"Talked to Ray. Two of the witnesses got scared. They were runaways to start with and took off. The names they gave Dunner led nowhere. Pretty sure they were fake. The other witness, a girl, came forward."

"Was it Tabby Atwood?"

He looked confused. "No. You're barking up the wrong tree."

"Who was it then?"

"I'll say it again: wrong tree, Ms. Reynolds."

Feeling like a pit bull, I came at it from another direction. "This all happened pretty late at night, didn't it?"

The handkerchief came out again. "Said they were communing with nature."

I snorted.

Inspector Schumaker nodded. "More likely they were partying."

"Would Dunner have allowed that?"

He tucked the handkerchief away. "The pastor was already asleep."

Hmm. "The newspaper said that the girl fell in, and then someone saved her. They didn't say who, though, only that she was still alive when they got her out, then she died on the way to the hospital."

"We were having a cold snap," he said. "It was bitter outside, had been for nearly a week. Some of the river was iced up."

"Not a place I'd choose to 'commune with nature.' "

He looked his agreement at me. "The girl's name was Gwen Miller. It sounds like you've read the newspaper account of what happened, so you probably already know that."

In fact, I'd read it again that morning before leaving the house. "It also said she

174

lived in Spring Creek. Was she a runaway?"

Schumaker shook his head. "Friend of the family. Dunner himself brought her in to the emergency room. It wasn't fast enough to save her, though."

"And there was an investigation."

"Of course. They concluded it was an accident."

"Why do I get the feeling you don't buy that?"

He shrugged. "It wasn't my case, but I have no reason to doubt the conclusion. Dunner closed up Rancho Sueño after it all happened and moved to town. Said the press coverage brought a lot of negative attention to what he was doing."

"And what was he doing?"

"From what we could tell? Occasionally providing a safe place for kids in unfortunate circumstances to catch their breath. It wasn't a formal nonprofit organization or anything. He just opened his home to them when they showed up. Sometimes there'd be half a dozen in the house, sometimes none." He leaned back, balancing on two legs of the chair, and laced his fingers over his abdomen. "We never found anything illegal, or even untoward. And believe me, we checked. Anytime kids are involved we take a look at the supervising adults."

175

I laid the well-worn copy of my brother's final missive that I'd been carrying for two days now on the conference table and sat back in my chair. Bracing myself, I forced out the words: "Do you think Bobby Lee had anything to do with what happened that night?"

He glanced down at the letter, but didn't touch it. "No."

Relief whooshed through me.

Wariness mixed with regret crossed his face. "I looked back through our files — and the city police files as well — after you showed me the letter yesterday. It certainly does imply he and Tabby might have been involved in something . . . unlawful."

I realized I was holding my breath.

"According to all accounts, he wasn't out at Rancho Sueño the night Gwen Miller fell in the river. In fact, there's a note in the file that he hadn't been there for almost six months."

The small smile came to my face automatically. Anna Belle would be delighted to know that.

"However, there is a case that's still open from that time."

My attention snapped back to Inspector Schumaker.

"A hit-and-run death. Guy on a bike, that

same night."

That had been one of the other articles I'd printed out. I hunched around the instant knot of dread that settled in my stomach.

"Ms. Reynolds, what kind of vehicle did your brother drive?"

Sixteen

I scrambled through my memory, searching for the answer to Schumaker's question. Then I had it.

"I don't remember," I lied. And, of course, the instant the words came out of my mouth the inspector's sharp eye saw right through me.

He held my gaze. "Your parents would know. Maybe I should ask them."

I sighed. "He drove a Honda Prelude. It was an awful, banana yellow." Bobby Lee had loved it. He'd saved for years, and then made a screaming deal on the sporty little car. He'd even liked the ugly color.

Now I watched as disappointment flickered behind Schumaker's eyes. Ha!

"I don't suppose your parents owned a pickup."

Ah — now I remembered. The guy on the bike had been conscious long enough to say he'd been hit by a dark-colored pickup.

"Nope," I practically crowed. "We've never had a pickup. I have, of course, but not when I lived here, and not anymore. It got smooshed and went to truck heaven a few months back. Now I drive a snazzy old Land Rover."

He stared at me, and I struggled to guide my thoughts back into line. "Sorry," I said. "Bobby Lee didn't have a pickup. He didn't hit that bicyclist."

One corner of his mouth quirked up ruefully. "Well," he said. "It was a long shot anyway."

I glared. "Funny, I think it's good news that my brother didn't kill someone and then run away."

"Sorry." He ducked his head and dragged out that dang handkerchief again. "Sometimes I get a little carried away with my job."

"Yeah. Well." It wasn't like I hadn't run roughshod over a few people in the past, in order to get to the truth. "It's okay. Are we done here?"

He nodded. "I'll let you know if we have any more questions."

Naturally.

Traveling east, I followed the retreating shimmer of late summer heat that rose from the highway. The dirt road that wound down

179

to the T&J Dairy seemed quiet after all the comings and goings from the day before. In the parking lot, I turned off the ignition and sat, unmoving, as heat filled the car.

So much death. Violent death. Were there simply those of us who attracted it into our lives? Some people only encountered death by disease or age or their own demise. To others violence was a job: emergency room doctors and nurses, policemen, paramedics. How on earth did I keep getting into these situations?

A thread of sweat trickled down my back.

I popped the door open and got out, unsure of what I'd find in the house on the hill. No doubt the mold-ripened cheese class was canceled. I checked the lotion bar and cuticle scrubber I'd brought as a weird kind of condolence offering to make sure they hadn't melted in the heat. But Tabby seemed like a practical woman; certainly she'd appreciate a useful gift.

Okay, I had to admit, all Inspector Schumaker's talk about Tabby having motive to kill Joe had piqued my curiosity just the teensiest, tiniest bit. However, even I knew this wasn't the time to quiz a grieving widow about the past.

Celeste came to the door, heavy disapproval weighing her features the moment

180

she saw me.

"Tabby's not here," she said by way of greeting.

"I see. Do you know when she'll be back?"

A young girl came up behind Celeste, her straight brown hair pulled back into a rough ponytail. Her nose was all puffy, and a streak of mascara ran from one red-rimmed eye down to her jaw line. "Mama's making cheese. She's out by the mold house."

Celeste put her arm around the girl and guided her back inside. "Delight, honey, you don't have to talk to anyone."

The door shut in my face.

Gosh, I'd only wanted to express my sympathies. Tabby's mom acted like I'd killed Joe myself.

My nose found the mold house. It was behind the barn, a small, metal trailer with the door open a few inches. That was enough to release the pungent, complex odor of cheese mold.

"You're a little early for class, aren't you Sophie Mae?"

I spun around to find Tabby right behind me, holding a large wheel of cheese. She stepped past me, opening the door all the way. The blast of stink made my eyes water, and I coughed.

An easy laugh echoed from within the

mold house, then Tabby reappeared looking amused. "It's a little much at first." She handed me a small round. "Here."

The outside of the round was hard and mottled white and charcoal-blue. The cheese had slumped in the middle, and it was surprisingly heavy. "What is it?"

"It's one of my varieties. I call it 'Poudre Bleu,' after the Cache la Poudre River that runs by here. It's great with walnuts, maybe a nice Sangiovese."

"Um, thanks." I was utterly flummoxed. Here I was, all ready to offer sympathy to a tragic figure after my encounter with the mourning generations on either side of her, and instead I find this woman smoothly coiffed and at ease, working away as if nothing had happened.

If I hadn't been the one to provide her alibi, I'd have suspected that she'd killed Joe, too.

At the very least she didn't miss him much. Though from what I'd seen, I couldn't exactly blame her. I mean, I wouldn't have wished the guy dead, but I could sure understand wishing him *gone.*

"Here. I brought you these." I held out the small bag. "The flat one in the shape of a leaf is a lotion bar. Good for really dry hands. The little container with the screw cap is cuticle smoother."

She took the bag and thanked me, motioning for me to follow her to the milking barn. A cow in the pasture lowed, long and deep, and another answered it in kind. I stood in the doorway as she went in and talked to a handsome Latino guy and a petite blonde woman who were sluicing down equipment with foamy liquid. I couldn't hear, but Tabby gestured and spoke for a while, and they nodded in understanding.

When she returned, I asked, "Your employees?"

"Eduardo and Gretchen. Couldn't run the place without them."

"Where were they yesterday? Did the sheriff interview them?"

"Eduardo had to drive down to Denver to get a part for one of the milking machines, and Gretchen had the day off. I try to manage it so I always have some help around, but I do a lot of the work here myself."

I guessed Joe didn't count as help. But it had been convenient for the murderer, I thought, that Eduardo wasn't at the dairy yesterday. Of course, there was enough to do in an operation like this that he might not have seen anything anyway.

"How often do you milk?"

"Twice a day, without fail." She seemed

pretty cheerful about it.

"Are you going to keep the dairy?"

Her head jerked back in surprise. "Of course! Why wouldn't I? It was my idea in the first place. I can hire a delivery driver now that Joe isn't out spending our profits on booze and poker and bail."

Wow.

"You seem to be doing all right," I said.

Her eyes cut sideways to mine, containing more sadness than I'd given her credit for. "I'm heartbroken for my daughter. Delight is just devastated, and I want to make it better for her, but I can't." The blue eyes welled. "But the animals still need to be cared for, and there's still a business to run. I don't have a choice."

"I see," I said, keeping my tone neutral. "And you're still teaching the cheese class?"

She shrugged. "Well, I wasn't planning on it, but if you want me to I will. Isn't that why you're here?"

"I came by to see how you're doing. I assumed you'd cancel the class." I didn't think I could take learning how to make more cheese after what I'd witnessed yesterday.

"Okay." She seemed distracted. Well, who wouldn't be?

"I signed my statement at the sheriff's department this morning," I said.

Her head was tipped back, her gaze directed at the sky. I looked up and saw a red-tailed hawk circling overhead.

"Inspector Schumaker and I ended up talking about Rancho Sueño."

The hawk screamed.

When I looked back at Tabby, her shoulders were hunched, and her lips had thinned into a grim line. "Why can't you just leave it alone?" she whispered.

Taken aback by the sudden change in her demeanor, I stammered, "Uh, it just came up, you know. Nothing to do with Joe. I'd heard Bobby Lee was involved with the Dunners, that's all."

Iron replaced the whisper. "He hated it out there. He only went because of me."

"Until he stopped going, right? Is that why you and Joe —" I stopped. Plunged on. "Did you and Joe get together after Bobby Lee was gone because of a shared interest in religion?"

Tabby let out a harsh, abrupt laugh at that. "Can you imagine Joe on the God-Squad? Please."

She had a point.

"So why did you go?"

Her smile held no humor. "Ray Dunner had good weed."

"What?"

185

Seventeen

"Son of a preacher man. You know the type."

"Is that why Bobby Lee went out there?"

"Nah. He was too straight-laced." Suddenly, she looked very afraid. "Please stop this, Sophie Mae. Please. No good can come of it."

Maybe no good for her. The way Tabby was acting made me question Inspector Schumaker's assertion that Bobby Lee's death had nothing to do with Rancho Sueño. Somebody had to get to the bottom of what happened, once and for all.

"Gwen Miller died," I said. "Do you remember that?"

Her eyes shot to the left, and she cleared her throat.

"Tabby?"

The fingers on her left hand fluttered up to her lips, but she still wouldn't look at me. Her gold wedding ring glinted even in the shade. "Of course I remember. It was terrible." The slightest tremor shook her voice.

"Were you there?"

Her chin swung back and forth in a negative.

"Tabby."

"What?" Her voice went up two octaves as the words tumbled out. "What do you want from me? It was a horrible thing that happened. And then Bobby Lee died. And now my husband has been murdered, and you just keep at it and keep at it. I can't help you, and even if I could, I don't want to!"

I cringed with dismay. Hadn't I told myself I wouldn't quiz a grieving widow? God, I was worse than Inspector Schumaker by a long shot.

"I'm so, so sorry."

She sniffed.

"I'll leave now."

"That might be best."

"Thanks again for the cheese." I began walking to my car.

"Sophie Mae?"

I stopped.

"I'm sorry, too." She strode purposefully back into the mold house and shut the door behind her.

Completely stymied, I continued down to the Subaru. I still felt like dirt. Tabby had been through so much. But I was also certain she was lying about something — if not everything. Is that what she had meant by, "I'm sorry"?

God, that woman was confusing.

I pulled onto the asphalt and considered my options. A glance at my watch reminded me that Barr would be landing in Denver any minute. This time of day it would probably be an hour and a half before he got to my parents' house.

Plenty of time to hunt for a few more clues in the library's microfilm.

A group of teenagers who were working on a homework project together destroyed the usual hushed calm in the library, despite regular attempts by the staff to quiet them down. However, I was soon oblivious, thoroughly engrossed in the news stories from the weeks after Bobby Lee's death.

First I discovered a follow-up to the hit-and-run accident. Spring Creek Police and the victim's family pled for witnesses or anyone with information on the driver of the pickup to come forward. It didn't look like anyone had stepped up, and, given Schumaker's questions about Bobby Lee's vehicle that morning, the case was still open after all these years.

Then I found two stories about Ogden Dunner and Rancho Sueño. Neither was about Gwen Miller's death. I made a couple of notes, then moved on. The fourth article took a lot longer to track down, and it was only a small blurb about Dunner saying he wouldn't be taking in any more stray teens at Rancho Sueño.

A glance at my watch made me swear under my breath. I'd skimmed all the articles on the hard-to-read screen and now tapped my foot as I waited for the pokey old printer to disgorge the pages. One of the high school girls at a nearby table pointed at me and giggled to her friend. Belatedly I realized I was drumming my fingers on a bookcase at the same time my foot tapped away. It must have looked like I suffered from multiple tics.

If I didn't hurry, Barr would arrive at the house before me. He'd have to face my parents — face Anna Belle — for the first time all by himself. Ack! Couldn't that thing print any faster?

I broke the speed limit all the way home, praying for lots of highway construction on Interstate 25. Anything to slow my dear fiancé's progress.

No such luck. A rental car sat in the driveway. I was too late to save him.

Barreling through the front door, I ran straight into Barr. He caught me, wrapped his long arms around me, and held me in silence for a long moment before tipping my head back and laying a big ol' I've-missed-the-heck-out-of-you smacker on me.

"Hi," he said and smiled.

"Hi," I said and smiled back.

"You're late," my mother said, but she was smiling, too, looking down on the great room from the kitchen counter. Everyone else, even Erin, was crowded behind her as if they were going to miss something vitally important.

Reddening, I flapped my hands at them all. "Show's over." And then to Barr, "I take it you've met my parents."

In the kitchen, no one had moved.

"We'll be right in," he called over his shoulder, and somehow that magically dispersed the whole group.

"I'm sorry I'm late."

"No problem," he said with a grin. "We were just talking flower arrangements."

I put my hand over my eyes. "Nooo . . ."

"How are you?" he asked. "You look great."

"I'm better now that you're here."

"Me, too." Another kiss. "Have you found out anything new?" Ah, my sweetie: my detective.

"Maybe," I said. "I'll tell you later."

He nodded his understanding. I wasn't ready to regale my parents with the information I'd gleaned that day until I could make a little more sense out of it myself. Arm around my shoulder, he guided me toward the kitchen where Anna Belle hovered over the stacks of bridal magazines, checklists, photos of wedding gowns, and invitation samples spread out all over the table.

I groaned. "What happened to simple?"

"Barr *likes* the gerbera daisies," she said.

"That's great!" I forced out, all bright and cheery.

He laughed and said, "I brought Scotch. Would you like one?"

I nodded so hard my neck popped.

EIGHTEEN

Thank heavens the wedding plans took a back seat at dinner, once more eaten on the patio, but for once not cooked on the grill. Dad brought out one of his reliable specialties: egg-battered chili rellenos stuffed with queso fresco, olives, and toasted pine nuts and drowned in his spicy pork green chili. Add a big side salad, fresh corn chips, garden salsa, and fresh guacamole, and it was a feast fit for royalty. The margaritas were classic, consisting only of aged tequila, Grand Marnier, and lime juice mixed with plenty of ice. After the single-malt Laphroaig Barr had offered, I limited myself to one.

We lingered over the food while my parents got to know Barr a little better, and he them. They asked about his work, about the changes we were making to the house, and about his family. He wanted to know more about their teaching careers and even managed to get my father to tell a few war stories from his reporting days.

When Dad brought out the dessert, we all groaned, but no one said no. Homemade angel food cake smothered in spiced peaches and heavy cream whipped with lots of vanilla.

"I'm not going to be able to move for a week," I said, settling back in my chair and closing my eyes.

"We'll do the dishes," Meghan said, reaching for her own plate.

I cracked one eye. She was such a tiny little thing, maybe tipping the scales to a hundred pounds with snow boots on, but she'd packed away a big portion of that wonderful food tonight and still felt frisky.

Kelly reached over and took her hand.

Oh. No wonder.

"You will do no such thing. It's my job to do the dishes when Calvin cooks," my mother said, immediately taking the plate from Meghan and motioning my father to his feet. He obeyed with alacrity.

"Oh, let them do it," I said to my parents. "They only got to spend the whole day together; don't deny them some kitchen time as well."

Kelly grinned.

"Nonsense," Anna Belle said and bustled

into the kitchen with Dad trailing behind her.

"They didn't get to spend the whole day alone, though. Not with me there," Erin said.

The trace of bitterness underlying her words made me open the other eye. Kelly regarded her with surprise, Meghan with concern. Beside me, Barr watched the tableau with one eyebrow slightly raised.

Erin saw us all watching her. She launched to her feet and ran inside.

"What," Kelly said, "was that all about? Did I do something wrong?"

Meghan looked after her daughter with a combination of bewilderment and guilt on her face. "Of course not."

"Does she resent me encroaching on your vacation?"

My housemate shook her head. "She seems to think she's the one encroaching."

Poor Bug, I thought. Eleven wasn't easy to start with, and there were a lot of changes going on around her these days.

The house wasn't set up for so many guests, but Anna Belle was surprisingly enthusiastic about having a houseful and had cheerfully made do. She'd made up a bed on the sofa in the basement for Kelly, and happily supplied a sleeping bag when Barr had requested to sleep in the backyard, under the stars. I'd protested, but she'd shushed me.

"All men like to revisit their youth once in a while. Besides, you two will have more privacy out there than anywhere in the house."

I'd gaped at her, but she just smiled and went to track down another pillow.

Now it was nearly midnight, and Barr and I sat out on the patio enjoying the cool air and talking. Cassiopeia rode her glittering throne overhead. A light breeze carried the scent of night-blooming nicotiana from the side of the house, and crickets chirped from under the bushes.

In low tones, I told Barr about what I'd learned — and hadn't learned — from Inspector Schumaker that morning, as well as Tabby's odd behavior at the dairy.

"It was really strange, how cool and collected she was. I tried to convince myself that Joe's death hadn't hit home yet, but I don't know if she misses him at all. Or maybe she's being stoic in order to keep it together for her daughter."

"People react to loss in different ways."

"I suppose so. But Tabby's all over the board. First she seemed willing to talk about Rancho Sueño, and then all of a sudden she reversed herself and wanted me to leave. All along she insisted none of it had anything to do with Bobby Lee. I'm positive she's lying about something, Barr."

"Of course she is," he said. "Everyone lies."

"I don't. At least not often."

"Sure you do. You just don't do it very well."

I punched him lightly on the arm, but didn't argue the point.

"Why didn't you want to tell your parents about any of this?" he asked.

"There's nothing to tell them, really. It's all more or less a lack of information, and I don't want to get their hopes up unless I find out something truly useful." My shoulders rose and fell. "Something isn't right about the whole Gwen Miller story, despite what Schumaker told me. I want to talk to the girl who was there, the one who spoke with the authorities at the hospital that night."

"Do you know who she is?"

I shook my head. "I didn't want to ask Schumaker. For one thing he probably wouldn't tell me anyway because he thinks I'm trying to solve Joe's murder — did I tell you he called and talked to Sergeant Zahn?"

Barr grimaced.

"I know. But I guess Zahn doesn't hate me as much as I thought he did. Anyway, the other reason I don't want to ask Schumaker is because he might start to think Bobby Lee really did have something to do with Miller's death. I mean, I showed him the note, so he knows Bobby Lee did *something* wrong."

"Or thought he did something wrong," Barr said.

"That would almost be worse." One corner of my mouth turned down. "Anyway, take a look at these." I handed him the printouts from the library. "These are why I was late, and you had to deal with my parents all by your lonesome right off the bat."

"I like your folks," he said, taking the papers. "You know I can't read these in the dark."

"Oh. Right. Well, they aren't that informative. The first is about how the hit-and-run driver hadn't been found yet; that's not really useful since Schumaker already indicated by his questions this morning that the case is still open eighteen years later."

"And doesn't seem to have anything to do with your brother," Barr said.

I nodded. "Then there are two stories about Rancho Sueño. Neither was written by the same reporter who first wrote about Gwen Miller's death. The first one mentions the accident, but merely as evidence that there was inadequate supervision at Rancho Sueño. The second came out about a month later, and was a weak attempt at an exposé. It cites some of the rules Dunner imposed on the kids who stayed there."

"Like what?"

"Oh, things like they had to pray with him before each meal, and everyone had daily chores. They grew a lot of their own food, and the teenagers who stayed there had to help. And if anyone was found with drugs or alcohol they had to leave."

"Except for Ray Dunner and his 'good weed,' " Barr said, referencing Tabby's stated reason for spending time at Rancho Sueño.

"Right. I wonder whether he shared it with everyone, or just Tabby and Joe?"

"I wonder where Tabby and Joe were the night the Miller girl fell in the water," Barr said.

"Me, too. And where Bobby Lee was that night, as well." I sighed. "It was all so long ago. Makes it extra hard to get information when people have to rely on memories that are eighteen years old."

"And when they don't want to tell you

something in the first place."

"Yeah, then there's that. Anyway, Dunner's place didn't sound that bad. I mean, I wouldn't have wanted to stay there, but I wasn't a desperate teenaged runaway looking for, as Schumaker put it, a place to catch my breath. He seemed to think Dunner was doing a good thing out there, though I could tell he didn't care much for Dunner's son."

"Maybe the sheriff's department knew about the drugs."

"Hmm. Maybe. For an exposé this sure doesn't seem very scintillating, yet when Dunner closed the doors to outsiders, it was supposedly because of poor publicity. There were kids involved, but other than Gwen Miller's death, nothing sordid or even sad. Dunner seemed to be the real thing — a man of God who wanted to do something good. Maybe a little more enthusiastic than some, but not a bad guy."

A flash of light near the horizon brought a smile to both our faces: heat lightning. Another flash followed immediately, and then another and another. We fell silent, mesmerized by the show. My hand crept over to Barr's and our fingers intertwined.

After a few minutes of dark sky, I asked, "Do you think Joe's murder had anything to do with what happened back then?"

Barr inhaled, thinking. "If I'd known the guy I might be able to speculate, but I really don't know enough about the situation to have an opinion."

"I guess I don't either. It'd be an awful strange coincidence if they were completely unrelated, is all."

"You're right about that." Another flicker of lightning on the horizon. "So whatever happened to Ogden Dunner?"

I turned to look at him, all shadowy handsome in the moonlight. "I wonder."

"We could —"

"Tomorrow," I said. "Right now I want to stop talking and try out that sleeping bag."

His teeth flashed white in the darkness. "Hard to argue with that."

Kitty Wampus had kindly deposited a present beside my bed during the night. My bare foot landed on the cold, wet hairball first thing Thursday morning, which did little to improve my reluctance to greet the day. Grumbling, I cleaned it up then shuffled down to the kitchen, still in my bathrobe and ducky slippers.

Barr sat at the kitchen table typing on his laptop. He had showered and dressed in a pair of khaki shorts, a polo shirt, and Birkenstocks. No cowboy boots or bolo ties on vacation, I guessed.

I sat down across from him and reached for the carafe of coffee.

He looked up and smiled. "Nice bed head."

My hand flew to my hair. I could feel it sticking up on one side of my head like a punk rocker with a bad stylist. "Thanks."

"Drink your coffee. Then we'll talk." He took a bite of the quiche wedge on the plate by his elbow and went back to his computer.

I sipped in silence, letting the caffeine take effect. It had been a late night — a late and active night.

"How long have you been up?" I still sounded pretty grumpy.

He peered at me from under his eyebrows and refilled my cup. "Couple of hours. Drink."

Obedient, I swallowed. He knew I didn't function well on a few hours of sleep, nor without a fair amount of caffeine in my system first thing in the morning. It didn't seem to bother him. Yet.

We'd see, though, how my morning crankiness went over on a daily basis. Who knew what irritating foibles each would encounter in the other? My first husband had left cupboard doors and drawers open in the kitchen and bathroom all the time. It had driven me crazy for the first two years we were married, until finally I realized he wasn't going to change so I'd better learn how to live with it.

I put my cup down. "Where is everyone?"

Barr took another bite of quiche and leaned back. He swallowed and said, "Kelly, Meghan, and Erin went to the bike library in Old Town. The plan was to check out some bikes and go for a long ride along the river. Your mother's at the gym, and your dad's downstairs."

"Meditating or yoga-ing or some such," I said. "How long has he been down there?"

"Hour or so." He got up and went to the counter where he sliced off a chunk of quiche and put it on a plate along with a pile of blueberries and brought it to me.

I leaned forward. Swiss cheese with bacon, broccoli and onion, no doubt on Dad's all-butter crust. Yum . . .

"Thanks," I said, as grateful to be waited on as I was for the food.

"You're welcome." Barr turned his laptop around so I could see the screen.

"What am I looking at?" I took a creamy, savory bite and chewed slowly, allowing the flavors to roll over my tongue. Between that first bite and two cups of coffee, I began to feel downright human. "Are you shopping for a new car?"

"Look at the name of the business."

"Dunner & Son Auto Sales. Oh, wow. So Ogden Dunner is still in town. Nice job!"

"Well, his business is still in town. He could have sold it, along with the name."

I pushed back from the table and stood. "I'm getting dressed, and then we're going down there and find out."

Barr nodded. "Okay, I'm game. But aren't you going to finish your breakfast first?"

The wedge of quiche, minus that single bite, beckoned. I sat down. "It's been eighteen years. I guess it can wait fifteen minutes more." The next bite contained a big chunk of bacon, verifying the wisdom of my decision.

"What are we going to say to him?" I asked after another sip of coffee.

Barr looked out the window and smiled. "We'll play it by ear."

I didn't know whether he was happy to be in on my little investigation or happy to be with me, but it didn't really matter. I was just glad to have him by my side and on my side.

NINETEEN

Instead of being on auto row south of Spring Creek, Dunner & Son Auto Sales was tucked off a side street in Old Town. It looked like a small operation, with only twenty-five or so cars in the lot, but they were all expensive foreign models: jaguars, BMWs, a beautifully restored MG in British racing green, and in one corner a stately looking vehicle Barr informed me was a Bentley.

Still, the place had a rundown, seedy look to it. Paint peeled from the exterior of the old building with the *Office* sign over the door, dust dulled the surfaces of the fancy vehicles, and thistles and bindweed flourished in the planting strips surrounding the lot.

My fingers curled around the old wrought-iron stair railing, and it rattled against the bolts that held it to the wooden stairs. The bars set into the windows matched the railing. Overall, the place radiated Old West grimness.

We went up the short stairway and through the door. The sudden dimness slowed my steps. The clammy air smelled of scorched coffee and Pine-Sol. Behind an unmanned reception counter, two desks faced each other from opposite sides of the room, and three windows, also heavily fortified, punctuated the back wall.

I turned to Barr. He shrugged.

The sound of a toilet flushing drifted through a closed door on the right. It opened to reveal a man about my age still hitching up his pants. He saw us and hurried to the counter.

Please God, don't let him try to shake my hand. No way had this guy taken the time to wash his hands.

"Hiya, hiya. Sorry, 'bout that," he said. "I'm here alone today, and you know, sometimes a man's just gotta do what a man's gotta do."

"No problem," Barr said.

I smiled, my radar on high alert. Something about this guy, just being in the same room with him, set my internal alarm bell to jangling.

"Are you Dunner or Son?" Barr asked in a light tone.

We both could see he wasn't old enough to be Ogden Dunner. But he looked to be about the right age to be his son.

"Ray Dunner, at your service."

I'd wanted to meet the father, but Ray would have to do, at least for now. And, after all, he'd been the one at the river when Gwen Miller fell in — though I didn't know how on earth I could bring up that painful incident with any finesse.

Barr started asking him questions about an XJ something-or-other. My eyes had adjusted to the difference in light, and now I perused Dunner's face while trying not to be obvious about it. He was short and stout, his considerable gut hanging over his belt buckle. His thinning blonde hair didn't stop the dandruff from sifting down to the shoulders of his dark blue shirt, and the broken capillaries on his nose and cheeks formed a complicated road map of dissolution. As Barr spoke, Dunner fidgeted, moving his head side to side as if trying to work out a crick, squinting and pursing his lips. All together the movements gave him the air of a teenager with ADD who didn't really care about anything the teacher was saying.

His eyes belayed any notion that he was stupid, though. Dark and watchful, they sent a cringe down my spine when they met mine.

"Let's go take a look at that beauty, then," Dunner said, leaning across the counter.

I tried not to wince as a wave of rank halitosis drifted over me.

"Oh, I'm not sure whether we're ready to buy yet," Barr said.

"Please, honey?" I said. "Pretty please? It's so cute." I had no idea which car they were talking about.

"Well, there ya go, buddy. The little lady has spoken." Dunner bustled out from behind the counter and opened the door to the lot.

"That's right," I said. My voice had gone up at least an octave.

Barr looked down at me. Raised one eyebrow, which Dunner couldn't see.

I grinned. He rolled his eyes.

We tagged after Ray Dunner, who glowed pale in the August sun and instantly began to sweat. Any sports this guy was interested in were on the screen in the corner of his living room. He led us to a low, sleek Jaguar, easily the sexiest car on the lot. Cute didn't even begin to describe it.

"This little lady of yours here has real good taste." He opened the driver's door.

"Lookit this interior — all leather. Soft as butter."

And hot as hell. Even with the old asphalt beneath our feet beginning to soften in the heat, the air coming out of the closed car felt like a blast furnace.

Dunner jingled the keys.

I sighed, long and loud.

"What's the matter?" he asked.

"It's just not quite right. I wanted one with a white interior."

Behind me, Barr snorted.

"White?" Dunner asked.

I nodded. "My friend, Tabby Bines, said you'd be the man to talk to." Too late I wondered whether Ray and Tabby were still in contact. I couldn't really tell from his reaction.

"Tabby. Bines."

I nodded again, adding extra vigor.

"Sent you out to see me."

"Well . . ." I scrambled for just the right words. What would Anna Belle do?

"She said you carried the kind of car little Sophie Mae here wants me to buy her."

My head whipped around so fast my neck hurt. Little Sophie Mae, indeed. It was one thing for me to let Ray Dunner refer to me like a second-class citizen, but Barr better not get any ideas. Amusement played across his features at my reaction.

I looked back at Dunner. Tried a wink. "You remember Tabby, don't you? From when she and my brother used to go out to your place, way back when?" That's what Anna Belle would do: charm, manipulate, and lie like a rug if she had to. So perhaps I had the gene for lying after all. I just needed to practice more.

"Who's your brother?" The words were flat, as was the gaze. His fidgeting quieted, too. I bet Dunner knew darn well who I was; Bobby Lee and I had looked too much alike for him to have missed the resemblance.

Beside me, Barr tensed. He didn't say anything, though, and I plunged on.

"Bobby Lee Watson. He's no longer with us, you know." Wide eyes. Big blink. I waited for the inevitable sympathy.

"I didn't know Bobby Lee had a sister. So you're friends with Tabitha Atwood."

"Bines," I said. "Tabby Bines."

"Right. Married." He lifted his left palm to the sky. "Or at least she was."

So he knew about Joe's murder. Of course, all that proved was that he read the paper or watched television. The story was all over the news.

"Terrible tragedy, what happened to Joe,"

209

I said. "Terrible."

Dunner blinked slowly. "Mm-hmm." The dark eyes in that pale face looked reptilian.

"I was there when it happened, you know." It wasn't hard to sound frightened.

"You don't say. Musta been awful," he said, rotating on his heel and moving back toward the air-conditioned office. Apparently he'd given up on us as potential customers. But we were right behind him. "You see who did it?" He tossed the question so casually over his shoulder that it took me a moment to realize what he was asking.

"What? Of course not. If I had, then the sheriff would've already arrested the killer."

He stumbled on my last word, paused, then went up the steps and opened the office door. Looking over his shoulder at me he said, "Depends on what you saw."

I trotted in after him, Barr silent beside me.

"Well, I didn't see anything."

Dunner regarded me with narrowed eyes from behind the counter. "Is that so. Well, now, you tell Tabitha hello from Ray Dunner. And tell her I'll be giving her a call soon, okay?"

Condolence call or threat?

"Listen," I said. "I want you to know that I think it's a real shame you all had to shut down your Rancho Sueño place. It sounds like it was a good thing while it lasted, and helped a lot of teens who were in serious trouble."

Dunner grew still again. "That was something my father did. I was just a kid."

I could feel the tension roll off Barr, and I glanced up at him. His poker face was impeccable, though, a mask of polite interest. He smiled at me. "Where was that place again?"

"You know, I'm not sure. Ray, it was out east of town, wasn't it?" I asked, all chatty-like. "Oh, my God. Are you okay?" His face had suffused with red so quickly I thought he was going to have some kind of attack. "Mr. Dunner? Ray?"

"Maybe you should ask your good friend *Tabitha* where our place was." He grated the words out.

"Ray." The single word came from the doorway, and Barr and I turned to find an older gentleman had joined us. He was rail-thin, with a gaunt, Lincolnesque face under bushy eyebrows. His brown eyes smiled at us both.

"Dad." Ray Dunner's tone held warning.

I glanced at Barr. So this was Ogden Dunner. Very unlike his son, it appeared.

Now he came into the office and intro-

211

duced himself. "Are you two looking for a new car?" he asked, then laughed. "Or a new old car? We've got both kinds here."

Barr spoke. "We were looking at one of your Jags, and then Sophie Mae and your son here got to talking about some people they knew back in the day."

Ogden's look contained interest and kindness. "You're Sophie Mae Watson, aren't you?"

Nonplussed, I said, "Used to be, yes."

"Well, dear, you have wonderful taste in cars. And you, sir," he said to Barr, "have wonderful taste in women."

If Ray Dunner had said that I would have been disgusted, but coming from his father, who gazed at us both as if he genuinely meant it, I found myself almost charmed. This guy was either a bona fide good guy or a terrific con artist. Either way, I found myself smiling.

"I'm afraid we're not quite ready to buy yet," Barr started.

"In fact, they were just leaving," Ray said.

"Really? That's too bad. I would've liked to try and convince you of all the positive attributes of the Jaguar. They're very nice machines."

"I'm sure they are. We'll be back if we decide to buy one," Barr said.

"That'd be fine. Well, you have yourselves a nice rest of the day, then." And darn it if he didn't seem to mean that with every fiber of his being.

We thanked him and left.

In the rental car again, I asked Barr, "Did Ogden get rid of us? Or did Ray?"

"Hard to tell." He shook his head. "So much for the pretty Jag."

"I have the best car ever, thanks to you," I said, and leaned over to kiss him on the cheek. A few months earlier, Barr had given me a used Land Rover when my little Toyota pickup had met with an unfortunate end. It was dark green, and I loved to drive it. It was also a very practical vehicle for running errands for my soap-making business.

"God, you do wade right in, don't you, Sophie Mae."

"What do you mean? I didn't ask either of them a single thing about Bobby Lee, didn't ask anything about Gwen Miller's death, didn't ask much of anything at all. But we did get a pretty good feeling for how Ray felt about Tabby, and Joe, too."

"Mr. Dunner the younger doesn't strike me as the nicest of men."

"That," I said, "is the understatement of the day. You know, I keep wondering . . ."

"What?"

"According to the newspaper there were three other people there when Gwen Miller fell into the river besides Ray Dunner. Inspector Schumaker said the same thing. One was the mystery girl I mentioned last night, the one who talked with the sheriff's department. He told me the other two were runaways staying at Rancho Sueño, that they got spooked and left before the authorities got involved. They couldn't track them down afterwards, and he thought they probably had given false names to Dunner. I went back and looked. The article said the authorities were looking for Tom and Jane Smith."

"Yeah, those names sound fake, all right. But it makes sense; runaways never give their real names to cops or social workers."

"Right. But the article in the paper didn't say who the girl who stuck around was. I wonder why."

"The law tends to protect kids. That's a good thing."

"Oh, I agree. But just because you're a teenager doesn't mean you're a child. They didn't say how old the runaway siblings were, but they wouldn't call them runaways if they were eighteen or older, right?"

Barr nodded.

"And I think Ray Dunner was nineteen. I'm surprised everyone was so protective of this one witness. After all, the paper was willing to publish the names of the brother and sister who hightailed it out of there, even if they were fake."

Speculation settled on Barr's face as he drove. "Maybe she was quite young. Plus, they were trying to track down the siblings who ran away, so publishing their names makes more sense. I don't know." He shook his head and glanced over at me. "Okay, so it does sound off. But all this happened almost two decades ago. There's just so much we don't know."

My shoulders slumped. "And can never know."

"Do you want me to ask your Inspector Schumaker about the mystery girl?" he asked.

"He's not my inspector. And no, I don't think so. I'm still leery about making it sound like Bobby Lee had something to do with the Miller girl."

"Do you think he did?"

"Bobby Lee? Not really. But if he did have anything to do with that girl's death, it would kill my parents."

"Doesn't sound like the brother you've described to me."

"Of course not. And there's no evidence at all that he was even there. Still, I can't believe he was involved with the Dunners or Rancho Sueño at all."

"A boy will do a lot for a girl," he said. "Love is blind."

"It better not be. You're not some crazed serial killer, are you?"

He grinned. "Maybe. The wife's always the last to know."

I rolled my eyes and looked out the window, watching a bicyclist riding toward us. He was about twenty, and took a long puff off his cigarette as he rode by. The irony distracted me for another couple of blocks. Barr turned on the radio and Neil Young's voice filled the car.

Down by the river . . .

I flicked it off, and silence returned. "The reporter would know," I said.

"Who the other girl was? Yeah. Probably. But why would he tell you?"

"She."

"Okay, why would she tell you?"

"She might not. But it was a long time ago, as everyone keeps saying. It can't hurt to try."

He made a left turn, heading back toward my parents' house. "The same argument you make for not pushing the sheriff's department for an answer applies here. You could just stir up trouble, make this reporter look for dirt on Bobby Lee."

"Maybe. But Schumaker's seen the letter and knows I'm trying to find out more about Bobby Lee. This woman would only know that I'm . . ." I wracked my brain for a good story.

"That you were a teenaged runaway and stayed at Rancho Sueño for a while, and now you're trying to track down someone you knew there."

"Wow. You're good at this stuff." Still, it felt like such a, well, a lie. Which, of course, it was. A lie I'd use if I had to.

TWENTY

The newspaper had no idea who I was talking about when I asked to speak to Carrie Romain, the reporter who had written the article about Gwen Miller. I was shuttled back and forth for a while, until it became obvious she didn't work there anymore. I hung up and frowned at Barr, sitting at the kitchen table across from me.

"Now why would I think a reporter would still be at the same job after all this time?" I stifled the urge to thump the heel of my hand against my forehead.

He took a bite of spicy zucchini bread spread with cream cheese and washed it down with a long swallow of iced tea. Cold droplets ran down the glass where his fingers had disturbed the condensation.

"You think she's still in town?"

"Who knows?" I grumped. "Probably not, the way people move around any more."

"Check the phone book, crankypants.

Romain isn't that common a name."

He was right. There was only one Romain listed. Grant Romain.

"She's moved," I said. "She could be anywhere." I picked up the phone and dialed the number, though. Perhaps Grant was a relative and could tell me where to find Carrie.

The man who answered confirmed that his name was Grant. When I told him I was looking for Carrie, there was long pause, and I wondered whether I'd happened into a family feud.

"Um, were you a friend of hers?"

I closed my eyes and covered them with my hand. *Were.* I'd done it again. Carrie Romain was deceased.

"My name is Sophie Mae Reynolds. I, uh, was trying to track down some information from one of her newspaper stories from several years ago, some information that wasn't included but that I thought she might have in her notes." I stopped and waited for him to tell me.

"I'm afraid Carrie passed away fourteen years ago. Cancer."

"I'm so very sorry. Are you . . . were you her husband?"

"Thank you. Yes, she was my wife. Um, perhaps if you tell me a little more about which story you were interested in, I could check her notes and get back to you? I still have all of them, and she was religious about keeping them in order."

Hope flickered on the edge of my awareness, but I kept my voice even as I said, "That's very generous of you, Mr. Romain. The story was about a girl who fell in the river east of town. She was rescued but then died on the way to the hospital. Hypothermia." I told him the date the story had appeared in the *Courier*.

A sharp intake of breath, and then its slow release. "Gwen Miller," he said.

The hope flared bright. "Yes."

"Why are you inquiring into her death?"

Lying was all well and good, but I usually had better luck with the truth. Besides, I wasn't on the defensive with a reporter or anyone in law enforcement here, merely talking to a widower. "My brother was involved with Rancho Sueño. He killed himself, and I'm trying to figure out why."

Barr's head jerked up at my bald words.

Grant Romain said, "Um, Sophie Mae?" Something in his voice.

Now trepidation bordering on dread swirled into my emotional mix. The hand holding the phone trembled, and the handset knocked gently against my ear. Barr's eyebrows furrowed and concern sharpened his gaze.

"Yes?"

"I think you'd better come to my house and see those notes for yourself."

Questions poured out of Barr as we drove to Romain's home.

"Yes, he seemed to know exactly what I was talking about," I said. "And I certainly got the feeling he had more information that he's willing to share, but other than that we just have to wait until we get there. Turn left at Cheyenne Avenue. We're almost there," I said, peering at the directions I'd scribbled down.

We pulled up in front of an older ranch-style home in the neighborhood known locally as Indian Hills. The lawn was neatly mowed, the landscape tidy, and flowerbeds along the front of the house shone forth in a flurry of brilliant color. Zinnias hovered behind delicate moss roses, and above them towered flirty hollyhocks. Roses were interspersed with freeform evergreen topiaries along the sides of the curving cement pathway leading from the public sidewalk in front. The beds on each side of the driveway boasted hardy perennials, among them wild geraniums, purple larkspur, yellow potentilla, brilliant California poppies and clumps of ornamental grass. An apple tree shaded the open garage. The air smelled green.

A tall woman with hair more salt than pepper answered the door. Her smile crinkled the skin around clear blue eyes, and her colorful East Indian print sundress set off a deep tan.

"Um, hi. I'm Sophie Reynolds," I said, stumbling over the words. "This is my fiancé, Barr Ambrose." I made a vague gesture to where he stood behind me.

"And you're here to see Grant," she finished for me. "I'm Lorrie Romain. Come on in."

I crossed the threshold, glancing down at the ring on her left hand. Well, people did get remarried, didn't they? I was, after all. My first husband, Mike Reynolds, had been gone six years now, and he wouldn't have wanted it any other way.

"He's down in the basement, going through Carrie's old files. Seemed pretty excited after you called. Follow me."

We did, down a short hallway painted red-orange and decorated floor to ceiling with funky African art and masks. At the bottom of the stairs we discovered an unfinished basement, surprisingly clean and dust free. Shelves all along the walls held boxes and bins with lids, each displaying a neat label marking the contents. Toward the back of the space a man stood hunched over a card table strewn with file folders.

"Grant, they're here," his wife said.

He looked up and waved us farther into the room. The impatient gesture was at odds with a man who looked like a cross between Jerry Garcia and Santa Claus. Cherub cheeks smiled under twinkling eyes and a thick, heavy mass of white hair. He wore denim shorts and a tie-dyed T-shirt with leather sandals.

"So you're Sophie Mae," he said. "Welcome to the archives."

"Thanks for being so willing to show me your, er, Carrie's notes. This is Barr Ambrose."

He shook Barr's hand vigorously, and then my own. "Pleasure to meet both of you." His arm stretched out over the table, encompassing all the paperwork. "These are all of Carrie's notes from the Miller girl's death and what she could find out about Rancho Sueño. I was just looking over them again to familiarize myself with the story."

"Grant was very interested in Carrie's work," Lorrie said. "She often discussed what she was writing and bounced ideas off him."

I looked at her, curious.

"Oh, Carrie and I were good friends. I miss her dearly. And her work fascinated me as well."

"This story was special, though," Grant said. "As soon as you mentioned Rancho Sueño and your brother, I knew I had to pass on the information she'd gathered. Carrie became ill shortly after she wrote it, and she had to leave the paper. But this story bothered her until she passed away."

In a careful tone, I asked, "Why was that?"

"Because enough things about it were fishy that she suspected there was a cover-up of some kind. She could never prove anything, though."

My pulse quickened. "Do you remember what she found 'fishy'?"

"There was a discrepancy between when the Miller girl went in the river and when she went to the hospital. Then two of the witnesses just up and left before talking to anyone, managing to disappear into thin air, despite the fact that they were teens on the run."

"The authorities tried to find them, figured they must have given Dunner false names."

"True, even believable. But it was still . . ."

"Fishy."

"Exactly."

"I'm interested in the time discrepancy you mention, between the accident and the hospital. That does sound suspicious. Is it possible it wasn't an accident at all? Why wouldn't the sheriff's department have pursued the investigation further?"

Romain's lips twisted ironically. "The problem kind of took care of itself."

I looked the question at him.

"Without the kids who took off before anyone could talk to them, the only witnesses were Ray Dunner, Ogden Dunner and another girl who was there."

"The mystery girl," I breathed.

He nodded. "Her story changed within an hour of getting to the hospital."

Intriguing. I plunged on. "Her name wasn't in any of your wife's articles. Did she know who she was?"

Grant Romain's head inclined a fraction. His next words seemed chosen with care. "According to Carrie's notes, the girl's name was Krista Jaikes."

It took a moment for that to sink in.

"Sheriff Jaikes' daughter." I glanced over at Barr.

"He wasn't sheriff then," Romain said. "He was a deputy. A deputy with ambition, but still a deputy."

My hand crept over my mouth. "Oh, my God. The sheriff covered something up, and . . ." My eyes welled. ". . . Bobby Lee —"

Romain held his hand up as Barr put his arm around my shoulder. "No, no, no. There's no proof of that at all. If there had been, Carrie would have gone with it. Krista was seventeen, so Carrie agreed to keep her name out of the article. And the sheriff's investigators believed her. It wasn't only her father."

"But it's still *fishy*."

He hesitated. "Yes. It was."

I leaned against Barr, reeling from this new information. It could be the key, the absolute key to everything.

Twenty-One

Grant handed us a stack of paper, saying, "I had time to copy the file notes, but not the two notebooks. Take those with you, if you'll promise to bring them back when you're done with them."

I was speechless in the face of his generosity.

"Thank you," Barr said with feeling. "This means a lot to us."

"It's what Carrie would have wanted," Lorrie said.

Romain nodded. "She's right. Carrie would have wanted you to have this information if there's any way it can bring you peace."

I managed to stammer out a thank you, and we took our leave loaded with more information from this one meeting than I'd managed to glean the whole time I'd been in Spring Creek.

In the passenger seat I rifled through the

paper the Romains had given us. "Let's get this stuff home and spread it out, see what else is here."

"Of course," Barr said, driving just as sedately as ever.

I was about to tell him to hurry, but when I looked over, the expression on his face stifled any thought I'd had about commenting on his old lady driving.

"What's wrong?" I asked.

He didn't say anything for a while. I waited, knowing he would eventually.

"Corrupt law enforcement pisses me off."

"Well, of course it does. But we don't know yet if that happened."

"If it did —"

"Then we'll deal with it when the time comes."

It wasn't his jurisdiction, and he didn't even live in the same state, but I knew if there was something awry in the local sheriff's department Barr would dive right in to fix it. I had to admit, the thought didn't exactly thrill me.

Maybe I'd change my mind if it turned out Sheriff Jaikes had jeopardized my brother.

When Dad walked into the living room, he found us sitting on the floor surrounded by the copies of Carrie Romain's notes. A lot of the information was repetitive; she'd kept her written notes even after she'd typed them up. It looked like she had actually used a typewriter for some of them. Others were dot matrix or laser printouts — presumably from a printer at home and another at work.

Dad spied the two reporter's notebooks and folded himself to the floor in front of them. "What do we have here?"

"These are the notes the reporter took who covered Gwen Miller's death."

His jaw slackened. "How on earth did you manage that?"

I explained about Grant and Lorrie Romain wanting to help us.

"Trust you to go with your instinct and have it turn out right, kiddo."

Barr smiled. I looked at the floor, pleased with the compliment but unwilling to say so.

"So let's see what we have here."

For the next forty-five minutes we sifted and sorted and read and commented. I told Dad about Krista Jaikes, but he didn't know what to make of that information any more than we did.

"We need more." He flipped a page in Carrie Romain's notebook.

"What about the time discrepancy that

Grant Romain mentioned?"

The three of us scooted together on the carpet, comparing notes. The official story was that the girl had fallen in the water, and Ray had rescued her. Everyone immediately hustled her back to Rancho Sueño. Tom and Jane Smith slipped away, but Ogden Dunner didn't have time to go after them. He'd loaded Gwen Miller into his truck and rushed to Spring Creek General.

But when Carrie Romain had talked to Krista Jaikes, the girl told her everyone had tried to get Miller warm at the house first. It hadn't worked. Krista had been sent to draw a warm bath for the girl, but when she came back the only ones left were Ray Dunner and his father. Mrs. Dunner was visiting her sister. They'd wrapped the girl up in blankets and were getting ready to take her into town.

Then Ray Dunner had pulled the Jaikes girl away, and the next thing the reporter knew the story was that Ogden Dunner had immediately bundled Miller up and driven her into town.

Other than that, most of the information wasn't new, or didn't seem important. We did get a fuller picture of Rancho Sueño, and a more well-rounded construction of the character of the man who owned it began to form in my mind.

Ogden Dunner was married to Constance Dunner, and they had one son, Ray. He'd been a pastor in a small church in Spring Creek for decades when he inherited a sizeable chunk of land east of Spring Creek. By selling off part of the land he was able to build Rancho Sueño, a home he'd dreamed of for years. It was big enough to host homeless teenagers, whether runaways, addicted, or abused. He wanted them to feel safe and to find a sense of community. Dunner also wanted them to come to Jesus, but even though he prayed with them before mealtimes, he didn't insist they convert. I found this last interesting, especially given what Anna Belle had said about him. It turned out the evangelist was more open-minded than I'd originally given him credit for. Before Gwen Miller died, he'd owned Rancho Sueño for three years without any kind of run-in with the law.

After she'd gathered so much information, it was too bad the *Courier* didn't have Carrie Romain write all the articles about Ogden Dunner. Of course, her husband said she'd fallen ill and left her job, so she hadn't had the chance.

"Whoa. This might be something," Dad said.

I dropped an interview with one of the Dunners' neighbors on the floor. "What?"

"According to this, Krista didn't only change her mind about what time Gwen Miller fell in the river. She also changed her mind about the relationship between Gwen and Ray Dunner."

I leaned back on my elbows on the carpet. Beside me Kitty Wampus erupted into a purr and stretched to his full length in a splash of afternoon sun.

"Do tell," I said.

Barr put down the file he was looking at, too, and watched my father with interest.

"At first she said Gwen was Ray's girl-friend," my dad said. "Then Ray denied that, and Krista changed her story. Said they were all just friends."

"Any other notes about that?"

"Only that no one wanted to talk to any reporters — not the family, and not Krista Jaikes. Romain was already at the hospital, following up on that story about the woman who beat up an intruder."

Right. The panty raider.

"When they brought in the Miller girl, Romain started asking questions about what happened. That's how she got the chance to talk to the Jaikes girl in the first place."

"Hmm." I smiled. "I wonder whether

Krista would talk to us now?"

My dad looked skeptical. "Wouldn't count on it. But you never know. I never would have thought you'd get all this information, either."

"I might not have if the reporter had still been alive."

"The point is that you did. Is Krista Jaikes still in Spring Creek?" Dad asked.

Barr already had the phone book out and answered him. "Not unless she has an unlisted number."

"Check the Web," Dad said.

I dutifully retrieved Barr's computer. Soon he was typing away. "At least it's a fairly rare name. I only show two of them when I do a search in the U.S. One is fifty-four years old, though. Ah, here we go: Krista Jaikes, thirty-two years old, listed both in Spring Creek and in —" He flourished with his left hand.

"You're killing me, here," I said.

"Youngstown, Ohio." More typing, and then he looked puzzled. "But she's not listed in the white pages there, either."

"Try a general search on her name. Use quotation marks around it," Dad said.

Clickety clack, clickety clack. Then, "Bingo. Here's an engagement announcement in the Youngstown *Vindicator*." His face glowed with the pleasure of the hunt. "She married Logan Madden five years ago."

Dad looked pretty happy, too. My two favorite guys had a lot in common. I, however, was more than a little creeped out by how easy it was to find people. But I didn't have anything to hide, and it sure made life easier when you were trying to track down someone from the past.

"Let me check the phone number . . . yep, here you go." He read off the digits.

Hurriedly, I copied it down.

Barr closed his laptop and looked over at me. "Okay. Now what do you want to do?"

I looked at my watch, surprised to find it was nearly five o'clock. "What's the time difference?"

"If I'm not mistaken, they're two hours ahead of us," Dad said. Meghan, Kelly, and Erin trooped through the front door. Everyone was getting a tan by now, after spending all that time in the Colorado sun, and Kelly and Meghan were breathless with praise for the bike-friendly community of Spring Creek.

"We spent all day riding the different trails, stopping by the river, having lunch. You can get anywhere you want to on a bike here," Meghan said.

Kelly nodded his agreement. "If one of the trails doesn't go where you want to be, all those wide streets and bike lanes sure make it easy."

My dad grinned. "It's pretty great, isn't it? Did you have fun, Erin?"

"Sure." She stomped up the stairway without another word. Her exit left a pall on the room.

"What happened?" Dad asked.

Kelly shook his head in bewilderment. "No idea. It seems to come and go with her. Say, what's all this?"

"Reporter's notes about Rancho Sueño and the girl who fell in the river there," I said.

He started to ask another question, then saw the look on Meghan's face. She was still upset about Erin. He gestured to her, and they excused themselves to go out to the backyard. Barr and I exchanged looks, and he grimaced. Erin wasn't making things easy on her mother and her new beau.

I'd check in with her later. Check in with Erin, too, for that matter.

We'd finished organizing all of Carrie Romain's notes when Anna Belle breezed in from an afternoon at the university terrorizing new students during orientation. We gathered in the kitchen, and I updated her

235

while Dad and Barr began dinner preparations. When I was done, my mother went up to her room to change out of her skirt.

I grabbed the cordless telephone handset and held it behind my back. Barr nodded at me, and I slipped around the corner and ran lightly up the stairs to the bedroom, the slip of paper with Krista Madden's phone number clutched in my hand.

TWENTY-TWO

"Hi!" The little girl who answered had a voice so soft and high I had to strain to hear it.

"Hello there. Is your mommy home?"

"Emily, give me that." The adult's voice was kind. I waited until it came on the line. "Hello?"

"Hi. Krista?"

She laughed. "Yeah, it's me. Sorry about that. Emily's new thing is to talk on the phone all the time — whether there's anyone on the other end or not. She called Australia last week. How are you?"

"Um, I'm fine, thank you."

Sudden silence, and then, "Who is this?" She'd obviously mistaken me for someone else.

"My name's Sophie Mae Reynolds. I'm calling you from Spring Creek, Colorado."

"I see. What can I do for you?"

"I've just learned that you were present

when a girl named Gwen Miller fell into the Cache la Poudre River eighteen years ago."

A sudden intake of breath was her only response.

"I wanted to ask you a few questions about that night, if I could."

"Who are you again?" The friendliness had vanished.

"Like I said, my name is Sophie Mae. Bobby Lee Watson was my brother." I took a deep breath and plunged on. "He killed himself not long after that incident, and he left a note that indicates his . . . decision . . . might have had something to do with what happened that night."

"Well, I don't see how that's possible."

"That he left a note?"

"No, that Gwen's death had anything to do with your brother's."

Disappointment settled into my bones. Yet another false trail. Nonetheless, I kept trudging along it.

"Can you tell me if Bobby Lee was there that night?"

"Listen, I don't know how you found out my name — it wasn't in the papers and my family protected me from the rest of the media — but dredging up all that old pain isn't going to do anyone any good."

I sighed. "Believe it or not, you're not the first person to tell me that. But can you tell me whether Bobby Lee was there that night?"

"No. He wasn't."

"Is that what you told the reporter?"

"I didn't talk to any reporters," she said quickly.

Liar.

"But you knew him?"

"To talk to, casually. We went to school together, but he was a year ahead of me. He went out to Rancho Sueño for a while, with that girlfriend of his, but then he pretty much stopped showing up."

"Can I ask why you went out there? You weren't exactly a runaway."

"No, I had a happy home life."

"Was it the drugs?"

Her laugh was sharp. "No."

Lots of negative answers, none of them helpful.

"Then why?" I pushed.

Her answer was almost a whisper. "Because Gwen Miller was my best friend, and she loved the place."

"I'm so sorry." And I was.

But I'd already come this far. "What about Tabby and Joe?"

"What about them?" Something in her

voice. A sharpness. Fear.

Instinct made me ask, "Were they there?"

"Why would you ask that?"

I continued to fly through the conversation by the seat of my pants. "Joe was killed a couple of days ago."

Krista Madden hung up on me.

I helloed at the phone a couple of times to make sure then stared at it in disbelief. Joe's death had certainly triggered a reaction. Interesting. I hadn't had a chance to ask her why her story about what had happened had changed at the hospital. Or whether she'd lied to her dad, the sheriff's deputy, about the death of her best friend.

But Krista hanging up on me extinguished my sympathy. I punched in the numbers again.

No one answered. When the answering machine came on, I hung up and punched them in again.

"What?" on the fourth ring, abrupt as all get out.

"You didn't answer my question."

"And I'm not going to. I don't have to answer any of your questions. Stop calling me."

"Maybe I should check with your father. The Sheriff."

Krista barked a laugh in my ear. "Good

240

luck with that."

She had a point. However, I could hear the fear thrumming through the telephone connection. If she wasn't afraid of her father, who was she afraid of?"

"Did the Dunners threaten you?"

"Please, stop," she said.

"I met them today, and neither of them seemed that scary to me." I was fishing.

"Then you weren't paying attention, Sophie Mae Reynolds. Because Ray Dunner was scary then, and he's scary now. I have to go. Don't call me back. I mean it."

"Wait!" I listened for the click. There wasn't one.

"Okay, listen," I said. "I understand that you're afraid, and that you don't know me from Eve. But you knew my brother, and he's dead. And so is the girl who you say was your best friend. I think you lied to your dad and everyone else about what happened, even though I don't understand why. All I ask is please, *please,* isn't there anything you can tell me?"

Krista's silence drew out so long I wondered whether she really had hung up on me again. Then she said, "Ask yourself how Joe and Tabby Bines managed to get the land for that dairy of theirs."

And then she did hang up.

What on earth?

And why was Krista so scared of Ray Dunner? Not just now, but for at least eighteen years.

My face must have been a picture of pure puzzlement when I walked out to the patio, because everyone immediately asked what was wrong.

"Nothing," I said. "At least nothing new." I told them who I'd been talking to and what she'd said. That led to having to catch Meghan and Kelly up on what Barr and I had done all day. The one thing I left out was Krista's parting comment. I wanted to talk to Barr about it first, before involving my parents. After all, it might be nothing, and I found myself oddly protective of them.

"Where's Erin?" I asked when I had finished.

Meghan's brow furrowed. "She says she's not feeling well. Went to bed."

"You're kidding." Erin never went to bed when she was sick. Instead she'd lie on the sofa and expect everyone to wait on her, hand and foot.

Never mind that I'd taught her to do that . . .

"I know," my housemate said. "Maybe she doesn't feel comfortable whining in someone else's house."

My mother snorted, then held up a finger. "I'll be right back."

Watching her retreat into the house, I said to my father, "I think she's relieved to have Krista Madden confirm Bobby Lee wasn't out at the Dunners' when Gwen Miller fell in the river."

"Of course she is. It also confirms that she was right about Bobby Lee staying away from the place after we talked to him."

I turned my head and looked at him.

He smiled. "And I'm glad to hear it, too."

I put my elbows on the table and sunk my chin into my hands. "Then what the heck does the letter mean?" Frustration raised my voice.

"You'll find out," he said. "I'm sure of it."

Kelly laughed. Beside me, Barr made a noise. "Maybe you shouldn't encourage her so much."

"And why not?"

My father and my fiancé exchanged amused glances. Once again I thought about how much they had in common — though I began to wonder whether that was a good thing or not.

Anna Belle returned bearing a platter of halved tomatoes that had been slow roasted with a sprinkle of sugar and a dash of olive oil. Chunks of cheese and finely minced basil, chives, and oregano topped off the rounds. The aroma was heavenly.

I reached for one as soon as she set them down. "Mmm. Is this the cheese I brought home?"

"It is. The flavor is quite subtle for a bleu."

"It's delicious," Meghan said, helping herself to another.

Kelly said, "I thought bleu cheese was bleu cheese."

I shook my head. "Nope. Or yes, it is, but there are lots of different kinds. Tabby calls this one Poudre Bleu." I toasted him with one of the tomatoes. "Gorgonzola is a bleu and so are Stilton and Roquefort. They're named after the location of the caves in which they're aged, like Burgundy and Champagne are named after the region where the grapes grow."

"Huh. That's actually interesting."

"Kelly!" Meghan said, giving him a light slap on the arm.

"I'm sorry," he said, and looked like he meant it.

I laughed. "Don't worry. Erin just comes right out and tells me I'm weird."

Meghan looked unhappy at the mention of her daughter's name.

"I want to know more about the caves,"

Dad said. "I know all bleus have some kind of penicillin in them, which is what causes the blue streaks to form, but why caves?"

"From what Tabby told me, it's all about the temperature and humidity that the mold thrives in. What's wrong, Kelly?"

"Mold?" he asked, a look of disgust on his face.

"Yep, you just ate mold. That's what gives bleu cheeses their distinctive flavors. And Dad's right — it's penicillin mold. The antibiotic wasn't discovered on bread, but in cheese."

"Well," he said. "If it cures pneumonia it can't be all bad." He took another off the platter, holding it carefully over the brightly colored paper napkins Anna Belle had provided. "And I do love the flavor."

The rest of dinner consisted of thick pork chops that had been sitting in salt and orange juice brine all day, then stuffed with wild rice, almonds, and dried apples, baby potatoes roasted in their jackets and slathered with cultured butter, and fresh green beans that Anna Belle had picked that afternoon. We ended with homemade vanilla ice cream, barely visible under a heap of late-season strawberries.

Despite the surfeit of food, I remembered to have a little bit of everything and to savor every bite. At the end of the meal Dad had the temerity to bring out a cheese course: Saga bleu cheese, walnuts, and dark ruby port served in my grandmother's tiny liqueur glasses. Everyone, even Barr, groaned when they saw more food come to the table. Oh, but we all had a few bites, a few sips, and the meal was all the better for the finishing touch.

After dinner Anna Belle went to her den to do a little work, but Dad asked if we wanted to watch a movie together.

"Big doings in Spring Creek." I immediately regretted the words when I saw the stricken look on his face.

"Of course you want to go out, have some fun!" he said. "We've gotten to be such homebodies that your mother and I just don't think about that. I'm sorry."

Luckily, Barr was standing right next to me when Dad went into his guilt-ridden diatribe, and stopped him in his tracks. "Please, Calvin, we enjoy spending time with you, we really do. It's why I'm here in the first place. Can Anna Belle join us for the movie?"

I nodded my agreement with Barr, and Dad looked relieved. "I'll check," he said and went to roust my mother out of her workaholism to join us for some quiet entertainment.

"I'm going to go up and see if Erin's awake," I said to Meghan. "If she is, I'm dragging her cranky butt down here to join us."

My friend looked worried. "She said she wasn't feeling well."

"And? Was she sick? Temperature, headache, throwing up, bleeding?"

She barely managed not to smile. "Well, go ahead and check. But don't make her come down if she doesn't want to."

"Deal," I went upstairs, leaving the movie selection to the others.

TWENTY-THREE

Erin's eyes were tightly closed, and the book she'd been reading had fallen open on her lap, still in her hands. Her breathing was deep, if a bit forced. When I looked closely, I saw the book was upside down. I stood by the bed for a minute, listening and watching and waiting.

Her eye cracked open the tiniest bit, checking to see if I was still there.

"Faker," I said.

The eye clamped shut, and she turned on her side with a murmur.

Uh huh. Nice try.

I flopped down on the bed beside her and put my face up close to hers. It didn't take long. Both eyes popped open, and she sat up.

"God, Sophie Mae!"

"Oh, good. You're awake." I sat up, too.

"I am now." A whine on the edge of her words.

"Oh, you were before. Now c'mon, Bug. Tell me what the heck is going on."

"Nothing."

"Horse poo. Something's up, and I've got to tell you, I'm getting pretty sick of wondering why you're so ticked off all the time. Your mom, too. Even Kelly thinks you're mad at him."

Unhappiness rose behind her eyes. "I'm not mad."

I inclined my head and waited.

"Not really," she said.

"You've been acting funny since before we got here. Back in Cadyville."

She picked at the bedspread with a ragged fingernail.

"About the time that all the construction started on the house."

Erin chewed gently on her lower lip. When she finally looked up, her eyes brimmed with unshed tears. "I'm sorry."

My heart melted. "Oh, Bug." I wrapped my arms around her. "It's okay. I bet all the changes lately have thrown you for a loop." Pulling back, I held her gaze. "We never really talked to you much about Barr moving in after we're married."

"But I'm happy about it!" she insisted through her tears.

"I know. But wanting to be happy about

249

something is one thing. Actually seeing all the changes happening around you is different." I was thinking out loud. "Your home is a mess, and now someone else will be living there. We're trying to keep things the same in many ways, but it'll be different in some ways, too."

Erin's shoulders slumped, and she whispered, "It's kind of scary."

I wanted to wrap this child up and keep her safe forever. But I couldn't. Erin was an only child, and while Meghan and I didn't exactly spoil her, she was still the center of attention a lot of the time. Barr was going to encroach on that, as might Kelly. No wonder she was taking some of her angst out on him.

"It is a little scary. For me, too."

Her eyes widened, and one big drop fell onto her cheek. "Really?"

"Sure. Change is always scary. It's just that the longer you live, the more you get used to it. Nothing ever stays the same, but after a while you get so that you believe in your own ability to deal with whatever happens."

Erin looked thoughtful. "So the more weird stuff you get in life, the better you are at coping?"

I laughed. "Something like that. You've

had some stuff happen already, right?"

"Yeah," she said. "I guess so."

For example, a degenerate gambler of a father who nearly got her killed, a wacky grandmother who should have been in jail, a newly discovered relative, and a hyper intelligence that made her a little too aware of what was going on around her sometimes.

"Like you finding dead bodies all the time?" she asked.

"Ha ha." That, too. "And it all turned out okay, right?"

She nodded.

"This will, too. I know you like Barr. We can't be sure exactly what it'll be like for us all to live together, but I bet it'll be fun."

The smile that ventured onto her face sent a bolt of relief through me. Our old Erin was on her way back.

"Will you come downstairs and watch a movie with us? Everyone wants you to."

"They do?" Her words were so tentative it made my heart ache.

"Yes. We do. Anna Belle thinks you're the slickest thing since sliced bread, your mom and I miss you, and Barr and Dad think you're pretty special, too. And Kelly?"

Her chin jerked up, and I saw another issue which had been bothering her. "Kelly

251

adores you." I leaned in. "You know what else?"

She feigned disinterest, putting her bookmark in her upside down book. "What?"

"No one, not Kelly, not anyone, is ever going to come between you and your mom."

She paused.

"Deep down, you know that, right?"

The eyes that met my gaze then were clear and bright. "Yeah. I guess I do."

"Okay then. Let's go see what movie they picked for us to watch and get you some dinner."

She slid off the bed. "Okay. Sophie Mae?"

I put my hand on her shoulder and hugged her against my side. "Yeah?"

"Thanks. For, you know, getting it and not hating me for being so mean to you. I didn't mean, I mean, I didn't want —"

"Silly Bug, I couldn't hate you."

She hugged me back.

"But don't you ever do that to me again," I said with fake menace.

Her laughter tumbled down the stairwell as we went to join the others.

Meghan pulled me aside after the movie to ask me what the heck I'd said to Erin. When I related our conversation she was more relieved than anything. Mother and daughter went up to bed, perhaps to talk some more. Kelly pleaded exhaustion after what had been nearly a full day of bike riding, and we left him in the basement to an early night. Anna Belle and Dad went to bed, too, which left Barr and me to our own devices.

As soon as we were alone I told him about what Krista Madden had said about the Bines' dairy.

"They come from money?" Barr asked, leaning back on the patio chair again.

He planned to leave the next day for a quick drive up to his parents' Wyoming ranch before flying back to Cadyville. I'd been hoping to join him, especially as I hadn't met his family face-to-face, but with only a few days to sort out Bobby Lee's letter, I couldn't spare the time.

"Tabby and Joe? Like, real money? Not that I know of. Joe's dad worked construction, and Tabby's folks didn't live high on the hog, either. I mean, everyone got by okay, but . . . how much does a dairy cost?"

"More than it sounds like they had."

"How do we find out more?"

"Public records, darlin'. Public records."

"Great," I grumped. "That'll take forever."

He grinned. "Naw, it won't." The laptop came open again. I snuggled onto the lounge chair with him and watched the screen light up.

As I marveled at his easy knowledge about how to gather information — though, granted, it *was* his job — he pulled up the address of the dairy, then the website of the county clerk's office. A few more clicks, and he pointed to the screen.

It took me a moment to decipher the entry, before realization dawned. Eighteen years ago, the T&J Dairy property belonged to Ogden and Constance Dunner.

I remembered how bitter Ray Dunner had been when we asked where Rancho Sueño had been located. How he'd said to ask Tabby.

The Cache la Poudre River that ran behind the dairy was the river that Gwen Miller had fallen into.

"Tabitha Bines' name isn't anywhere on this real estate transaction," Barr said. "Do you know when they got married?"

"No, but it looks like Joe bought the land from Ogden Dunner and his wife when they closed up Rancho Sueño. That was only a year or so after the Miller girl died. Dad told me Joe and Tabby started dating a few months after Bobby Lee died, but they didn't get married for a while. Still, it seems kind of odd that he never put her name on the deed after they were married."

"She doesn't own any part of the dairy, then."

"Well," I said. "She might own the whole thing, now that Joe's dead."

A night bird squawked from a nearby tree, followed by the sound of an automatic sprinkler turning on in the neighbor's yard.

"I wonder how Joe managed to afford that land," I said. "He was barely twenty years old."

"He didn't," Barr said.

"Didn't what?"

He pointed to a notation on the website: *QC.* "He didn't have to afford it. The land was quit claimed to him."

"Quit claimed?"

From eight inches away, Barr's eyes twinkled in the faint light of the laptop screen. "Essentially, that means the Dunners *gave* the land to Joe Bines."

"Gave . . . ?" Oh. Wow.

Krista Madden had been a gold mine of information after all. The only reason you'd give a parcel of land to Joe Bines would be if he had something really incriminating on you.

"We have to tell the sheriff," I said.

Barr nodded, then rested his chin on top of my head. From above me he said, "I think I'd rather talk to your Inspector Schumaker, if you don't mind. Get a better feel for this Jaikes fellow before talking to him directly."

I craned my head back to look at him. "What about the trip to see your family?"

A slight shrug against my cheek. "I'll leave a little later. We'll track down Schumaker first thing in the morning."

The tiny shudder of excitement that ran down my back was partly because of Barr's proximity, and partly due to the feeling that we were finally making some real discoveries about what had happened eighteen years ago.

Turned out that my father and my fiancé weren't the only ones who enjoyed the hunt.

TWENTY-FOUR

The cacophony of trills, cheeps, and whistles outside my open window jolted me awake just before six on Friday morning. Fifteen minutes later it became evident that further sleep would be impossible, and I swung my feet to the floor. Padding across the room, I opened the blinds and peered through the screen, expecting to find the entire avian cast from *The Birds* had taken up residence in the big old cottonwood tree next door. Instead, less than a dozen feathery creatures contributed to the racket. Below, Barr stood by my mother's kitchen garden and examined the bean vines climbing to the top of the trellis. He was already fully dressed.

The birds hadn't been kind to his slumber, either.

A shower later, I donned a floral sundress and strappy sandals and left my hair to air dry. For most of the summer my tan was my makeup, so it only took fifteen minutes to put myself together and tiptoe downstairs to make coffee.

As it brewed, I jotted notes on the pad by the telephone. I still didn't know if we'd found out anything substantial about Rancho Sueño or the Bineses. Correction: I was pretty sure we'd discovered some nicely orchestrated blackmail, but I wasn't sure that it had anything to do with Bobby Lee's death. Despite my assorted juicy and sordid discoveries, no one had placed Bobby Lee anywhere near Rancho Sueño the night Gwen Miller died, or had said anything about him spending time there in the weeks preceding the incident.

There was still a lot we didn't know. I'd felt like this before — completely bewildered, yet on the cusp of something. First came the ferreting out of information, the gathering of facts, discovery of secrets. But much of that turned out to be irrelevant or tangential to the bigger puzzle. Next I had to eliminate from consideration the bits that weren't important in order to piece together the bits that were significant into a cohesive, meaningful solution.

Sighing, I crinkled my notes into a ball and threw it in the garbage under the sink. That wonderful, left-brained idea of narrowing in only on the correct information and then extrapolating the truth was all fine and dandy in theory. Too bad real life wasn't so black and white, but rather so many shades of gray there weren't names for them all.

I poured coffee and took a cup out to Barr.

The sky was high and bright, and the early morning air still felt cool. Soon temperatures would shift, signaling the onset of a Rocky Mountain fall — swift and often surprising. It was not unheard of for snow to fall in September, followed by a month of glorious Indian summer.

He took the steaming mug with a smile. "Morning, you."

"Morning back," I said.

We spent the next forty-five minutes sitting on the garden bench, sipping our coffee and occasionally talking, but for the most part content to be together in silence. The ease with which we could do that was one of the many things I loved about Barr. He was the guy for me, forever.

Then Anna Belle stepped out of the house, followed by Meghan and Erin. Our quiet time was over, but as we joined them, I realized how much I loved all of them. My family, both original and made. The contentment that settled across my psyche at the thought lessened my frustration at not knowing why my brother had died.

Kelly joined the group, and we gathered on the patio for another signature Cal Watson breakfast: cheese blintzes covered with gooey cinnamon-blueberry sauce, savory sausage made in Boulder and freshly squeezed grapefruit juice. I gave the delectable menu short shrift, though, anxious to call Cyan and catch up on my business e-mail. If I didn't stay on top of my inbox, it would rapidly get out of control, and I'd start losing business.

Then I called Inspector Schumaker, reaching him at the sheriff's office.

"I need to talk to you," I said. "When would be a good time?"

"The sooner, the better."

"Excuse me?"

"I was just about to call you. We found something at the crime scene that I want you to see."

Well, that piqued my curiosity all right.

"Can you come right now?" he asked.

I assured him I'd leave immediately, not mentioning that I was bringing Barr with me. He'd find out soon enough.

"Barr, we need to get going," I said from the doorway, tote bag already hanging from my shoulder.

Anna Belle looked up in surprise. "Where

are you going?"

"I wanted Barr to meet the inspector who interviewed me at the dairy when Joe was killed."

"Why?" Blunt, but reasonable.

"When I spoke with Krista Madden, née Jaikes, she said something about how Joe had managed to buy the land the dairy is on."

"And?" Patience was not my mother's strong suit.

"And Barr and I looked up the real estate records at the county clerk's office on the computer last night."

My father looked delighted, Meghan and Kelly listened with interest, and even Erin seemed intrigued. Anna Belle tapped her foot.

"The dairy used to be Rancho Sueño."

Dad leaned forward. "Really? I went out there once, when Bobby Lee was first interested in the place, but I've never been to the dairy."

My mother sat back. "Could it be a co-incidence?"

"I don't think so," I said. "Especially since Joe didn't buy the land. The Dunners essentially *gave* it to him through a quit claim deed."

Kelly whistled. "Wonder what your Mr.

261

Bines had on the Dunner family."

"Exactly," I said. "We thought perhaps Inspector Schumaker could help us with that. Unfortunately, he's going to be leaving the office in less than an hour."

Barr stood. "We'd better get over there, then." He turned to my father. "Thanks for another amazing meal, Cal. I can see Sophie Mae inherited her kitchen smarts from both sides."

Dad and Anna Belle both smiled, and we went out to Barr's rented car.

"Silver-tongued devil," I said.

He waggled his eyebrows and gave me a kiss. "You better believe it."

As we were going into the squat, square building that housed the sheriff's department, the man himself was coming out.

"Good morning, Sheriff," I said.

He held the door open for us. "Morning." Barr received a hard look as we walked by. I was surprised when Jaikes turned around and followed us inside. "Investigator Schumaker's right back here. I think I'll join you."

Alarmed, I glanced up at Barr. What was going on?

Jaikes led us to the same conference room where I'd signed my statement. Schumaker looked up when we walked in. Dark sweat circles had already formed under his arms despite the air-conditioning set to "frigid." He sat bent over the paperwork and files that covered the table, his legs folded awkwardly beneath the molded plastic chair.

"Sir?" he said when Jaikes ushered us into the room and shut the door.

"Sit down," the sheriff . . . invited? Sounded more like a command.

Slowly, I slid onto a chair. Barr sat beside me. Jaikes leaned against the wall with his arms crossed in front of him. One finger tapped against his elbow.

"You the lawyer?" the sheriff asked him. Tap. Tap.

Barr raised one eyebrow. "No."

"Then who are you?"

"I'm the fiancé."

Recognition flashed across Schumaker's face, and I remembered that he'd talked to Barr's superior when he'd been checking up on me. He probably knew Barr was a detective on the Cadyville force. Did that mean he'd be on my side or not? After all, he'd expressly told me to stay out of his way after Sergeant Zahn told him about my investigative adventures back home.

When he heard Barr wasn't a lawyer, pleased surprise settled into Jaike's little blue eyes. "Well, then. I'm afraid you're going to have to leave."

"No," I said. "He stays, or we both go."

"That's not how it works."

"Sure it is," Barr said in an easy tone. "Unless she's under arrest. Is she under arrest?"

No one looked happy. My heart skipped a beat. "Not yet," Jaikes finally responded.

What on earth? I caught Schumaker's eye and looked the question at him. He sighed and reached for a plastic bag in front of him. A neatly sealed evidence bag. He held it up so I could see the contents.

"Recognize this?"

"Sure," I said. "It's lip balm."

"Made by a company called Winding Road," he said. "Your company."

"Well, of course it is. That one's cinnamon flavored, if you read the label. Where did you find it?"

"At the dairy."

"Well, I sort of figured that, or else you wouldn't have it in that little bag. But where at the dairy?"

Jaikes stepped in. "Funny you should ask that. We found it under Joe Bines."

I blinked.

"You have any idea how it got there?" he asked.

"My lip balm? Under a dead body?" Yuck. I shook my head. "No idea."

"Well, it turns out I do have an idea, Ms. Reynolds. I do indeed." Jaikes seemed to savor the words.

"Oh, now, c'mon," I protested. "You know I didn't kill him. Why would I? I hardly knew the guy."

"So you say. Funny how you were there when he died, though."

Beside me, Barr sighed.

Instantly I felt guilty. And angry. "I wasn't *there* when he was murdered. I was up at the house with Tabby."

"Again: so you say."

"Listen, I know how I lost the lip balm in the first place." I tried to keep the desperation out of my voice. Did these people really think I could have killed Joe? "When the billy goat butted me, my tote bag and everything in it went flying. I must have missed that little tube when I was picking it all up. Maybe Joe found it and then dropped it when, well, you know, someone dropped him."

Jaikes went still. "Goat? What goat?"

Schumaker said, "She says a goat hit her from behind and knocked her down when she was on her way up to the house that day. I asked her about the dirt and scratches

265

at the time. Show us your hands."

I held them out for inspection like a little kid. The minor scrapes on my palms were healing quickly, but still looked recent. "I hope you don't expect me to show you the bruise on my behind."

Schumaker smiled. His boss pointedly did not.

"Anything else?" Barr said. "Because she's cooperated so far. If we're going to dance around like this some more, though, it's lawyer time. Your choice."

The sheriff glared at him. My sweetie's return gaze was implacable.

"You're free to go." Jaikes opened the door and stalked out of the room. Instantly, the charge in the air dissipated, and I let out a whoosh of air. A moment later we saw Jaikes walk out to the parking lot, climb into a Suburban with the county logo on the side, and drive away.

"Thanks for remembering about the goat," I said to Schumaker.

He snorted. "Like I could forget a thing like that. Besides, it's in your statement." He turned to Barr. "You're Detective Ambrose?"

"Sure am." Barr held out his hand, and the inspector shook it.

Rather than leaving, we settled back into

our chairs. Schumaker watched us. Irritation vied with curiosity on his face.

"How well do you know the sheriff?" I asked.

He cocked his head to one side. "Now why would you ask a question like that?"

"Because we found out a couple of things about Gwen Miller's death that weren't advertised. One of those things involves a quit claim deed. The other one is the identity of the mystery girl at Ran—."

His eyes flicked up, and he gave an infinitesimal shake of his head.

Barr touched my arm, cutting me off, and stood. "Good to meet you. I'd love to grab a coffee sometime, exchange war stories." He pulled me to my feet, though I resisted.

Schumaker stood as well. "That'd be good."

"Any suggestions for a good place to get a cup?"

What the heck?

Schumaker hesitated. Looked at his watch. "Zillah's Café is good. I go there most days for lunch."

"Sounds good. Let's go, Sophie Mae."

"What? Wait a minute . . ."

He took my arm and gently steered me to the half-open door. "We're going to be late."

Late for what?

Out in the parking lot, I started to demand why we had to leave before quizzing Schumaker about Krista Jaikes and the quit claim deed, but he shushed me.

"Camera," he said once we were in the car. "There'll be one in this parking lot, too."

Oh.

I felt like an idiot. Jaikes might have left the building, but it still was a lousy place to talk about him.

"We'll have to wait until lunchtime," Barr said.

Ah. The coffee discussion made sense now. Mr. Ambrose was a rather clever bear.

TWENTY-FIVE

Apparently some secret cop signal had flashed between them, because Barr assured me Schumaker would be at Zillah's Café at noon. So we had over an hour to kill before lunch. I talked him into going to the health food store with me to pick up ingredients for the body butter I wanted to make later for my mother. Anna Belle had complained the evening before about how the high desert sun dried her skin, so I was going to whip up a concoction that would cure the problem in no time.

Supplied with olive oil, shea butter, and vitamin E oil, we found the café and parked. Inside, we discovered a large space which had been broken up into sections delineated by low glass walls and cushy furniture groupings. The seating areas were private enough that it was the perfect place to talk, and if the cooking smells were any indica-tion, the place served a lot more than coffee. The large blackboard behind the register listed menu offerings.

I ordered coffee drinks and sandwiches at the counter while Barr commandeered an arrangement of chairs in a back corner. Meatball submarine for him, grilled Reuben for me. Schumaker came in as I loaded our lunches on a tray. Our eyes met and I indicated the back of the café with my chin. He saw Barr sitting there and nodded.

Soon we were all ensconced in the ultra-comfortable seating. Barr and I were munching and sipping away, but the sheriff's investigator had only ordered coffee.

"Thanks for coming —" I began.

Schumaker cut me off. "Let me make something perfectly clear. You are still a person of interest in this case, Ms. Reynolds. I am not here to discuss any part of it with you. Nor am I here to buddy up with another cop. I met you here for two reasons: to clear up any misunderstanding about the sheriff's daughter and the death at Rancho Sueño, and to find out what the heck you were talking about regarding a quit claim deed."

He sat back with an expectant air. Took a sip from his Grande whatever.

"I respect that," Barr said.

I nodded. The last thing I wanted to do

was compromise a murder investigation or get Schumaker in trouble. He'd been a pretty good guy considering how he'd met me.

"Okay. Who quit claimed what to whom?"

"Ogden Dunner quit claimed the Rancho Sueño property to Joe Bines two years after Gwen Miller died," I said.

His lips came together as if he was going to whistle, and he looked at Barr. "No kidding."

"Two years after Gwen Miller and Bobby Lee died, and one year after he shut down Rancho Sueño. Joe was only twenty years old."

Schumaker had taken a small notebook out and began scribbling.

"Blackmail is a good motive for murder," I said.

His glance was sharp. "Not, repeat not, discussing the Bines murder case with you." But his eyes softened then, and he said, "However, I do indeed thank you for this information. Of course I knew the dairy was located on the old Dunner property, but didn't know the particulars of the real estate transaction. This does change things a bit."

I smiled. "It also links the current case, which we are definitely not discussing right now, to what happened eighteen years ago."

"Perhaps," he conceded.

"Is Ray Dunner a suspect?"

The inspector wagged his finger at me. "Maybe. Maybe not."

Barr said, "Then there's that other connection between the current sheriff and a certain girl who was present the night Gwen Miller died."

"Who was Gwen Miller's best friend, actually," I said.

Schumaker frowned and swept the room with his gaze before answering. "Yes. About that. How did you find out she was there?"

"She talked to a reporter at the hospital that night. Carrie Romain. But only briefly, until Ray Dunner pulled her away, and then Krista's whole story changed."

He looked surprised. "Now where the heck did you come up with that crazy idea?"

"I saw the reporter's notes. She never went to press with the alternate story — prevented by her editor, I'm guessing, since she was also asked not to reveal Krista's name."

"Krista was only seventeen."

"We understand that," Barr said. "But she was also the daughter of a sheriff's deputy who had political goals. If she were anyone else her name would have been right there in print for the world to see. Now, what

272

were you going to tell us that would clear up any 'misunderstandings' we might have about Krista's involvement?"

I could feel the tension rolling off him as he spoke. I wondered whether Schumaker could, too.

"Krista Jaikes was only seventeen," Schumaker said again. "But she knew what she had to do. She sat down and told sheriff's investigators everything she knew."

"How do you know that?"

"It's all in the case file," he said, impatient.

"How about the fact that Gwen Miller and Ray Dunner were more than friends. She was his girlfriend."

He shook his head. "After you were asking about that incident in relation to your brother, I went over the file. There was nothing about those two being involved romantically."

"Nonetheless," I said.

"Miller's parents would have known if they were dating, don't you think?"

"Maybe. Believe me, if I were dating him, I wouldn't have dared to tell my mother. She would've thrown a fit." I couldn't imagine dating a jerk like that anyway. Ray Dunner or Joe Bines. Now those two I would have expected to be best friends, not Joe and Bobby Lee. "But I would have told my best friend."

The inspector shook his head. "Why would Krista Jaikes have lied?"

"Well, I talked to her on the phone, and even after all these years Ray Dunner's name still terrifies her. And she actually hung up on me when I told her Joe had been murdered."

"*You talked to her on the phone?* Are you crazy? What were you thinking? Sheriff Jaikes is going to come after you with both barrels if he finds out you've been harassing his daughter. Finding your lip balm under Bines' body is nothing compared to that."

I put down my half-finished sandwich and leaned forward. Barr touched my arm, but I shook him off. "Oh, for heaven's sake. I asked her some questions about my brother — there's no crime in that. She's a grown woman, and perfectly capable of deciding whether she wants to talk to me or not. By the way, she mostly chose 'not.' She certainly doesn't need Daddy watching out for her anymore." I pointed at him. "But you make a good point. I bet Deputy Jaikes would have done a lot to protect his little girl."

Anger narrowed Schumaker's eyes. He stood up. "This conversation is over. I understand that you're trying to heal an old wound, but you're going about it the wrong way. If and when you step on the sheriff's toes too hard, don't expect me to be on your side." He slammed his coffee cup on the table and strode out the door.

I turned to Barr. "Oops."

"No. Not oops. You gave him a lot of valid information, and while I understand his reticence to rat on his boss, I'm a little surprised he's not more interested in following up on it."

"He'll follow up on the quit claim. I'm sure of it. For one thing, it's relevant to the case he's working now."

"And that might lead to more information about the past," Barr said. "At least I hope so. You've only got until day after tomorrow, and if you don't figure out what happened with your brother I think your head might explode."

"A slight exaggeration," I said.

"Not by much."

Barr promised to call that evening, and left on the five-hour drive up to see his family. My parents were both at the university again, and who knew where Kelly, Meghan, and Erin had gone off to this time. It was a perfect opportunity to make the body butter for Anna Belle.

First I melted the olive oil and shea butter together over low heat. Once they were combined, I set the pan on the counter to cool and dug out Dad's stick blender. I spent an hour catching up on e-mail, then checked the oils. They were cooling nicely, and barely starting to solidify. Upstairs, I dug through the essential oils I'd brought with me, deciding on the jasmine since Anna Belle had such a preference for loud floral scents. A call to check in with Cyan relieved my mind about Winding Road Bath Products, and by the time I was done, it was time to finish up the body butter.

I stirred in the vitamin E oil and essential oil first, then hit it with the stick blender. The result was a fluffy, emollient mixture the color of heavy cream with a slight green-ish tinge from the extra virgin olive oil. The jasmine was a little overpowering, but Anna Belle would love it.

Time for a walk 'n' think. Cadyville was small enough that I walked many places, though I didn't think about it as exercise. However, while everyone else had been riding their bikes and going on hikes, I'd been driving around Spring Creek. It made me feel sluggish; I needed some movement and some time outside to organize my thoughts.

The weather had cooled to the mid-eighties. At that temperature the dry air actually did make a difference, and I hardly broke a sweat as I power-walked down to the park. It wasn't very large, taking up only one city block, and I circled it once, admiring the gardens and smiling at the children who played on the swings. Three college-age boys were throwing a Frisbee, and an elderly couple sat on a bench holding hands. I could only hope Barr and I were still so affectionate in our eighties.

As I continued, my steps fell into a steady rhythm, and soon my brain was clicking along at the same pace. Bobby Lee did something he was ashamed of. Took part in something he was ashamed of. A girl died after falling in a frozen river. Everyone said Bobby Lee wasn't at the river that night. But something happened, something everyone was lying about. Had Gwen Miller's plunge been more than an accident? What was Ogden Dunner's role in the whole thing?

Speaking of more than an accident: Who the heck killed Joe Bines? He wasn't the nicest guy in the world, and I wouldn't be surprised to learn that he'd angered someone enough for them to kill him. Like maybe someone he blackmailed. Someone with a temper. Someone like Ray Dunner.

Or maybe Joe's death was, if not random, at least unrelated to past events or my family. Still, if that were the case then the sheriff's investigators would have discovered something by now, and I didn't get the impression from Schumaker that they had.

Granted, he wasn't one to share whether they had developed any leads or not, but I couldn't shake the idea that whoever bashed Joe over the head did it because of something that happened eighteen years ago.

Which meant that I might be partly responsible.

Was that true? Really? Had I started something in motion by asking so many questions?

I sighed, and my steps slowed. I'd come as far as College Avenue, and the cars whizzed by. I walked south for a block and started toward the house again. My parents' neighborhood hadn't changed much over the years, though the trees in the front yards had certainly matured. Most of the homes had been built in the sixties and seventies, everyone took care of their yards, and all the streets were named after universities: Tulane, Harvard, Stanford, Duke, etc.

Joe and Tabby had blackmailed the Dunners. Or at least Joe had. I was sure of it.

But they hadn't been there the night Gwen Miller died. Or had they? Were they Tom and Jane Smith? Or, if the blackmail was unrelated to the girl in the river incident, then what the heck did they have on the Dunners that would be incriminating enough for Ogden to give up on his dream of Rancho Sueño?

The walk helped me to organize my questions, but did little to provide answers. At least my blood circulated through my veins with more enthusiasm as I neared the house. That counted for something.

A large black pickup was parked on the street in front of the house, and I could see in through the screen door to the great room. Someone was home.

Then I saw the bumper sticker on the truck: Dunner & Son Auto Sales.

Twenty-Six

The hair on the back of my neck and arms stood on end when I saw Ray Dunner sitting on my parents' sofa in the great room, red soda can dangling from his fingers. He wore jeans and a T-shirt and thick work boots. As soon as I came in the door, Erin jumped up from where she'd been sitting in Dad's big recliner and ran to me.

"This man is here to see you, Sophie Mae."

Dunner glowered up at me from his seated position but didn't say a word.

I put my hand on her shoulder. "Thanks, Bug. I'll take it from here."

She craned her head to look up at me. Her eyes were scared.

"Go outside and play," I said.

Bless her heart, she didn't take umbrage at being told to go out and play like a third grader, and she didn't hesitate, either. I waited until I heard the sliding door in the kitchen open and close, then came farther into the room.

"Mr. Dunner," I said. "What can I do for you?"

He swished the Coke in the bottom of the can and took a final swig. Leaned forward and put the empty can on the carpet, then made himself comfortable on the sofa again. He stretched out one booted foot and put it on the coffee table, the picture of insolence. As much as I wanted to knock it off, my hand remained steady at my side. He still hadn't spoken.

I shrugged. "Well, if you just came over to drink my folks' soda, I guess you're done."

He picked at his teeth with a thumbnail and regarded me with dark eyes. "Tabitha tells me you have a letter of hers."

My stomach swooped. Trying to appear casual, I walked to the window and looked out. "I'm not sure what you're referring to." Anna Belle and Dad were still at the university. Meghan and Kelly were gone.

Erin had been here alone with Ray Dunner.

His answer was a snort. "I want to see it."

I faced him. "Sorry I can't accommodate you."

His foot came off the coffee table, and he leaned forward in one sudden, smooth motion. "It wasn't a request."

My heart was beating so hard I could hardly hear him. I didn't say anything.

He stood up, and I jumped.

"I don't have it!" I said.

"Sure you do."

"I don't! My mother put it in her safe deposit box."

"That's crap." But he looked unsure.

I took a deep breath, encouraged by my own lie. "Tabby saw the letter. Didn't she tell you what was in it?"

He scowled. "Give it to me."

She hadn't told him. Or she had told him, and he didn't believe her.

"Seriously." I forced myself to walk toward him. "I don't have it. And I don't know why you'd care about it anyway. It was just a love note from my brother to his girlfriend."

A tiny flicker of relief crossed his face at that. I could tell he really wanted to believe the letter was innocent.

"What did you think it said?"

Now he looked scared. Oh, how I ached to ask him how Joe had blackmailed his father. But I didn't dare, not all alone with him like this.

Keeping my voice calm and low, I said, "I really am sorry you came over here for nothing. I showed the letter to Tabby because it was written to her. Her mother sent it back before she saw it. But it's the last thing Bobby Lee wrote, the last thing he said to anyone that we know of, and for that reason my mother values it more than anything."

All of that was true, and it all pointed to the idea that Anna Belle would put the letter in her safe deposit box, without repeating the lie. Maybe that was the trick: Tell as much of the truth as possible when you're lying.

But he took a determined step toward me. "You have a copy — Tabby told me. Show me that."

I shook my head, mentally scrambling. Would it be so bad to show him, after all? I mean, it didn't say anything incriminating, not really. Heck, maybe he could tell me what Bobby Lee was talking about. At least it would get him out of the house.

Oh, but I didn't want to give Bobby Lee's letter to this man, not when I didn't know what it meant.

Anger flared behind Dunner's eyes, and he took another step. I backed away. "You have it. Show me!"

"Hi, there," Kelly said from the top of the steps.

Ray's nostrils flared.

I spun around. "Hi!"

"I'm Kelly O'Connell." He came down the three shallow steps and walked right up to our guest.

Dunner had been a salesman for a long time; clasping Kelly's outstretched hand was automatic. "Ray Dunner."

Kelly didn't give any indication that he knew the name, just looked at him expectantly.

"Came to see Sophie Mae here."

"Uh huh." Didn't give him an inch.

I tamped down a grin. "Good to see you, Ray. Sorry you have to go." Opened the front door. Kelly took a step forward, crowding Dunner.

"Uh. Right. But I'll check back with you about that thing we were talking about, Sophie Mae."

"Oh, that's okay. You needn't bother."

His parting look from the front sidewalk dripped with malice.

"Buh bye." I closed the door and locked it. Turned to Kelly and gave him a humongous hug. "Oh, God, thank you. I was about to give him the letter just to get him out of here. Have you been home this whole time?"

"Yeah, I was down in the basement. Meghan ran to the grocery store to get a few things for dinner and left Erin with me.

I didn't even know Dunner was here until she came and told me."

I looked up to see Erin standing in the kitchen. "You little scamp. You didn't go outside at all, did you?"

She grinned and shook her head. "Opened and shut the door then tippy-toed down to the basement. That guy was spooky."

I was glad to hear her internal alarm was in good working order.

"Took you long enough to get up here," I said to Kelly, now that my heart rate had returned to normal.

"I came right up. Thought I'd let things play out a little, see what he said."

"Nice. Well, I feel a lot better now, knowing you were here all along. It's frustrating, though, because we didn't learn anything except that he wants to read the letter."

"Which means your friend Tabby didn't share the contents with him."

"I was thinking that. Why would she tell him about the letter at all? And once she did, why not tell him what was in it?"

He smiled. "Maybe you should ask her that."

"Sure — and then she can give me more non-answers. It's her specialty."

Meghan came in then, calling for help with the groceries. Erin hopped to, but before Kelly went he put his hand on my arm. "You need to be careful. Dunner threatened to come back, you know."

"I know. I'm calling Inspector Schumaker right now."

"That's a start."

Schumaker found Ray Dunner's visit interesting, but it turned out there wasn't much he could do to help us. Dunner hadn't actually done anything except ask to see a letter, and his threat to me had been so subtle that he could easily deny it.

"You be careful, Sophie Mae," Schumaker warned. "He has a mean streak and a history of violence. Ran off three wives over the years and is known for getting into fights at some of the local drinking establishments."

"Fights with people like Joe Bines?" I couldn't help but ask.

"A few times," Schumaker acquiesced. One visit from Ray Dunner had sweetened the inspector's attitude toward me. "Dunner had a thing for Tabitha for a lot of years. Didn't like that she married Joe."

Oh, brother. Why wasn't Ray in custody?

"Sounds like motive to me," I said.

Schumaker sighed. "There's a lot of that around. We're still sorting it all out. Just be careful, okay?"

I assured him that I would and hung up the phone feeling less safe than I had before making the call. That creep had been alone with Erin. Down in the basement, Kelly hadn't realized she'd let him in. I'd asked her about that, too. We didn't encourage her to be afraid of people, but she wasn't stupid and she knew how to deal with strangers. When Dunner had knocked, she'd opened the interior door and left the screen door closed. He'd opened it and let himself in. Meghan tried to hide her distress when Erin told us that, but I saw her hand shaking as she reached for her glass of tea.

The law couldn't protect us, but Kelly had already intimidated him once and would have no qualms about getting physical if he had to. Plus, there were six of us in the house. We'd lock up carefully tonight, including the windows my parents usually left open in the summer. I dreaded telling them what happened, but they needed to know, and maybe they'd have some ideas.

In the meantime, there was another person Ray Dunner had responded to: his father. Ratting him out to his dad might not work, but it seemed worth a try.

Ogden Dunner had an unlisted number, and I couldn't find his address online. I didn't want to run into his son again, but Ray hadn't been dressed for work. My bet was that Ogden was holding down the fort at the new-and-used luxury car lot.

But when I told Meghan what I wanted to do, she didn't like my idea one little bit. "No. Absolutely not."

Dad came in then, all sweaty and pumped up from riding home from the university on his bike. I related what happened all over again.

He reacted with more speculation than fear. "So Ray Dunner thinks Bobby Lee wrote something about him eighteen years ago. Which means Bobby Lee knew something about him that he doesn't want advertised."

"Or he *thinks* Bobby Lee knew something. Either way, it fits the Dunners being blackmailed."

"Ray sounds desperate. That makes him dangerous," Dad said.

"I want to go talk to Ogden, see if he can call his son off."

"He could be just as dangerous. After all, he was the one who signed over the family land to Joe Bines, not Ray."

"Will you come with me?" I asked.

"I insist on it. Let me get changed." My father, the former investigative reporter, looked downright excited to get in on some of the action.

Meghan gave in since I wasn't going by myself — and she couldn't very well tell Dad what to do. Still, her face was pinched with worry when we left.

TWENTY-SEVEN

Dad drove. We parked on the street, and he walked onto the lot while I stayed in the car and watched. If I was wrong and Ray Dunner was manning the store, he didn't know what my father looked like.

But it was Ogden who opened the office door and descended the rickety steps. He wore a dark suit utterly inappropriate for the weather. It made him look like an undertaker. I got out of the car and joined them.

He smiled when he saw me approaching. Close up I could see the dark half-moons under his eyes like twin bruises. I wondered when he'd last slept. If anything, the gauntness of his face had increased since Barr and I had first seen him, and his skin had a gray tinge to it.

Oh, but those dark eyes still crinkled with benevolence, and his voice betrayed nothing. "Sophie Mae, how nice to see you again. Have you come to test drive that Jaguar?"

I shook my head. "No. I'm sorry, but we're not here about a car."

"Oh. So you're with this gentleman?"

"This is my father, Calvin Watson."

"I'm very pleased to make your acquaintance, sir."

"Likewise," Dad said.

Ogden regarded me. "So if this isn't about a car, how can I help you?"

I glanced at Dad then back at Ogden. Took a deep breath. "I need you to talk to your son."

I didn't think the older man could look more tired, but I was wrong. He slowly raised his eyebrows in question.

"He came by my parents' house today. My housemate's eleven-year-old daughter was there alone, and he opened the door and walked right in." Okay, so it was a slight exaggeration. Sue me.

"He didn't hurt her." But the statement sounded like a question. Not encouraging to know Ogden thought his son capable of hurting a little girl.

"No, thank goodness, but she didn't invite him in, either. He wanted to talk to me." I stopped. How much should I tell this man? Ogden was, after all, up to his bushy eyebrows in whatever was going on. "Mr. Dunner, Ray wanted to know the contents of a letter my brother wrote before he died. He was very insistent, threatening even. He frightened me."

His shoulders slumped under an unseen burden.

I continued, "Now, why does your son think my brother knew something incriminating about him?"

His large hands came up to rub his face. "I'm so sorry. I'll talk to him."

"Thank you."

The hands fell to his side. "My son's not a bad man."

Neither Dad nor I responded.

"He's had some problems, I admit. His mother left us. I never gave up on him, though. Never."

"I understand," my father said.

I did, too. And I was positive this man was telling the truth. He'd quite possibly saved his son's life. But at what cost to himself?

"I just don't want him to come back," I said. "Will you please assure him that Bobby Lee said nothing, absolutely nothing, about him in that letter?"

Relief washed across Ogden's face, and I realized he'd been worried about what might be in the letter, too. I was pretty sure this was the first he'd heard of it.

"I'll tell him. You don't have to worry," he said.

"Thank you," I said again. "Mr. Dunner?"

"Yes?"

"What happened that night at Rancho Sueño? The night Gwen Miller died?"

His face continued to emanate that intense melancholy. "A girl died. And a dream was lost."

I'd been hoping for a little less drama and a little more detail.

Dad said, "A boy died, too."

Ogden nodded. "It's a terrible thing to lose a son. I'm so very sorry."

Sorry sympathy? Or sorry apology?

But we never got a chance to ask because Mr. Dunner said, "I'll call Ray now," and went up the stairs and into the office, leaving us alone in the car lot.

He moved like he was a hundred years old.

A few minutes later, we were back in the car. Dad sat behind the steering wheel without turning on the ignition. Staring at the Auto Sales office door.

"Do you think I should have asked him more questions while I had the chance?" I asked.

He shook his head. "He wouldn't have told you anything else. But I can tell you one thing: whatever happened that night has stayed with him like a waking nightmare all these years, and yet he manages to still care about other people. That's a rare gift."

"Or a curse," I said.

Meghan was determined to give Dad and Anna Belle a night off from the kitchen and had taken over the dinner preparations. When we entered the house the scents of sage and fried onions greeted us. We hurried to join the others in the kitchen.

Anna Belle had found the jasmine body butter I'd left for her, and the heavy floral scent surrounded her like a cloud. The smell reminded me of my friend Tootie Hanover, Erin's great-grandmother, who wore jasmine every day, though on a much lighter scale.

"How does your skin feel?" I asked her.

"Like velvet," she said with a smile. "Thank you."

Kelly and Meghan had filled her in on Ray Dunner's visit when she got home, and now she demanded to know how Ogden reacted to his son's threats.

"He said he'd talk to him," Dad said.

"And if he does I think Ray will listen," I said. "When Barr and I were at the car lot yesterday, Ray backed off when his father came in." That reminded me of how much I missed Barr. He'd be getting close to the Ambrose family's Horseshoe Ranch by now, if he hadn't already arrived.

My mother snorted. "But then he came over here and scared you and Erin, didn't he?"

I grimaced. "True. Well, if you have any other ideas, please share. The sheriff's investigator didn't seem to think they could do anything based on what Dunner did."

"I'm not surprised." She huffed her disgust at the vagaries of law enforcement.

Good thing I hadn't told them that Jaikes had braced me about the lip balm they found under Joe's body.

Ick.

"So what are you making?" Dad couldn't help but ask Meghan.

"Nothing all that special. My summer version of chicken pot pie and a big salad. I took a look at the garden to see what I could use from it. You've got a wonderful selection of goodies out there. Then I saw the sage, and that made the decision for me. I only needed to buy the chicken and puff pastry."

Yum. Meghan made the best pot pie ever. In the winter it was surrounded by a savory, flaky crust made with home-rendered lard, but in hotter weather she simply topped it with store-bought puff pastry and added a few more vegetables to lighten it up.

"Dessert?" I asked. We didn't often eat dessert at home, but we sure had while on vacation.

Vacation. Ha!

Anyway, I hoped it wouldn't be too heavy. My walk earlier had reminded me I had a wedding coming up, and I needed to watch my waistline.

"Chocolate-dipped strawberries."

"Perfect." I could nibble on one, get a nice little dose of chocolate, and still feel relatively virtuous.

I checked my e-mail and voice-mail, and did a little work before dinner. Barr still hadn't called, but he also hadn't seen his family for a while. I understood. They had a lot to catch up on.

We were digging into the mounds of creamy chicken, carrots, onions, peas, zucchini, and new potatoes on our plates when the doorbell rang. I got up to answer it, swearing under my breath at people who dropped by during the dinner hour.

Just in case Ray Dunner had decided to grace us with his presence twice in one day, I flicked the shade to see who was on the front step.

Not Ray.

Ogden, still in his black suit and fidgeting with his tie.

Slowly, I went to the door and opened it. "Mr. Dunner." I stepped out to the front step, reluctant to let him enter the house.

"Miss Watson."

"Reynolds," I said. "Ms. Reynolds."

"Oh. Of course. I'm sorry."

"That's okay." I waited.

"Um, I was wondering whether I might be able to see that letter you were telling me about, the one your brother wrote to Tabitha Bines."

I stared at him. Was he kidding?

"I might be able to help you," he said.

"It was a love letter. That's all."

"That's not exactly what Tabitha told my son."

"So you talked to Ray. Is he going to leave us alone?" My tone was flat.

"Yes. I promise. But I promised him I'd look at the letter if you'd let me. To assure him he doesn't have anything to worry about."

You can't promise someone else will behave, but I'd take what I could get.

"Worry about? Like what?" I asked. "What is he so afraid of?"

Ogden shook his head. "Nothing real.

Believe me."

Right. Now Ray was paranoid. Good Lord. Why couldn't anyone just give me a straight answer?

Behind me, Anna Belle's voice lilted. "Hello. Won't you please come in?"

Surprised, I turned around. She ignored me and held the door open to Ogden Dunner. He walked past me into the great room. I followed, my eyes drifting up to the open beam above. What was she thinking?

"Wait here," she said, and disappeared into her den. When she returned she held Bobby Lee's letter. The real one, not the copy I'd been carrying around in my tote bag. Everyone had drifted in from the kitchen and stood around awkwardly. Ogden cleared his throat and darted a glance at me. I felt my nostrils flare.

He reached out and took the letter. Unfolded it and began to read.

As he took in the contents his shoulders began to relax. When he raised his head, he was the picture of bewilderment. Intense disappointment clogged my throat when I saw that, and I realized I'd thought maybe he really could help, despite my reluctance to show him the letter at all.

"I have no idea what this means," he said.

Anna Belle sighed. My father went and

put his arm around her. Meghan sat down on the step and Erin perched behind her. Kelly continued to lean against the wall.

"I hadn't seen Bobby Lee for months before he died. I thought . . ." He looked down and closed his eyes briefly, then looked back up. "I thought perhaps I could put your minds to rest. But I'm afraid I'm less than useless at clearing this up."

"Tell me," I said. "What did Tabby say my brother wrote?" Because if she had told the truth then there would have been no reason to get so upset. Or was there? I was so confused I was starting to wonder if I'd ever figure this thing out.

Ogden hesitated. "I'm afraid I don't know. Whatever it was bothered him, but I believe I was able to put his mind to rest." He handed the letter back to my mother. "I'm sorry to interrupt your evening. I only wanted to help."

"We appreciate that," Anna Belle said in her most gracious tone.

I walked Ogden out. He said goodnight in an apologetic tone and got in the MG I'd seen at the lot, the one painted British racing green.

Back inside the house no one had moved.

"C'mon people," Anna Belle said with false enthusiasm. "We were in the middle of a perfectly fabulous meal."

We trudged back to the table and sat down.

"Dad, do you believe he doesn't know what that letter is all about?"

My father shook his head. "It doesn't make sense to trust him. Something is going on, or was going on, and he's involved. I certainly don't think he wanted to see that letter just to help us. If it incriminated his son he would have kept that to himself."

I swallowed a bite of chicken. Poor Meghan, having her wonderful dinner grow cold on the table. "I agree. But he really did seem clueless when he read it. Anna Belle, I was surprised you showed it to him. You sounded so contemptuous when you first spoke of him."

"Contemptuous? Yes, perhaps. I didn't like what he did out there at the Rancho Sueño. Or at least what I thought he was doing. Perhaps I was wrong."

Everyone stopped eating and stared at her.

"What? I can't admit I was wrong? Maybe the place wasn't so bad. Calvin told me about what that reporter had in her notes, and it sounds like Mr. Dunner was really trying to help people. I still don't like forcing religion on kids when they're down on their luck." For someone who was admitting she might be wrong, she sure sounded defensive.

But still: Wow.

"The point is," Anna Belle continued, "I wanted to know if he could explain Bobby Lee's letter." I could tell she felt the same disappointment I did.

I picked my fork back up. "Well, I'm going out to the dairy in the morning to talk to Tabby. She sicced Ray Dunner on us, and I want to know whether it was accidental or intentional. And if it was the latter, I damn well want to know why."

Not only that, but Tabby seemed to be the only one with the answers to my questions — had been from the very beginning. Tomorrow I'd go at her with a little more ammunition than I'd had before — like the quit claim deed and the information I'd gathered from Carrie Romain's notes.

"Oh, that won't work," Anna Belle said. "Not in the morning. I've made an appointment at Ginger's Bridal downtown. I'm hoping you'll see something you like and we can get started with a fitting."

Across from me, Meghan ducked her head to hide her amusement.

"But —"

"You can go talk to Tabby afterward," my mother said. "The answers she gives you

won't be any different in the afternoon."
And that was the end of that.

The chocolate-covered strawberries were huge. I ate five of them.

Twenty-Eight

"My mother's planned the menu, and she's blocked out all the cabins for the whole week, so there'll be plenty of room for people to stay. Of course, you'll have final say on the food, but I can't imagine you won't love it." Barr had finally called from Wyoming.

"That's great," I said, my voice weak. "Tomorrow I'm going shopping for a dress with my mother."

"Anything you pick out will look beautiful on you. Remember that it'll be November, though. Of course, we'll be inside, so you don't need to actually dress for the weather." It was the closest Barr had ever come to babbling.

"I'll keep that in mind." I sat cross-legged on the bed with Kitty Wampus on my lap. He stretched and purred. I'd finally given in after he refused to stop sleeping on my pillow, even after I'd covered it with a cloth soaked with peppermint oil. Felines usually hate peppermint, but not this one. I had to give him credit for persistence.

"At least we've decided on rings," he said. "We can cross that off the list."

I wasn't much on diamonds, so we'd commissioned a jeweler in Cadyville to make us one-of-a-kind platinum rings with Montana sapphires in them.

"Cross them right off," I repeated, amazed.

"Say, I've asked Randall to be my best man," Barr said.

Uh oh. Randall was Barr's brother. Who was currently dating Barr's ex-wife.

"Does that mean Hannah needs to be in the wedding party?" I hated even asking the question out loud.

"Oh, God no. I've already explained that would be too weird for you, and she completely understands. She's offered to tend bar at the reception, though."

Too weird for *me*. Great. Tend bar. Excellent. She'd just better not think she could tend Barr, if she knew what was good for her.

"Um, speaking of the reception, just how many people do you think we should invite? Anna Belle is getting all het up about the guest list and sending out invitations."

"I thought about that as I drove. I've got at least fifteen people I'd like to come, if they can. How about you?"

I sighed, low so he couldn't hear it over the phone. Surely it was a good sign that I was more excited about being married than the actual wedding, right? I mean, my vision of the wedding had been down-to-earth and very simple. But if this was going to make everybody happy, I'd be happy, too.

"I'd invite a few people from Cadyville, but I doubt most of them would come out to Wyoming in November for a wedding."

Silence greeted my words, and I realized how I must have sounded. "They just won't know what they're missing. And I'll be sure to talk Tootie into it. She's the most important one besides Meghan and Erin." Petunia Hanover was Erin's great grandmother, and a close friend.

"I'll pay for her and Felix, both. Make sure you tell her that." Felix was Tootie's ninety-something-year-old boyfriend.

I laughed. "Okay. Enough with the wedding details. I've had a full, rich day since you left. Listen to this." And I proceeded to tell him about the various interactions with the Dunner family.

When I was done, he whistled. "That Ogden is a conundrum, isn't he? You feel okay about his son now? Or are you still worried?"

"Well, father-son talk or not, we're locking the house up tight tonight, and I'll be sleeping lightly."

And we did, battening down the Watson hatches from attic to basement.

Since I'd be trying on fancy dresses, I stuck to a bowl of berries for breakfast on Saturday morning. Our appointment at the bridal shop was for ten o'clock.

"What kind of a place is this that you have to make an appointment?"

My mother sniffed. "Exclusive, that's what kind. Ginger carries the most unique dresses. You'll love them."

"Hmmph."

"Oh, for heaven's sake! It's your wedding."

"Sorry."

I liked to play dress up as much as any female; it was Anna Belle's machinations that bothered me. It was silly, of course. Would Erin be the same way with Meghan, caught in that struggle to break away and be her own adult? I hoped not. Silently, I vowed to stop resisting and count myself lucky to have a mother who actually enjoyed event planning. Running my own business was my forte, but organizing special occasions was not. Left to me, we'd end up with a pile of Twinkies bought at the last minute instead of a real wedding cake.

Mmm . . . cake.

"How about carrot cake?" I asked.

"You're hungry?"

"No. For the wedding cake."

Anna Belle's face lit up. "Of course. That's a wonderful idea. I'll call Cassie and —" She looked at her watch. "No, it'll have to wait until we get back. We'd better get going."

In the car, I related some of my conversation with Barr the evening before, including his excitement regarding the reception menu his mother had in mind.

"Well, he ought to be excited. She wants to serve filet mignon," Anna Belle said.

"Yum. With garlic mashed sweet potatoes, too. Starting with roasted red pepper bisque. Oh, and the appetizers! Okay, I'm officially into this whole wedding thing."

She didn't clap her hands, but then again, she was driving.

The little bridal shop was in a converted house on Mulberry Street. Small and quaint on the outside, it was elegant but friendly inside. Ginger met us at the door and had several dresses ready for me to look at. A couple of them were white, fluffy affairs, but the one I immediately fell in love with had a fitted lace bodice and low neckline. The long sleeves reflected the flowing skirt sans train, and it was a dark purple-brown.

"This color is crazy for a wedding dress, but it's so beautiful." I fingered the layered skirt.

Anna Belle frowned. "Don't you think it's a bit dark?"

"Aubergine is very chic," Ginger said. "It's wonderful with your skin, and makes your green eyes positively glow. Try it on."

I did, and loved it even more.

"Well, it does look quite nice on you," my mother said, pursing her lips. "And you are getting married late in the year."

"I'll take it," I said. "No, wait. How much is it?"

Ginger cited the amount so casually it took a moment to register. When it did, the blood drained out of my face.

"Oh. Well. I, uh . . ."

"We'll take it." Anna Belle shook her head and consulted the ceiling. "Most women would take hours to choose the right dress, but trust you to pick the first one you try on."

I bristled.

But her smile was good natured. "Very efficient of you." She tugged at the dress fabric. "It could use a small tuck in the waist and a bit of letting out around the bust."

"Not a problem," Ginger assured us and opened the armoire in the corner which held her measuring tape and pins.

"Anna Belle," I whispered. "It costs too much." Actually, Barr could afford it, but I hated to ask him to dip into the money he'd inherited from his uncle earlier that year, especially for a dress I'd only wear once. And I sure couldn't afford that extravagantly beautiful garment on my own.

"This is my present to you."

"But —"

"No 'buts.' "

"I can't let you do that."

She looked stricken. "Please? It can be your something new."

Desire warred with guilt, but when she put it like that, how could I say no?

The brief coolness of the early morning had vanished, leaving a heavy feel to the air and blazing temperatures that threatened to climb even higher as the afternoon wore on. Clouds hovered on the northeastern horizon. Virga wisped down from their undersides like gray fur, the potential rain evaporating before it hit the ground. It was not a phenomenon I'd ever seen in the Pacific Northwest. Here, precipitation teased the parched land below. At least the spreading clouds might offer some relief from the heat.

My flight to Seattle would leave the following afternoon. This was my last chance to get answers from Tabby, my last chance to give my parents some closure. I wondered whether she knew who had killed her husband, then reminded myself that was Schumaker's problem. My focus had to be on my family in the limited time I had remaining in Spring Creek, however frustrating it was to leave while Joe's murder remained unsolved.

Now that I knew about the quit claim deed, Tabby might spill what had happened. At least I hoped so. Was she as skilled a liar as she was a cheese maker, or could it be that she really didn't know Joe had blackmailed Ogden Dunner? The latter was pretty hard to believe. As the Subaru seemed to find its own way down the county road, I thought about Tabby's face when she spoke of her daughter and cared for her animals. She might have decided never to fall for another man after Bobby Lee's death, but her love for Delight radiated a fierce intensity.

A similar expression had settled on her

face when she spoke of Bobby Lee. Her refusal to help me get to the bottom of what had happened eighteen years ago made me want to shake her until her teeth rattled, but it was hard to truly dislike someone who felt that way about my brother.

I'd expected to see more vehicles in the T&J Dairy parking lot, but found only the milk delivery truck and Tabby's Jeep. Merry yellow streamers of crime scene tape festooned the area behind the classroom where we'd learned to make mozzarella, but a rattle and clank from within the building alerted me to someone's presence inside. Leaving my heavy tote bag in the car, I walked the few steps to the door. It was ajar a few inches, and I pushed it open. Inside, I discovered Tabby stacking crates of empty bottles along one wall.

Photographs, scissors, a glue stick, and an assortment of scrapbooking supplies covered the long table in the center of the room. At one end a large poster board stood on an easel, already half covered with pictures of Joe Bines.

"Hi," I said.

She whirled to face me, one hand over her chest. "Oh. Sophie Mae. You scared me."

"Sorry. Didn't mean to sneak up on you." I pointed to the poster board. "Joe's life in pictures?"

"It's for the memorial service."

Leaning in, I saw the collage captured a progression in time. Joe as a baby sitting on his mother's lap. His third-grade picture, already showing a devilish glint in his eye. Around fourteen, posing in a baseball uniform and grinning high, wide and handsome. A similar grin as he leaned against the door of a forest green pickup, *First Truck* in fancy script across the bottom of the picture. He'd been almost good looking as a young man, before the hard living and tobacco chewing. Before the blackmail and bar fights.

Tabby watched me from the other side of the table.

Straightening, I took a deep, bracing breath. This wasn't going to be easy. I folded my arms and considered her. "That letter really threw a monkey wrench into things, didn't it?"

She sighed. "Why are you here?"

"Did you hire someone to kill Joe?" It was the first time I'd really thought of that; just my luck the brakes between my brain and my mouth chose the perfect moment to fail. Again.

She blanched under her tan. "I don't have to listen to your wild accusations. I think you should leave."

"No."

Anger flared across her features, widening her eyes and her nostrils. Her lips parted to reveal even white teeth.

"You do have to listen to this," I said. "I'm sick and tired of getting the runaround. Nice and reasonable haven't worked with you, Tabby. Now I'm simply at the end of my rope. You're going to answer my questions, or else you're going to answer Sheriff Jaikes' questions about that letter." I shrugged. "It's up to you."

"Why do you think I know something about Bobby Lee? I *don't*." She blinked rapidly as sudden tears threatened to spill down her cheeks.

"You do. Damn it, Tabby, I know you do." I heard the pleading tone in my voice and stopped. Cleared my throat and tried again. "I know a few other things, too. For example, that Ogden Dunner quit claimed this land to Joe. Then lo and behold, you married him even though you admitted to me you never loved him. But you got the dairy you always wanted, didn't you? Were you behind the blackmail? What did Joe have on Dunner that could make a man give up his family's land?"

Her throat worked as she tried to swallow.

"I didn't have anything to do with it. Joe and I weren't even married then."

"But you knew about it, didn't you? You told me the other day this dairy was your idea, and that you love it. As far as the daily work went, Joe was more of a detriment than a help. But Tabby, your name isn't even on the deed. Is that how you run a business?"

"It's mine now." Her chin raised in defiance. "Stop looking at me like that. You don't know as much as you think you do. I didn't kill Joe, but this place belongs to me now that he's dead."

"Of course you didn't kill him. I'm your alibi, for heaven's sake. That still begs the question of why Ogden Dunner gave Joe this land."

Her chin swung back and forth. "I don't know."

"You loved Bobby Lee. So did I. You owe me an explanation if this involves him."

The anger flared again. "I don't owe you a thing, Sophie Mae. You're the one who started this whole mess."

"Oh, no you don't. This mess — your mess — was here all along. I just wanted some answers about my brother, and you could have simply told me the truth. He wrote that letter to *you*. Only you understand what he meant by 'it wasn't your fault,' and 'don't blame yourself.

"But then you had to tell Ray Dunner there was something about him in that letter. Something incriminating. Did you know that jerk showed up at my parents' home yesterday, forced his way past an eleven-year-old girl and waited inside until I came home?"

Tabby's eyes widened at my mention of Erin.

"Then he demanded the letter. He even threatened me."

Her jaw set. "I had nothing to do with any of that. He called me because you came into his car lot and acted like I'd sent you there. How dare you involve me in your lies, Sophie Mae? I had to tell him something. So guess what? I told him the truth. I told him you were trying to find out what Bobby Lee meant in that stupid letter. It's not my fault if Ray came to the conclusion that you tracked him down because of something your brother wrote. You poked that bear, and he came after you. What did you expect?"

I stared at her, speechless. Then my fist came crashing down on the table. The collage supplies jumped. So did Tabby.

Ow.

"I may have poked that bear, but you *sent* him after me. To get me to stop asking questions? Did you sic him on Joe, too?"

Her eyes widened.

"I talked to Krista Jaikes." Frustration lent a rasp to my words. "She told me about that night." I gestured behind me. "Down there, by that river. You've lived where it happened all this time. How does that make you feel?"

Her fingers crept over her mouth.

"She knows there weren't any runaway siblings, no Tom and Jane Smith. She knows who was really there."

I was half-fishing, though I'd thought about it a lot. The look in Tabby's eyes said I was on the right track. "There was Tabitha Atwood and . . . Joe Bines." It could have been Bobby Lee, but he wasn't the one who blackmailed Ogden Dunner.

"They're going to reopen Gwen Miller's case." Yes, a flat-out lie. Tabby didn't notice. I didn't have any qualms about telling it, and I wished to God it were true. Maybe that was the key: needing to believe your own lie. "And they'll be asking questions. Lots of questions."

She still didn't say anything.

"Tabby! Gwen Miller is dead. Bobby Lee is dead. Joe is dead. They have to be connected."

Fear shone from her eyes.

"Aren't you frightened?"

And I could tell I'd hit home. Tabby Bines was downright terrified.

"Please, please: tell me what happened. Was Bobby Lee there? Was Gwen Miller the reason he killed himself?"

"No," she whispered. "He came later. To pick us up. I called him. I was scared."

TWENTY-NINE

So she had been there. And Bobby Lee hadn't been, at least not until later. I wanted to crow over this small victory, this tiny bit of information I'd finally managed to extract.

But I kept my voice even when I said, "Thank you for finally admitting that. I mean it."

She gave a tiny nod in response.

"So Joe was there with you? Why couldn't he take you home?"

Her shoulders slumped, and she covered her face with both hands as something inside of her let go. She half-sat on the table. Her arms fell to her sides, knocking photographs of her dead husband to the floor. Tabby didn't seem to notice. Red-rimmed eyes regarded me for a long moment then her gaze shunted away.

"We came out here with Gwen and Krista. In Krista's car. I wanted to leave, but she wouldn't take me home." Her words were hesitant, heavy with memory.

As gently as I could, I asked, "What happened that night, Tabby?"

She looked out the window behind me, toward the river. I followed her gaze. The water she was remembering was invisible from where we were, but I could see the thunderheads, gray and threatening, stacked high on the horizon. The hay in the field undulated in waves as the wind picked up. Distant rumblings through the thick summer air gave fair warning of an impending storm.

"It was late." Her voice had a dreamy quality to it. "The cold was bitter, raw. We didn't care — we were just stupid kids, goofing around, joking and smoking. A little snow had fallen, and the moon was almost full. It was almost as bright as daylight, but everything was in black and white. It was so beautiful."

She licked her lips. "Then Gwen screamed. From behind me. She . . . she fell in the water, slipped and went under. It wasn't that deep, but she couldn't get out. Maybe she hit her head. I don't know. So Joe waded in and took hold of her arm and dragged her to the riverbank. God." She closed her eyes and rubbed her forehead.

Opened her eyes. "Gwen was so cold. So was Joe, but he hadn't been in the water as long as she had, and he was only wet to his thighs. We tried to walk her back to the house, but she kept falling. Joe and Ray had to carry her between them. Krista ran ahead to get Ray's dad out of bed."

"What did Ogden do?" I asked when she paused.

"He met us in the yard, helped get her inside. Tried to get her warm. Wrapped her in blankets, put heating pads around her, rubbed her hands and feet."

"He didn't take her straight to the hospital then."

Hesitation, then, "Not right away. He tried to save her, tried really hard. Her lips were blue. I could see she wasn't going to make it."

"Is that what scared you?"

"Yeah. That and Ray. He was so angry, yelling at her to wake up, telling her how stupid she was to fall in like that." She licked her lips. "Krista wasn't going to leave her friend, but I wanted to leave. Joe's feet were in bad shape, too, from wading in the freezing water, but no one paid any attention to him. So I called Bobby Lee to come get us."

"You called him at home? That late?"

"I told him I'd call when I got home that night. As long as we planned it ahead of time your parents never woke up when the phone rang."

I knew why, too. I'd taught Bobby Lee how to unplug all the phones in the house except the one in the basement when he was expecting a phone call after Dad and Anna Belle went to bed.

"And he came and got you?"

She nodded. "By then they were talking about taking Gwen to the hospital. There wasn't room for us in the car anyway, with her lying in the backseat. Joe pulled Ogden aside and talked to him for a few minutes. Then everyone else left, and we waited until Bobby Lee showed up."

"Why didn't you follow them to the hospital in Krista's car?"

Tabby looked out the window. "We didn't want to be involved. Joe had been in some trouble with the police — minor stuff, but only a few weeks before. And there wasn't anything I could do to help. There was no reason for us to go to the hospital."

I didn't know what to say. Their behavior wouldn't win them any awards for bravery, but I could understand it, too. They were kids — not little children, but not adults, either. And there was an adult present who was supposed to know what to do in emergencies. Plus, it didn't help that they'd probably been sampling some of Ray Dunner's illegal offerings.

What I still didn't understand was why no one had admitted Tabby and Joe had been there in the first place. Why the story about the runaway siblings?

Tires crunched on gravel outside.

Tabby whirled and peered out the window. Her eyes widened. "Oh, no."

I joined her. The same big black pickup that had been parked in front of my parents' house when I'd come home from my walk had pulled in next to the dairy's delivery van.

Her fingers closed on my arm. "He's here for me."

Ray Dunner climbed down from the driver's seat and slammed the door. His ruddy face was visible from our vantage. He stood with his fists on his hips and surveyed the area.

"Here for you?" I asked, even though I knew.

Her fingers tightened, and I winced. "To kill me."

Hearing the words sent a trill of terror through my veins, but there was a part of me that resisted panic, too busy trying to figure out the rest of the puzzle. "I don't get it. Nothing you told me — wait a minute, what about the blackmail? Was it completely unrelated to Gwen Miller's death?"

Ray walked over and looked in the window of Anna Belle's car.

Tabby whispered, "Joe saw Ray push her in."

My mind scrambled to make sense of her words. Ray had killed Gwen. Joe witnessed it and made a deal with Ogden, who had given up his dream to protect his son. It explained the antagonism between Ray and Joe, the frequent fights. Joe got the land and the girl with the pretty blue eyes; Ray got to work in a rundown car dealership and wake up every day to the knowledge of his father's sacrifice. It all added up to more than enough motive for murder.

Ray opened the door of the Audi and pulled out my tote bag. I groaned as I saw him take the car keys out and put them in his pocket. My cell phone followed, and then he rifled my wallet. Holding it up to the light, he eyeballed my driver's license. Then he took the cash out and stuffed that in his pocket, too.

What a jerk.

That'll teach you not to leave your keys in the car, small town or no small town.

Ray started up the little hill to the house. As he walked, he reached around to the small of his back and pulled something out of his waistband. It glinted in the odd gray light of the oncoming storm.

"Gun," I said without thinking.

Beside me, Tabby nodded.

She was right about Ray's lethal intentions. This time there would be no spur-of-the-moment use of whatever weapon came to hand; this time he'd come prepared. Whether or not she had been directly involved, Tabby knew Joe had blackmailed Ogden. Ray had crossed the line when he killed Joe, and for someone with such a violent nature, my bet was that the second time it would be easier. Make that the third time, since he'd been responsible for Gwen Miller's death as well.

A new reason for panic surfaced. "Is Delight up there?" I asked.

Tabby shook her head. "She's at my mom's."

Gently, I tried to pry her grasp from my arm. "Where are Gretchen and Eduardo?"

"Eduardo's day off. Gretchen wasn't feeling well, so I sent her home early."

"We're here alone?"

Tabby nodded, and I heard her swallow. "I should have known. Why didn't I think to bring it with me?" Her voice rose.

"Shh. Bring what?"

"My gun. It's up at the house. On the kitchen counter." Fear laced the words.

My jaw slackened as the realization struck me. Good Lord. She'd been expecting something like this. It was why Delight wasn't home. It was probably why her help wasn't here either.

And I'd walked right into it.

"You've known all along who killed Joe," I breathed. Turned to look at her.

Her face was a mask of hard determination, but her chin swung back and forth. "I only suspected. They had a history."

Well, that was true enough. Even Schumaker had admitted that.

"We have to get my gun," she said.

"I'd rather get a phone. Or get out of here," I said. "Do you have the keys to your Jeep on you? Or to the delivery truck?"

Her response was an impatient shake of her head.

"Cell phone?"

"Not with me."

Crap. "Then we'd better leave before he comes back out of the house. Run down to the county road and flag someone down."

She looked at me and bit her lip, indecision all over her face.

"Let the authorities take care of Ray Dunner."

Tabby still didn't move.

"We have to get out of here. *Now.*"

"Right. Okay." She put her hand on the door handle. "Let's go." Her hip brushed against one of the crates stacked against the wall. The empty milk bottles inside rattled and clanked against each other.

The crate began to tip. Tabby opened the door.

My hand flew out to steady the crate.

Not in time.

It fell to the floor with an unholy crash audible in Kansas. If Ray Dunner hadn't known where we were before, he certainly did now.

I grabbed her hand. "Come on!"

"Tabitha . . ." Ray's voice drifted in from the parking lot, and he walked around the back of the delivery van to find us half out of the doorway. We hadn't seen him return from the house.

He smiled and held up a hand gun. "This yours, Tabby?"

Thunder rolled across the sky as we ducked back into the classroom. I slammed the door shut and threw the bolt lock.

"Now, what did you go and do that for?" His voice drew closer.

Tabby and I stared at each other like scared rabbits. I swear my nose twitched with fright.

"Enough is enough, Tabitha," Ray yelled from the other side of the door. "You have our land. You can't have anything else. I'm putting a stop to it."

"I don't want anything from your family," Tabby called. "I never asked for anything in the first place. That was all Joe."

Ray kicked the door, and we jumped.

"Stop antagonizing him," I hissed.

Barr was going to kill me when he found out about this — if I weren't dead already. The thought galvanized me. I was going to get married, damn it, and I wasn't about to die at the hands of this violent nutcase. My gaze swept the room, weighing the options. Hoping.

There.

I hurried to the window in the back and slid it open. It was three feet wide and low to the ground. Piece of cake to climb out. The wind blasted in, scattering the photos of Joe around the room. I hiked one leg over the sill and lifted myself through.

Tabby was right behind me. The sound of the front window breaking followed us as we veered to the right and ran up toward the house. The sky loomed above, packed with volatile potential. A few fat drops of rain splatted down. We reached the front door, and I turned to see Ray lumbering up the hill.

"Do you have another gun?" I yelled to Tabby, my heart loud in my ears. Why weren't we inside yet?

"That son of a — he locked the door!"

"Don't you keep a spare key out here?"

She shook her head in disgust. Together, we launched off the step and sprinted around to the rear of the house. Tabby started for the back door, but I grabbed her arm and pulled her toward the barn. If he'd locked the front door, he'd probably locked the back one, too.

We zig-zagged to the far side of the milking barn and stood with our backs flat against it. The small herd of dairy cows crowded into the covered area near the doors. I didn't know whether it was time for them to be milked, or if they didn't like the weather. The temperature had dropped, and the wind had a bite to it. The rain came down faster. Bigger.

Harder. Rounder.

Great.

"We have to get inside the barn," I shouted as the hail increased in intensity. The ground around us squirmed with half-inch ice pellets.

"No. He'll look there, and we can't keep him out. Come on." She took off toward the trailer that housed the mold-ripened cheeses.

I followed, the hail bouncing off my skull, striking the bare flesh of my arms and shoulders. The smooth soles of my sandals slid on the slippery ground, and I went down on the same knee I'd scraped when Billy the goat sent me flying.

Ow.

We stumbled in through the door. Tabby slammed the door closed and twisted the dead bolt home.

THIRTY

The sudden darkness made me blink. Humid air brushed clammy fingers against my cheek. Hailstones pummeled the metal roof above, an inescapable, earsplitting roar of pure sound. The concentrated odor of mold lodged in my throat and sinuses. I gagged. My arms, neck, and back tingled and stung from a hundred tiny blows, and my damp clothes clung to my skin. Shivers ran from my scalp all the way to my toes, and I clamped my jaw shut so my teeth would stop chattering.

I took a step and ran into a table. Turned the other direction and earned another bruise. Something grabbed at my arm, and I shrieked, flailing. The greater cacophony buried my screams. Whatever it was, it let go.

Sinking to the floor, I sat huddled, rocking. Waiting. I couldn't see, couldn't hear, and could barely breathe. Tears streamed down my face from the smell.

At least I blamed the smell.

Oh, and I was probably going to die, too.

A curtain twitched at the end of the trailer. The tiniest bit of light seeped in, granting instant vision to my fully dilated eyes. Tabby stood by a small square of window. Thick black plastic covered most of it, but she'd worked the staples out of one corner.

Mold grew better in the dark and the wet. Hence the caves. Of course. We were in a simulated cave.

I shook my head and stood, trying to orient myself. Shelves stacked with rounds of cheese ran down both sides of a narrow aisle. Strips of plastic sheeting hung from the ceiling to provide crude cover. One of them must have touched my arm in the dark.

Nice, Sophie Mae. Panicked by a sneeze guard.

Like a pan of popcorn cooking on the stove, the hail slowed, gave a few more raps on the roof, and ceased. An eerie silence descended for a long moment. Then a crack of thunder split the air, and my slowing heartbeat jumped again.

My hands were shaking. But nothing had grabbed me. We were still alive. I could hear myself think. My nose was becoming inured to the odor of mold, and we had enough cheese to survive in here for months.

So why did the light from the window reveal such intense fear on Tabby's face?

I lurched to her side, scanning the artificial twilight outside for danger. No sign of Ray Dunner.

She pointed up.

Dark gray clouds scudded overhead, but to the northeast the sky loomed an evil slate-green. A flash rent the rumpled flannel, then another. Constant, almost conversational thunder rolled all around us. Staying in a metal building during a nasty thunderstorm wouldn't be terribly smart. At least the hail seemed to be over.

Tabby swirled her finger in the air. I frowned, and then my eyes widened in comprehension.

Uh oh.

The thunderhead spread dark fingers toward the landscape, and, while we watched, a spiral of clouds slowly tightened. A hailstorm was one thing, but a tornado? In August? That was a whole different can of worms.

"This isn't necessary." It was a man's voice.

We jerked back from the window.

"You have to trust me, son. Just go on home."

I almost wept again. We were going to be all right. "It's Ogden Dunner," I whispered.

Tabby put her hand on my arm and bent close to my ear. "Wait."

Well, I hadn't been planning to run right out and hug him.

"Give me the gun," Ogden said. A pause, then, "Okay, good."

A grin spread across my face, and I gave Tabby a thumbs-up. Slowly, I pulled up the corner of the window covering again. A quick peek revealed more dark, rotating clouds, but neither of the Dunners were visible. The voices had come from below us and to the right.

Leaning forward, Tabby whispered into my ear. "Ray has my thirty-eight, too. He may not have given both of them to his dad."

Ogden's voice again. "Now go. I'll take care of this."

"What are you going to do?" Ray asked. He sounded angry, but I didn't think it was at his father. "Once Tabitha's gone, we won't have to worry anymore. No one else knows anything."

"We can't count on that," his father said.

"But you said there was nothing in Watson's letter." Ray's tone had a whiny edge to it.

"His sister's asking a lot of questions, and now the sheriff's people are looking into everything that has to do with this property again, digging up old relationships. They're investigating you. It's my fault, I know. But Joe didn't exactly give me a choice. I'm afraid I've backed us into a real corner, son."

Tabby's shaking hand still gripped my arm. I watched the sky and listened.

"We can't keep trying to patch this mess. Trying only made it worse," Ogden continued. "You haven't killed anyone yet. At least not that anyone can prove. I've thought long and hard about what to tell the authorities about the Miller girl, and I don't think you'll have to serve time. Or at least not much time. After what I did, I don't think I'll be so lucky."

Holy crap: Ogden Dunner had killed Joe! I strained to hear more.

"I'm not serving any time, old man." Ray's voice dripped with disgust. "Not then, and not now. Gwen's death was an accident. You were so ready to believe Joe, to believe I'd hurt her, that you gave away everything we had."

"Ray —"

"You were a fool then and you're a fool

334

now if you think I'm going to jail."

"They think you killed Joe."

"But we know better, don't we . . ." Ray's voice faded as the pair walked away.

Tabby's grip on my arm was starting to cut off blood flow. I pulled away. "What were you thinking, trying to blackmail the Dunners all over again?"

She shook her head. "I wasn't. Ray thought I was, but I never wanted anything from them. The blackmail was all Joe's doing. I didn't even see Gwen go in the river that night; I told you that."

"You wanted the dairy," I said. "More than anything."

"But by the time I married him, Joe already had this land."

"Is that the reason you married him?"

She licked her lips and looked away. "Partly."

"And you knew how he got the Rancho Sueño property, didn't you."

"Well . . . yeah."

Whatever look crossed my face made her flinch.

Outside, something hit the mold house with a loud crunching noise. The trailer rocked, and we stumbled. Rounds of cheese flew off the shelf, and I ducked as one narrowly missed my head. Tabby tore the blackout covering from the window, exposing the fully formed funnel cloud now dancing across the landscape. It was still miles away, and it was unclear which direction it was moving. In the artificial gloaming, the muscular twister conveyed power and malevolence.

I'd grown up in this area. May and June dinners were often eaten in the basement because of tornado warnings. Old hat, but that thing still scared the bejesus out of me.

Frightened me more, even, than the two men with guns searching the dairy for Tabitha Bines and yours truly.

"We have to get out of here," I said, no longer trying to be quiet. "Where?" This wouldn't be Tabby's first experience with a tornado, either. She'd know the best place to hunker down.

"We always go in the basement when there's a warning, but if the house is still locked we can't get in."

"Nowhere else? Storage under the barn?"

"Barn's right on the ground. Too open. The classroom has those big windows."

Not to mention all the glass bottles.

"What about the river cut bank?" she suggested.

A cut bank was where the river had eaten away at the soil, leaving a vertical drop to the water. "How deep?" I asked.

"Maybe three feet in places."

I shook my head. "Might be enough, but there are all those cottonwoods, and with the lightning it's better to avoid the water. We'll try for the basement."

My hand grasped the doorknob. A short nod from Tabby, and I turned it.

The wind yanked the door away and slammed it against the metal exterior of the trailer with a loud report. We dashed into the maelstrom.

Gusts tore at our hair and clothes. The yard was littered with detritus. I dodged a four-foot tumbleweed and turned to see a mountain of them towering above us, piled against the side of the barn and held there by the force of the wind. The temperature had dropped even more, and stray raindrops struck my bare arms and legs. A low roar reverberated through the gloom, punctuated by cows lowing in panic.

I shivered from cold and fear. Thought of Barr. Of my family. Of my friends. I just had to weather this storm — and avoid two killers — and everything would be all right. I'd wear that amazing dress. I'd marry the love of my life. I'd live happily ever after.

Keeping one eye on the funnel cloud and the other out for the Dunners, I started for the house.

Tabby went the opposite direction.

I sprinted back and spun her around. "What are you doing?" I yelled in her face. "Don't be stupid."

"I have to get the cows inside," she yelled back. "Too much debris flying around, and they're terrified. They'll feel safer in the barn."

Crap. "I'll help you."

But she shook her head and pushed me away. "They don't know you, and you don't know anything about cattle. You'll just make things worse. Get to the house. Break a window if you have to and get inside. I'll be there as soon as I can." She plunged back into the wind, toward her bellowing charges.

The fact that I didn't trust her as far as I could throw her didn't stop me from turning back toward the house. And she was right — I didn't have the first idea of how to get a frightened bovine to do anything.

I stopped and looked around the corner of the barn. Billy the goat led the three kids around to the southwest side of the chicken house to shelter from the wind. The hens had already gone to roost as if the day were done. I didn't see the Dunners anywhere, so I started for the back of the Bines' house.

The explosion of a gunshot down the hill

gave my feet wings.

As I ran I glimpsed the parking lot below. A surge of hope coursed through me when I saw the new arrival: a white Suburban with a light bar and county logo on the side.

The cavalry had arrived.

THIRTY-ONE

The back door was indeed locked. I started toward the side of the house, but the crash of breaking glass stopped me dead in my tracks. Leaning around the corner, I saw father and son Dunners standing deep in a basement window well, clearing glass shards from around the sill.

Just because you lock a door doesn't mean you have the key to get back in.

So much for weathering the storm in the basement. I had a feeling I wouldn't be happy with my roommates.

Ray Dunner suddenly looked up, and for a split second our eyes met. The gun in his hand rose, and I ducked back. I was already fleeing when the second gunshot of the afternoon sounded. Back to the barn, and around the other side. Tabby urged the penultimate cow inside the structure. I grabbed the halter thingie on the last one and gave it a mighty tug. The big girl's eyes rolled, but she trotted along willingly enough. Tabby met us and took over.

She peered over my shoulder, clearly expecting pursuit. "Which one is shooting?" I could hardly hear her over the howl of the wind.

"Ray Dunner. Don't know about the first shot. But there's a sheriff's SUV in the parking lot. Come on, let's get down there."

But Tabby shook her head. "I have a few things to button up here. You get down to lower ground. I'll be right behind you."

The dark column reaching down from the clouds swayed and turned as if swinging its hips in a do-si-do. It was definitely closer, and on a direct line toward us. The house was on a hill; the barn slightly lower. The cheese classroom shed was the lowest-lying building on the dairy property.

"Are you crazy? Come *on*. I know you love these animals, but you can't sacrifice your life for them."

"They are my life. And my living. Don't worry, I'll make it down there."

My fingers tightened around her arm. "I mean it. Don't you dare die on me today, Tabby Bines."

She shook me off. "Let me get to work, then."

I hated leaving her again, but I wasn't going to get caught out in the open by a tornado just because she was stubborn. "I'll meet you at the classroom," I yelled, and then took off like my hair was on fire.

The Dunners were temporarily out of the way, hiding in the house. I reached the parking lot and ran up to the SUV. It looked like the one I'd seen Sheriff Jaikes drive, but the man was nowhere to be seen. I reached in the Audi and grabbed my tote bag as if it were some kind of security blanket, muttered a curse at Ray for taking my cell phone, and headed for the squat, square building.

Jaikes' head jerked up when I entered. He saw it was me and returned to his task. Positioned by the open back window where he could keep an eye on the approaching tornado, he was trying to fasten a towel around his arm.

I went to his side. "Shouldn't we leave? We might be able to outrun the storm. Oh, God, is that blood?"

"Just a flesh wound," he said, all macho-like. "Help me out."

Quickly I pulled the towel taut around the bloody wound on his upper left arm and tied it. Made me feel queasy, though it didn't actually look too bad. "Who shot you?"

"Not sure — came from behind the chicken coop when I was still in the parking lot. Ran the plates on the vehicles out there; both Ray and Ogden Dunner are here."

"I know. Ray shot at me. But Ogden has a gun, too. He killed Joe."

His head jerked around. "How do you know that?"

"We overheard them talking. Listen, Tabby's up at the milking barn, but she'll be here any second. Then we can go."

"Too late to outrun it," he said. "We'll have to hunker down."

Hope of escape had lightened the panic that scrabbled for purchase in the back of my mind. Now the fear clawed its way back, and I had to clench my fists to stop my hands from trembling.

"Stay in here?" I gestured at the milk bottles stacked in crates against the wall. "That'd be suicide."

"Be better to get up to the house."

"Ray and his dad are already settled in there," I said. "I doubt they'd welcome our company."

Tabby ran in the door, and Jaikes' hand flew to his gun. The holster was already unsnapped.

Without a word, she pointed out the window behind him. The tornado had halved the distance, and we could see how fast it was moving now. As one, we turned and dashed out the door toward the drainage ditch that ran along the driveway into the dairy. Jaikes slipped down the side and landed on his wounded arm, swearing loudly. I slithered down behind him, and Tabby followed.

Prone on our stomachs, we tucked our heads and put our hands over the backs of our necks. I squeezed my eyes shut and whispered disjointed prayers as the insanely loud rumbling of an approaching freight train bore down.

An eternity later, quiet returned. I raised my head above the edge of the ditch and surveyed the damage. Pieces of fencing littered the parking lot. A metal barrel had shattered one of the windows in the classroom, and part of the chicken house roof had up and disappeared. But as I watched, a rooster strutted out and crowed his defiance at the receding storm. My old friend Billy the goat peered around a corner, already chewing on God-knew-what. But all the buildings still stood, whole and largely unharmed.

The twister had passed us by. Not by much, but by enough.

Relief flooded through me.

The sound of frightened cows echoed down from the barn. Tabby leapt to her feet and raced back up the hill. Jaikes yelled at her to come back, but either she didn't hear him or didn't care. The roar of an engine made us turn our heads. A car careened down the driveway toward us, dodging tumbleweeds and crunching over cottonwood branches. The door opened and Investigator Schumaker was out of the cruiser almost before it stopped.

Sheesh. Was this crazy afternoon ever going to end?

I was on my knees, still half in the ditch. The stiff dry grass poked into my skin, which was already sore from the hailstones. I wondered whether I'd have dozens of perfectly round little bruises tomorrow.

Tomorrow. There would be a tomorrow after all. That thought drove me to my feet.

Schumaker paused when he saw me, then immediately turned to Jaikes. "Everyone all right, sir?"

"Far as we know. The Dunners are holed up in the house. Apparently they're both armed. One of them shot me."

The investigator's eyes narrowed as he took in his boss' towel-wrapped arm. "How bad?"

"Not too bad. I'm functional."

"Well, then. Let's go get them."

"So you already knew Ogden killed Joe?" I asked. "Forensic evidence? Blood spatter?"

Schumaker shuffled his feet. "Er . . ."

"We didn't know," Jaikes said. "I came out here to talk to Tabby Bines."

"On your own time." When Schumaker spoke, their eyes locked and something passed between the two men.

"I talked to Krista last night." The sheriff frowned at me. "She told me you called her."

"Yes." And I wasn't about to apologize for it.

The third gunshot of the afternoon reverberated through the air.

"Tabby," I said in alarm. "I thought she went back up to the barn to check on her cows."

"Stay here!" Schumaker yelled at me, and both men took off at a run.

Fat chance.

I slogged up the hill after them. And here I'd been complaining about not getting enough exercise in Colorado. Still, I'd specifically told Tabby not to die today, and I meant it. She still hadn't answered my most important question about Bobby Lee.

The two men went to the back of the house, disappearing from my view. As I approached loud voices reached my ears, then a scream I recognized as Tabby's. Unlike her scream of horror when she'd discovered Joe lying in a pool of blood and cream, this scream held raw fury. I slowed and carefully eased my head around the corner.

Tabby and Ogden Dunner were in the dirt, rolling and kicking and punching like twelve-year-olds on the playground. They seemed to be evenly matched, neither gaining the upper hand. Ray stood over them, pointing a wavering gun as he looked for an opening to shoot.

"Freeze!"

Feet wide apart, a sweating and disheveled Inspector Schumaker trained his own gun on Ray Dunner like a caricature out of a bad movie. And Ray froze.

I joined the group. Beside me, Sheriff Jaikes sighed, walked over to Ray, wrested the gun from his hand and put it in his pocket.

"Stop acting like kids and get up," he said to the pair on the ground.

Tabby rolled off Ogden and got to her feet. Mud smeared her jeans and T-shirt and arms. A streak of it smudged her cheek. Grass stuck out of her hair, which had come loose from its ponytail and now curled around a bloody scrape on her jaw.

I joined the party. Other than a disapproving glance from Schumaker, no one seemed to notice.

Jaikes helped Ogden up, then held out his right hand. Sheepishly, the older man reached into his own pocket and gave him the gun. "I don't even know how to use it."

"Guess that means you're the one who shot me?" The sheriff glared at Ray, who winced. "Hmph. And is that why you bashed Joe Bines over the head with a bottle of cream, Ogden? 'Cause you didn't know how to shoot a gun?"

Tabby's eyes blazed and she took a step forward. Jaikes shook his head without looking at her. She stopped. Waited.

Ogden Dunner slumped, and he looked down at the ground. After several seconds he straightened and raised his head. The heaviness seemed to lift from his shoulders. A calm settled into his eyes.

"If you're asking if I killed him, the answer is yes."

"Dad." Ray took a step. Schumaker grabbed his arms and quickly cuffed his hands behind his back. The younger Dunner looked surprised for a moment, before his familiar angry expression returned.

"No, Son. This is best," Ogden said. "Confession is good for the soul, and God knows my soul could use some good." He held out his wrists to the sheriff.

"Is that necessary?" Jaikes asked.

"No."

"Well, then: You have the right to remain . . ."

The sheriff Mirandized Ogden Dunner and then did the same to Ray Dunner. Ogden hadn't seemed like a killer, but now I could see he possessed considerably more mettle than his blowhard son. Ray huffed and puffed and turned red in the face, while Ogden appeared to be almost relieved.

Jaikes finished, and silence fell upon the motley crew gathered behind the house. A few intrepid bovines exited the barn and ambled around to eyeball us with dull curiosity. Tabby must have opened the barn doors before stumbling on the Dunners exiting the house.

"Why did you kill Joe?" I asked Ogden before anyone could stop me.

THIRTY-TWO

The sheriff glared at me. Schumaker opened his mouth to speak, but closed it again when Ogden nodded and took a deep breath.

"I'm sorry, Son."

"Shut up, old man."

Resignation tempered Ogden's obvious regret. "No. It's time." His gaze flicked from one face to another, settled on mine. "The night Gwen Miller died, Joe pulled me aside. He told me she hadn't fallen in the river by accident. Ray had become angry and pushed her in, on purpose."

"That's a lie!" Ray said. Schumaker's grip on his arm tightened, and he gave him a little shake. Ray ignored him. "You were always ready to believe the worst about me. You never took my side."

Ogden's eyes cut to his son. "I took your side more often than I should have." He sighed and looked back at me. "Joe said he'd keep what he saw to himself if we'd leave him and Tabby out of the whole thing. I didn't know what to think, but I agreed and made up a couple of runaways named Tom and Jane Smith."

Something must have shown on my face, because he smiled. "I know. Not very original. But it wasn't like I had a great plan to cover everything up. Just reacted to the circumstances. In fact, I wouldn't have mentioned them to the authorities at all if I hadn't heard Krista say someone else rescued Gwen when we got to the hospital. Then we had to scramble to get our stories straight, and to convince Krista to go along with it."

Jaikes glowered at this mention of his daughter. "So Ray threatened to kill her? What kind of a preacher were you, getting your son to do that?"

"I guess I wasn't a very good preacher, was I? But I didn't know about any threats. Ray told me Krista went along with the story because she was afraid she'd get in trouble for drinking." He cocked his head to one side and considered his son. "You threatened to *kill* her?"

"Of course not. See. There you go again, willing to believe anything anyone says about me."

The naked anger shining in Jaike's eyes

betrayed his own personal stake in Ogden's tale. "Krista told me last night that she'd also seen your son push the Miller girl into the river. That was why he threatened her — to keep her from saying anything."

Ogden rubbed his hand over his face. "I'm sorry he frightened her, Sheriff. I didn't know."

Ray made a sound in the back of his throat.

"I thought that was the end of it, but Joe came back," Ogden said. "He wanted more after he found out Gwen actually died. I was afraid Ray would be convicted of killing her. I didn't want him to go to prison, but I didn't have any money. Joe told me he'd take this land in exchange for his silence. It couldn't happen right away, though, or people might put two and two together. He was willing to wait for two years. I accepted the deal and thanked God for sparing my son's freedom."

Ray's shoulders sagged, and he stared at the ground. Schumaker shuffled his feet and looked impatient. Tabby watched with a blank face as the lies she'd so carefully built her life upon came to light.

"But I didn't know the full story, Sheriff," Ogden continued. "I didn't know your daughter had also seen Ray push that girl

352

into the river. I didn't know he'd threatened her into silence. And I didn't know that Ray would probably only have been charged with manslaughter. He hadn't tried to kill her; he'd only been playing around. Isn't that true, son? It was actually all just an accident?"

I didn't know whether he was trying to convince us or himself.

"I didn't mean to kill her," Ray said in a dull monotone.

"You didn't kill her. The hypothermia did. In fact, I'm to blame as much as anyone because I didn't take her straight to the hospital. If I had, they might have saved her. But I was weak. I wanted to keep the incident quiet, and I blame myself for that girl dying."

"Is that another reason you gave the land away?" I asked as gently as I could. "To punish yourself?"

His lips turned up in a slight smile. "You know, Ms. Reynolds, I think that might be true, though giving up that land was easier than I thought it would be. The dream was gone. And it didn't seem right to continue as pastor at my little church, so I gave that up, too. Took out a loan, and started the car lot.

"I filed the quit claim deed. When Ray

found out, he told me he hadn't meant to kill Gwen Miller. That it was an accident."

Oh brother, I thought. Ogden might understand his son's true nature, but he was still willing to protect him whenever he could.

"But it was done," he continued, "and there was no way to reverse it. So I took it as God's will, and we went on with our lives."

"Until Joe called you again recently," I guessed.

"Until he called and said there was more evidence, concrete evidence, that implicated everyone that night in the Miller girl's death as well as your brother's death. He told me to bring all the money I could lay my hands on."

I shook my head. "Tabby, why would Joe think that? He hadn't even seen the letter."

"I don't know. What did you tell him it said?" Accusation dripped from her words.

I tried to remember. "I said it was very revealing. He jumped on that, said Bobby Lee was a liar. But I never said anything about Rancho Sueño or —"

Or any of the other stories I'd found in the newspaper. The rest of the puzzle pieces snapped into place with an almost audible snap.

Holy cow.

"— or anything else that could possibly be taken as incriminating. It was almost as if his guilty conscience took control. Ogden, did Joe want cash?"

He nodded. "As much as I could get within the hour. He said it would be just this once. Of course, I'd heard that twice before, so I didn't believe him. But what was I going to do? So I grabbed all the cash we had in the store and withdrew a couple hundred dollars from the ATM. When I got here, he told me it wasn't enough. Said he was going to the authorities, bring everything to light."

"Including his own blackmail?" I asked. Another part of my mind was working out the timing. Ogden must have left the dairy mere minutes before Tabby and I came out of the house. If I'd left a little earlier we might have prevented his death.

If, if, if.

He closed his eyes and covered them with his hands. "I told him he would just have to go ahead, then. That I didn't have anything else to give, and that he'd be revealing himself as a blackmailer. He was frantic. He pushed me against the wall. Said he'd kill me, kill my son if we said anything. Came right out and said that. Said he knew I could get more money, that he needed it now. He was acting like a crazy man. I panicked, grabbed the first thing that came to hand, and . . . I hit him with it."

He swallowed and licked his lips. "I didn't mean to kill him. But that hardly matters now, does it?"

Actually, it might make a very real difference in how he would be charged and sentenced.

I looked into Tabby's clear blue eyes. "Do you have any idea why Joe wanted cash right away?"

Slowly, she shook her head. I held her gaze, though, and saw the awareness surface as she thought about it. She quickly turned her head and appeared to examine the devastation the storm had left behind.

"Because I think I do." I turned to Jaikes. "He was going to run away and leave his wife to deal with all the fallout. Did your daughter tell you Tabby and Joe were at Rancho Sueño the night Ray here pushed his girlfriend in the freezing cold river?"

The sheriff's lips pressed together. "Why, yes. As a matter of fact, she did." He walked over to Ray Dunner, who flinched at his approach. "You made my own daughter lie to me, on the most traumatic night of her life," he grated out. "But now she's willing to testify against your sorry ass. As am I."

It was a good thing Inspector Schumaker was standing there, or else his boss might have flattened the suspect then and there.

I was proud of his daughter's willingness to come forward after living in terror of Ray Dunner for so long. I wondered whether she'd called her father because I'd called her, or whether Schumaker had related what I'd told him in Zillah's Café and Jaikes had contacted her. In the end, though, it hardly mattered which.

"Could I show you something, Sheriff?" I asked. "You, too, Inspector."

"What?"

"It's in the classroom. And Tabby? I think you'd better come along as well."

"What's this all about?" Inspector Schumaker sounded downright grouchy for a guy who had just solved a murder case.

"Sheesh — will you just trust me for once?" I asked.

The Dunners waited in the parking lot, Ogden in the back of the sheriff's Suburban and Ray in the inspector's prowler. The air was cooler after the big storm, but still felt heavy and muggy.

"I need to go call my mom," Tabby said. "Delight's terrified of tornadoes."

"Here, call her on my cell," I said and handed her the phone Schumaker had kindly retrieved from Ray Dunner's pocket, along with my cash.

"I need to go up to the house," she repeated and turned to go.

"Don't let her leave," I said, the words chopped and urgent.

Sheriff Jaikes stepped in front of her. "Use that phone to check on your daughter. We'll wait." Apparently he was willing to trust me — at least for now. Still, he looked weary. His wounded arm must have throbbed like the dickens.

Tabby moved a few feet away. She dialed and then spoke into the phone, all the while darting glances my way. When she was satisfied everything was all right at her mother's, she handed the phone back to me without so much as a thank you.

"Okay. Come on in here." I led the way into the classroom, picking my way among the shards of window glass on the floor. "You can stay in the doorway, actually. It's a mess in here."

The photos of Joe Bines were scattered all over the room, and the poster board collage for his memorial had fallen to the floor. I retrieved it and returned to where Tabby stood with the two lawmen. Holding it up, I pointed to the picture of Joe with the script *First Truck* pasted under it.

"Was this the vehicle Joe drove eighteen years ago?"

Tabby didn't answer.

I put my face next to hers. She shrank back. "Is it? They can find out, you know. Just tell us."

Earlier the fight had gone out of her when she'd finally confessed that she and Joe had been at Rancho Sueño the night Gwen Miller died. Then in the process of escaping the Dunners and surviving the storm she'd regained her composure. But now, as I pointed to the picture of Joe and his dark green truck, it leaked away again.

In a quiet voice she said, "Yes. That was what he drove."

"But not that night, out here by the river."

"No. We rode out with Krista and Gwen."

"Why?"

Sheriff Jaikes cocked his head to one side. Inspector Schumaker inclined his. Both intrigued.

"Why didn't you and Joe drive here in his truck?" I asked.

"Because . . ." She sighed. "Because Bobby Lee had borrowed it."

The inspector's eyes widened as understanding began to dawn.

She continued, "I don't even remember what he needed it for, but that's what he drove that night when he came to get us."

"Did you tell him about Gwen?"

Hesitation, then she nodded. "He wanted to go to the hospital to check on her."

That sounded like my baby brother. "Then why didn't you?"

Silence. God, this woman was an expert at silence.

"Tabby."

"Joe said we shouldn't. They were arguing."

"He and Bobby Lee?"

"Yes."

"And then?"

"Something happened."

Something. Talk about an understatement.

I chose my next words with great care. "Who was driving when Joe's truck hit that bicyclist?"

Sheriff Jaikes' eyebrows climbed to the top of his forehead.

Tabby's eyes filled with tears. I leaned in to hear her whispered response: "I was."

THIRTY-THREE

Anna Belle had been frantically trying to track me down all afternoon as news of the tornadoes east of town blared from the newscasts. Apparently my cell phone had vibrated in Ray Dunner's pocket over and over, and he'd either ignored it or had been too distracted to notice. There were thirteen voice-mail messages from my mother by the time I got around to checking it.

I'd called her and rushed home. Finally, I had some answers for my parents.

Now Dad, Anna Belle, Meghan, Kelly, and even Erin sat in the great room, watching me pace back and forth in front of them as I related the events of the day.

First I told them about the tornado veering so close to the dairy. About how Joe had blackmailed Ogden Dunner, and then when he turned violent during the last attempt Ogden had killed him in self-defense. About how Tabby had assumed from the moment we found Joe's body that Ray had killed him because of their long and checkered history.

Had I caused Joe's death? I'd been deliberately vague when I'd related the contents of Bobby Lee's letter. I had to admit that could have been a catalyst for what followed. But I wasn't about to hold myself responsible for Joe Bines' paranoia and violent nature. That family had built a precarious life around lies and greed and death. It was bound to implode sometime.

As for Tabby, it didn't look like her happily-ever-after was in the cards, either. If charged with first-degree vehicular homicide she was facing a possible three- to fifteen-year sentence, Schumaker told me. If they went with negligent homicide, she might get a year in jail or even probation. For Delight's sake I should have hoped for the latter.

I didn't, though. Tabby's decisions, even influenced as they had been by Joe, had placed Bobby Lee in an untenable moral quandary. His love for her warred equally against his own guilt. My sweet eighteen-year-old brother had taken the only way out he could see.

So I told my family what Tabby had revealed about the night Gwen Miller died, and Bobby Lee's role in the whole mess.

"When I heard Ogden say Joe wanted cash and wanted it fast, it sounded like he was desperate. Like he needed the money to run," I said. "And then I remembered the picture of the truck and put it together with the other newspaper story and Schumaker's questions about what kind of vehicle Bobby Lee drove. That was when I realized how the two incidents were connected, and finally I understood what Bobby Lee had meant in his letter. He'd helped Tabby cover up what happened, but then he couldn't live with it."

I asked my parents if they knew why Bobby Lee had borrowed Joe's truck. Anna Belle looked puzzled, but Dad's expression was thoughtful.

"He was helping an older neighbor put in some new landscaping," he said. "I bet he borrowed it to haul compost."

Anna Belle said, "I didn't even know he was gone from the house. I wonder how many times he left and we never knew."

My father put his arm around her. "He was eighteen, and we'd lifted his curfew altogether by then."

"Maybe we should have —" but Anna Belle cut herself off. Self-recrimination was useless now. His arm tightened around her.

"After rescuing Gwen, Joe's feet were

messed up from going in the river," I continued. "He had a couple of frostbitten toes and couldn't walk very well. So when Bobby Lee got there he helped Joe into the truck, and Tabby went around to the driver's side. At first the plan was to go to the hospital, but Joe didn't want to. He and Bobby Lee argued. Now we know Ogden had agreed to keep quiet about Joe and Tabby's presence at Rancho Sueño, but at the time Tabby had no idea. She just thought Joe didn't want to get in trouble."

"Makes sense. By then he'd already had a few run-ins with the law," my dad said.

I went on with the story as I'd heard it. Tabby had said the boy on the bike came out of nowhere. The snow and cold no doubt had something to do with why he swerved out of the bike lane and in front of the truck. Maybe he'd been avoiding an ice patch, or had hit one and slid out of control. It had been early morning by then, two or three o'clock, and a cyclist on the streets at that hour and in that weather was unusual but not unheard of in bike-crazy Spring Creek.

Tabby had sideswiped him. Instead of stopping, she'd roared away. Bobby Lee had wanted to go back; Joe didn't. He said he saw the cyclist getting up behind them.

He'd be fine, and they were already in enough trouble. So she drove them to Joe's apartment. The next morning, Joe's feet were better but not great. He dropped Tabby and Bobby Lee off at our house after Anna Belle and Dad left for work.

My parents had no idea Bobby Lee wasn't in his bed. That he had been gone all night.

I had to wonder whether that night didn't give Joe leverage over Tabby as well as Ogden. After all, he obviously didn't have a problem with using a little blackmail to get his way. He'd always been sweet on Tabby, but she was Bobby Lee's girl. After Bobby Lee was gone — however tragic the circumstances — she was available. At least in theory. She didn't love Joe, but between the land for the dairy and the fact that he knew her secret, I could see how he had persuaded her to marry him. She'd spoken of a "bond" between them. Indeed. And what a complicated thing that bond had been.

But I hadn't had a chance to ask Tabby whether any of that was true, so I didn't mention it. I also left out what I'd been thinking about as I drove home from the dairy. If the hit-and-run victim had lived, or maybe even if he'd been killed instantly, perhaps my brother would still be alive. If Bobby Lee'd had a chance to anonymously call 911 and get an ambulance to the site of the accident, maybe his guilt would have been assuaged. But Tabby had been terribly upset, and Joe insisted the cyclist had only been bruised. So Bobby Lee never made that call.

"So much death in order to cover the crimes of others," Meghan murmured.

"None of the deaths were intentional," I said. "Well, Ray shoved Gwen Miller in the river in a fit of anger, but we can't know that he meant to kill her. Ogden will certainly argue that he didn't. Tabby will be tried for killing that young man so many years ago and for leaving the scene of the hit-and-run. But if she'd stayed and called the police when it happened, she likely wouldn't have gone to jail. Even Ogden Dunner realized after he'd given in to Joe's blackmail demands that the law wouldn't have done much to his son if they had all told the truth in the first place. And in the end, Ogden killed Joe in self-defense."

It was all so sad. However, now that we knew the truth, a weight had been lifted from my shoulders. I hadn't even realized how heavy it had become after all those years. When Tabby revealed that she'd been the one driving, I'd been surprised at first. I really had thought it was Joe. But it made perfect sense. Joe was my brother's best friend. Bobby Lee was as loyal as they came. Though mystified as to the connection between them, I could just barely understand why Bobby Lee would cover up for Joe. But it made oodles of sense when I realized he was covering up for Tabby, the girl he was head-over-heels in love with.

The girl with the ice-blue eyes.

The subject of protecting others for their own good came up later as Dad and I worked together in the kitchen. We'd grilled steaks with peppers, onions, zucchini, and tomatoes for dinner, as well as a foil-wrapped loaf of crispy garlic bread, so washing the dishes was a snap.

"Everybody was protecting someone, weren't they?" I leaned down to put another plate in the dishwasher then stood and faced him. "Ogden protecting Ray. Sheriff Jaikes wanting to protect his daughter. Bobby Lee protecting Tabby. Celeste protecting Tabby. And you, protecting Anna Belle."

My father blinked. "I'm not sure I —"

"There's no other explanation. Celeste Atwood returned Bobby Lee's letter as soon as she got it. You happened to see it before Anna Belle did. And you kept it from her all these years."

He licked his lips.

"Why, Dad?"

Hesitation. Then he nodded. "You weren't here. You don't know what your brother's death did to her. She couldn't have taken it then."

"Did you read it?"

Eyes shiny with tears, he shook his head. "I couldn't." His voice broke on the second word.

I put my arms around my father. He hadn't just been protecting Anna Belle; he'd been protecting himself as well.

"You have to tell her, you know."

He nodded, and I felt the day's stubble on his chin catch in my hair. "I guess maybe I'd better go do that right now, huh?"

I gave him another squeeze and let him go.

"I love you," I said to his retreating back. "So does she."

He paused. Without turning around he said, "I know."

Snow drifted to the ground as night fell outside the main lodge at the Horseshoe Guest Ranch. Flames crackled around four-foot logs in the oversized fireplace, and guests perched on the elevated hearth and the eight-foot sofa in front of the fire. Others stood talking in small groups. The jazz quartet in the corner accompanied conversations as people munched and sipped. Tantalizing food smells issued from the depths of the kitchen and from the appetizer buffet along the back wall. Elk, moose, deer, and antelope heads mounted high on the walls looked down upon the festivities, but no one seemed to mind their skulking.

There were clusters of orange gerbera daisies everywhere.

Meghan shot a look at the grandfather clock and raised her eyebrows. I nodded, and she began quietly assembling the wedding party.

A quick and simple ceremony in the middle of a reception, then a sit-down dinner later.

Starting with the reception was a bassackwards way to do it, Cassie Ambrose said. But Barr's mother wasn't opposed to doing things a little differently, and I loved the idea of getting married in the middle of a party rather than making a big production out of the vows. Everyone, including me, was relaxed and enjoying themselves, and that had to be a good sign.

And Anna Belle was having a fantastic time, moving from guest to guest, pouring Southern charm over them like honey. She wore a svelte, wine-colored suit and a matching pair of smashing Italian leather pumps. Dad stood by the fireplace in a sedate black suit and watched her with an adoring gaze. Their relationship had rekindled over the last few months to the degree that I'd had to ask my mother to stop sharing details over the phone.

I hadn't dictated what any of my attendants wore, figuring they were smart enough to figure it out on their own. I wasn't disappointed. Meghan was my maid of honor, of course, and wore a stylish blue silk sheath. Erin had wanted to be my flower girl, but I'd nixed the idea. The disappointment on her face lifted when I asked her to be one of my bridesmaids instead. She looked beautiful in a light blue dress with a soft, twirly skirt.

My other bridesmaid was my good friend Tootie Hanover. The cold Wyoming weather wasn't good for her severe arthritis, but she was cheerful even in her wheelchair. She was elegant as always, tonight in a deep green satin tunic and long black skirt. Her boyfriend, Felix, hovered constantly at her side, and I wondered whether he was planning to stand up with me during the actual wedding, as well.

From behind the bar, Hannah Ambrose,

Barr's ex-wife and possible future sister-in-law, flashed a bright grin and waved when I looked her way. I bared my teeth at her — I think it came across as a smile. But if it didn't, that was okay, too.

My deep purple lace dress was something new, but I'd also tucked the key to our newly renovated house under my garter. The key wasn't new, but the house and living situation would be.

I'd borrowed a lace handkerchief from Erin that her Nana Tootie had given her. I figured that covered both old and borrowed. Then Barr's mother had given me the string of pearls around my neck. They'd belonged to her mother, and I was pleased to wear them in honor of being welcomed into the Ambrose family.

As for the something blue, it was really something bleu. And no, I wasn't wearing it. Meghan and I had started making our own fresh cheeses after returning to Cadyville from that adventurous week in Spring Creek, but my father had turned his culinary passion to serious cheese making. He'd supplied two small wheels of a young bleu he'd made, as well as flying in some of the well-aged good stuff from an artisan cheese house in New York. They were among the appetizers on the buffet table. The dinner menu also included bleu cheese dressing for the salad and guests would have the option of adding a dollop of bleu cheese butter on top of their filet mignon.

A friend of the Ambrose family, a local judge, waited to marry us. Meghan spoke to him, and he began moving toward the area in front of the fireplace where we'd decided to exchange vows. The rest of us followed. The quartet quieted, and the ceremony began.

Barr and I had written our own simple promises to love each other and stick out the rough times. Yes, Barr's actually said that. As long as he meant it, I didn't care how he put it.

Just before the exchange of rings, the judge asked if I wanted this man to be my husband.

I said, "I do."

And I really, really did.

ABOUT THE AUTHOR

Cricket McRae's interest in traditional colonial skills is reflected in her contemporary Home Crafting Mysteries. Set in the Pacific Northwest, they feature everything from soap making to food preservation, spinning to cheese making. For recipes and more information about Cricket go to her website, www.cricketmcrae.com http:// www.cricketmcrae.com/, or her blog, www .hearthcricket.com.

We hope you have enjoyed this Large Print book. Other Thorndike, Wheeler, Kennebec, and Chivers Press Large Print books are available at your library or directly from the publishers.

For information about current and upcoming titles, please call or write, without obligation, to:

Publisher
Thorndike Press
295 Kennedy Memorial Drive
Waterville, ME 04901
Tel. (800) 223-1244

or visit our Web site at:

http://gale.cengage.com/thorndike

OR

Chivers Large Print
published by AudioGO Ltd
St James House, The Square
Lower Bristol Road
Bath BA2 3BH
England
Tel. +44(0) 800 136919
email: info@audiogo.co.uk
www.audiogo.co.uk

All our Large Print titles are designed for easy reading, and all our books are made to last.